PENGUIN BOOKS

Dawn

EVE EDWARDS has a doctorate from Oxford University
and thinks researching is a large part of the fun in writing
historical fiction. She lives in Oxford and is married with
three children.

eve-edwards.com

Dawn

EVE EDWARDS

PENGUIN BOOKS

PENGUIN BOOKS

Published by the Penguin Group
Penguin Books Ltd, 80 Strand, London WC2R 0RL, England
Penguin Group (USA) Inc., 375 Hudson Street, New York, New York 10014, USA
Penguin Group (Canada), 90 Eglinton Avenue East, Suite 700, Toronto, Ontario, Canada M4P 2Y3
(a division of Pearson Penguin Canada Inc.)
Penguin Ireland, 25 St Stephen's Green, Dublin 2, Ireland (a division of Penguin Books Ltd)
Penguin Group (Australia), 707 Collins Street, Melbourne, Victoria 3008, Australia
(a division of Pearson Australia Group Pty Ltd)
Penguin Books India Pvt Ltd, 11 Community Centre, Panchsheel Park, New Delhi – 110 017, India
Penguin Group (NZ), 67 Apollo Drive, Rosedale, Auckland 0632, New Zealand
(a division of Pearson New Zealand Ltd)
Penguin Books (South Africa) (Pty) Ltd, Block D, Rosebank Office Park,
181 Jan Smuts Avenue, Parktown North, Gauteng 2193, South Africa

Penguin Books Ltd, Registered Offices: 80 Strand, London WC2R 0RL, England

www.penguin.com

First published 2014
001

Text copyright © Eve Edwards, 2014
Illustrations by Carole Golding
All rights reserved

The moral right of the author and illustrator has been asserted

Set in 12.5/16pt Bembo Book MT Std by Palimpsest Book Production Ltd, Falkirk, Stirlingshire
Typeset by Jouve (UK), Milton Keynes
Printed in Great Britain by Clays Ltd, St Ives plc

British Library Cataloguing in Publication Data
A CIP catalogue record for this book is available from the British Library

ISBN: 978-0-141-33740-1

www.greenpenguin.co.uk

Penguin Books is committed to a sustainable
future for our business, our readers and our planet.
This book is made from Forest Stewardship
Council™ certified paper.

For Hannah and Sam Bickersteth

We are the dead. Short days ago
We lived, felt dawn, saw sunset glow,
Loved and were loved, and now we lie
In Flanders fields.

– John McCrae (May 1915)

PART ONE

Paper Lanterns

I

London Docks, 13 June 1917

Blue skies had become a curse in London.

Helen Sandford knelt to the pavement and kissed the little girl goodbye before ushering her through the gates at the Upper North Street School, near East India Dock.

'Your mum will be along to fetch you later, Joanie.'

Joan bit her bottom lip, looking like she wanted to bolt for cover rather than join the cluster of children by the doors.

'Don't look so sad. It'll be fun. You're making lanterns today – the teacher told me yesterday.' Joan's glum face brightened. 'Be good, won't you?'

Joan gave her a shy 'thank you' and ran to join her fellow infants near the door to her classroom. There was little danger of Joan making any trouble in lessons, as she would barely say boo to a goose. Helen stood for a moment, thinking that she looked so achingly vulnerable with her pink cheeks and wide blue eyes, hardly ready for the rough-and-tumble of the gritty playground in the poorest part of London. Joan only came out of her shell when Kitty, her best friend, took her hand, tugging her to sit on a bench. Helen smiled as she saw the two, heads together, exchanging the tender secrets of a five year-old. The crown of Joan's blonde head glowed in the morning sunshine like a miraculous gold coin dropped in the concrete and brick of London's grimy East End.

'She yours, love?' asked a matronly woman with the yellowed complexion of a munitions worker who handled TNT, a regular at the school gate like her. Helen had noticed she had just sent her son off with a clip round the ear for some cheek. Rough love: standard round here.

'No. She's my landlady's – second eldest of five.' Helen turned to leave for work; the woman fell into step with her, heading for the same bus stop.

The woman smiled, displaying a set of crooked teeth. 'I should've known. You look a mite young to have one of your own. My next guess was that you were her sister.' She chuckled as her son leapfrogged another boy, pushing him over. 'Can't say I'm sorry to leave mine here each morning – they run me ragged at home. I think the teachers deserve a medal putting up with them all day.'

'That they do.' Helen knew from experience how a small house in Poplar could feel like it was bursting at the seams with young ones rattling around inside. Life felt scraped to the bone with washing drying in the communal yard, shared outhouse lavatory and water tap. The air smelt of the ever-present tang of chimney smoke and too many people living too close together. Pot plants struggled on windowsills; thin, mean cats haunted the alleys. 'I take one look and envy sardines for their roomy tins.'

The woman gave her a sharp glance. 'Not from these parts, are you, love?'

Her pulse tripped over a beat; she shouldn't have tried to be witty. Ever since she had been hounded out of a military hospital for her German blood, she had hated any enquiry into her origins. She aimed for calm unconcern. This was hardly the first time she had been asked. 'That's right.'

The woman hadn't lost interest. 'Can't place the accent though.'

Helen gestured vaguely to the north, over the rooftops and curls of smoke. 'I'm from Suffolk. A country girl.'

The woman nodded but clearly she had little concept of the rest of the country beyond the end of the Central line. 'You must think me nosy. I'm Lizzie, by the way: Lizzie Morris. My old man's on the front. I think he left for a bit of peace and quiet as we've four boys at home.'

'Pleased to meet you, Mrs Morris.' Helen had got used over her months in the East End to the openness of the people there. Though the streets and docks were crowded with people, they were a close-knit society, the majority thinking everyone else's business was theirs to know and comment on freely. It was a good thing her landlady was excellent at keeping secrets. Helen's German half from her mother's side would get her in trouble in minutes.

'Whereabouts is your husband?' Helen kept the conversation focused on the chatty Lizzie and away from the minefield of her own past.

'Not sure exactly, dearie, but he's an artilleryman, near

a place called Albert last I heard.' That was very close to Helen's old hospital but she gave a vague smile as if all French place-names were the same to her. 'What about your young man?' Lizzie nudged her in the ribs. 'I take it that a pretty little thing like you has a suitor?' She cackled good-humouredly at Helen's blush. 'Thought as much.'

Helen was not sure how to answer. It always took her by surprise when someone inferred she was pretty; her heart-shaped face, heavy long brown hair and full figure seemed the epitome of ordinary to her eyes, far from the blonde fairylike waifs that were the beauties of stage and screen. And as for suitors, her relationship with Sebastian Trewby was complicated, not something for gossip. Yet to make a fuss about her reply would only make the woman even more curious and, as meetings at the school gate were a feature of her life now, she couldn't afford to seem mysterious. 'Oh, he was wounded last year but has gone back in service.'

'Eager to do his bit, eh?' The woman looked down the street as the omnibus approached; the motor vehicle was held up behind a drayman's cart, horses' heads hanging low in the harness as they pulled a heavy load along. 'Mind you, these days it seems as dangerous living here as in France. Can't stand these fine mornings.' She scowled at the blue sky. 'Sittin' ducks, we are.'

The war had taken an even uglier turn of late as the Germans had developed bomber planes capable of reaching London. With no way of defending the civilians from the airborne menace, a new front line had opened up right on the doorstep of the government. The German High Command made no secret of the fact that its intent was to demoralize the English and force them to seek a settlement to the stalemate of the trenches. And Lizzie was right to be worried. If one of the German bombs fell on her place of work, there would be no part of London that wouldn't hear the explosion and a family of four boys would be left without a mother.

'I wish they could do something,' Helen said, echoing the sentiment on everyone's lips. Just because all were saying it, it did not mean it was any less heartfelt.

'If they can't work out a way of defending us, there'll be a bloody revolution in the East End, you mark my words. The Tsar went pretty quick once his people set their mind on it. We're not going to put up with it much longer.' Lizzie climbed aboard the omnibus first with a cheery good morning to the woman checking tickets, her grim words left on the pavement to linger with Helen.

When Helen got off the bus, she had to run the last few streets in order to be on time for her shift. After the disaster of being expelled from France under false accusations of stealing medical supplies, she had found anonymous employment as a machinist at the factory manufacturing blouses. All her months of sewing and mending for her glamorous older sister, Flora, at the Palace Theatre, had paid off and she was already recognized as a skilled hand at the more complicated patterns.

She ducked through the door and punched her card just as the clock struck nine.

'Cutting it fine, Miss Ford,' called the formidable head machinist, a woman with the bearing of a drill sergeant and less compassion.

'Good morning, Mrs Hopper.' *Mrs Hopper kept them on the hop* – that was what the women said about her behind her back. Helen hung her hat on a peg and stripped off her cotton gloves. Around her, six other women were already bent over their work, crouched over the machines like machine-gunners, doing their bit for the war effort on fabric rather than the fields of Flanders.

'Finish the batch for the Red Cross, then start on the mechanics.'

'Yes, Mrs Hopper.' Helen picked up where she had left off at the end of her last shift. The cavernous factory that had once fashioned silk and fine linen blouses for ladies was fully occupied providing uniform shirts for women who had taken over the roles formerly done by men in many of the support services.

The working day under way, the normal chatter ebbed and flowed in the rows of women between the more intense moments of machining. Helen let the patchwork of voices roll past her; the hands knew better than to try and include her, accepting that she was reserved, not quite one of them.

'Daylight robbery, it is: mutton, twenty-one shillings a pound, an' that only scrag end that's barely fit to eat! Nobody round here can afford that.'

'Can't believe there's nothing the government can do to stop these raids. If it was Mayfair being targeted, they'd do something at the double.'

'Bloody shambles, the whole thing.'

'That Mrs Thomas won't keep the blackout curtains closed – leaves us exposed with her house like a bloomin' lighthouse. The police have had words with her but no good – she's gone daft since her sons died.'

'Six mistakes, Miss King. Undo the whole seam. You can stay late to make up. There is a war on, you know!'

Then one conversation bubbled up from the mass, making everyone else fall silent. Nelly Carpenter, a stout woman from Hoxton who sat two places over from Helen, had a voice that could gut fish. Each sentence was punctuated by the clatter of the machine or the snip-snap of scissors.

'She was walking out with a chap called Jan Kleine.' *Brrrrrrr*. 'Well, we got suspicious, as you would. Laid down the law to her, we did.' *Brrrrr*. 'Finish with him or you're out. So, to her credit, she did.' *Snip*. 'Couldn't leave it there though. The boys took Herr Kleine behind the pub and taught him a lesson in the King's English,' *brrrrrr*, 'of knuckles and fists. He got the message that we don't want Germans on our patch.' *Snap-snap*.

'But, Nelly, I thought you said before that your sister's man was from Belgium?' said her neighbour, a slight woman with the bulky name of Bernadette O'Callaghan. She shook out the blouse she was working on like a flag of surrender.

'That's what he *said*.'

'Oh, I see.'

'Sent him packing, we did.'

'Good for you.'

Nelly chuckled. 'They turned him away at the hospital when they heard his name.'

'So they should.' Bernadette rethreaded her machine. 'Those beds are for us – too many of us, thanks to the bombs. Did you hear what happened at Folkestone? Ninety-five dead – old men, women and children. Devil take the Kaiser and roast him in the hottest fires of Hell, I say.'

'Give him a taste of his own medicine: drop one of his bombs on him in his palace.'

'As much as I admire your sentiments, ladies, can we have less chat and more work, please?' interrupted Mrs Hopper.

Helen sat over her machine, chilled to the core, her fingers locked on the controls but the orders from her brain to press the pedal weren't reaching her foot.

'Something the matter with your machine, Miss Ford?'

'No.' She pushed her toes down. The machine began to eat up the fabric. 'Did it not matter that he might've been Belgian? I thought we went into the war to save "plucky" Belgium?' At least that was what the papers had claimed a few years ago.

Nelly looked up. 'Are you talking to me?'

'I was just asking a question. Your Mr Kleine could've been one of the refugees.'

'With a name like that?' scoffed Nelly.

'I'm under the impression that is a common name in Belgium as well as Germany.' Helen could tell her words were falling on hostile ground but she had to put down a little marker for the truth or feel ashamed for remaining silent.

'Exactly, so he could hide among us.'

'And I'm *under the impression*, Miss Ford, that you are here to work, not debate matters which are far above your understanding,' cut in Mrs Hopper. 'When I was eighteen, I didn't question my elders.'

The women nodded in agreement. Helen was by far the youngest among them and her skill had gained her tolerance but few friends.

Helen could not risk sounding too sympathetic to anyone German in case her own origins were examined. 'I'm sorry, Mrs Hopper, I was just curious.'

The overseer walked on to examine the work going on at the far end of the room. Nelly chucked a finished garment on the pile next to her chair. 'You're right, my girl. Could've been a mistake, I suppose, but better safe than sorry, eh?' Nelly wasn't a bad sort under normal circumstances but the bombing campaign had made all the East End virulent haters of anything Germanic.

Bernadette chuckled. 'Good point. There's a war on, you know!' She parroted Mrs Hopper's favourite saying.

Helen looked down at her perfect straight seam. 'Yes, I do know.'

Sebastian eased the joystick back to take his plane through a canyon between clouds, great white walls rearing up on a scale larger than anything the land could offer. It was like Jack and the Beanstalk: the cloudland being on giant scale compared to what lay below. He smiled with satisfaction as the aircraft responded to the least nudge of the steering column. These new Sopwith Pups were a huge improvement on the Rumpties and Hunguffins he had trained on; those crates at the flying schools in England had been already outdated pre-war models that needed more nursing than a newborn to keep in the air. The Pup, by contrast, practically flew itself.

Tipping his wing, he looked over the side. Two other pilots from his squadron circled under him, the perspective like swimming in deep clear water and seeing fish swimming below, the bubbling clouds the river channel.

A splatter of castor oil smeared his goggles. He used the end of his scarf to wipe it away. The sun came out, ricocheting off the fuselage in spikes of light. Cheeks chilled by the breeze, lips numbed, body shaken by the vibration from the engine, Sebastian had never felt more alive or closer to death, not even on the battlefield of the Somme. In the trenches last year, he had thought the airmen looping above were like Icarus – their fall significant and poetic compared to the maggot existence of the common soldier. It had been a large factor in his decision to re-enlist as a pilot in the Royal Flying Corps rather than resume his place in his regiment. The other had been his desire to do something when he had been stuck in misery, unable to find Helen. Now, up at five thousand feet, he knew he had been right. He was born for this. The pilots all knew they faced a short life expectancy but were buoyed by the optimism that it would be the other chap who bought it; pilots reached a state of acceptance of their fate that was pretty much religious.

So *carpe diem* – seize the day.

Sebastian laughed. It was a ridiculous sensation, the exhilaration of flight; he marvelled at the impossible physics that allowed him to soar at a hundred miles an hour in a craft made of little more than piano wire, wood, linen, paint and engine. Flying a plane made travelling by express train seem dull sport. The double wings stretched out either side of him, extensions of his own limbs, shuddering slightly in the flex of the wind. The propeller in front was just a blur, invisible while rotating at top speed. Few men had been granted this godlike view on the world. Even the war, grinding away on the ground a few miles away, seemed very distant. In the trenches the shells had deafened him; up here there was no sound but the hum of the engine and the roar of the wind. He could set his nose in any direction and keep on flying if he so wished – until his fuel ran out. Freedom was absolute.

The illusion of it, at least. He was still tied to the earth by his bonds of duty and love. By happy chance he was facing England. If he carried on flying, he could cross the Channel and drop in to find Helen in an hour.

And be court-martialled for dereliction of duty.

Sebastian turned his joystick to bank to the left, putting temptation behind him. He had a job to do and, now the clouds were breaking up, he should have decent visibility to complete the mission over German lines. Now he had gained the right altitude, he had to join his flight and give protection to the two-seater craft whose observers were to photograph the lines. The enemy had to be mapped for the artillery; targets located and destroyed. No time to think about them as men – they were wiggles of fortifications in farmland; scratches of railways; veins of canals; scars of roads; puffs of anti-aircraft fire. These used to be solo missions but since the Germans had gained air superiority over the winter with their flying circus under Manfred von Richthofen, the Red Baron, the British had started sending their planes out in groups for mutual defence.

Sebastian tilted his wings and slipped into his position at the end of the left flank of planes, like the last goose in the migration. Time to fight a war.

2

Helen took her break in the sunshine and sat on the steps outside the factory. Brick walls loomed around her; nothing grew in this space, no birds visited, no insects buzzed. It was the opposite of everything she loved. She leant back on her hands and turned her face to the light, feeling the cramp in her back unknot. She sensed rather than saw someone come and sit beside her.

'You all right, love?' It was Nelly.

'Yes, thank you.'

'I hope I didn't upset you earlier with what I said about that German bloke.'

She had, but there was no point in admitting it. 'I'm fine. Don't worry about me.'

'You're too young to know what's what. I expect you think the best of everyone but I've learned to be suspicious.'

'I see.'

'We know the Germans have spies here so we have to be wary of outsiders.'

Such attitudes had cost Helen her profession. She hated

15

the casual prejudice. 'I would've thought spies might hide better than that man you mentioned.' The remark skated on the edge of what was safe to say; this had been the very assumption made by the army doctors – that her hidden origin made her guilty.

'Maybe. But his loyalty was suspect, wasn't it?' The fact that Nelly hadn't let the subject drop suggested she wasn't entirely at ease with what she and her neighbours had done.

'Isn't it better to judge people by what they do rather than what they are?'

Nelly offered her a cigarette. Helen shook her head.

'You're an odd fish, aren't you, dear?'

'We're all odd in Suffolk.'

Nelly laughed, inspecting her chilblained fingers. 'What are you doing down here with German bombs falling on your head when you could be up there safe at home?'

Helen shrugged. 'My bit, I suppose. I've friends here, none left where I grew up.' And home wasn't always safe.

'I can't help wondering if there'll be any of us left when this war finishes.' Nelly chucked her cigarette butt on the pavement. 'Still, no rest for the wicked, eh?' With a heave on the iron banister, she got up and returned to her machine. Helen snatched a second's more peace, following the progress of a wisp of white cloud, winding like a silken Chinese dragon over the chimney-pots. Her hand clenched the silver locket she wore, a curl of hair and a photograph kept close at all times. She didn't have to open it to see in her imagination Sebastian's poet's face, sensitive mouth and dark expressive eyes, crop of chestnut hair, and stubborn jaw gazing back at her with a hint of a smile. She had been apart from Sebastian too long. She missed him so much it hurt; it felt like a void in her chest, a pebble of compressed nothingness right under her ribs. The last time she had felt this alone was when she had run out of his family home in October, having failed to get through the wall of relatives and friends keeping their boy from the disgraced nurse. It wasn't hard to conjure up the memory of that scared girl who had ended up homeless, friendless and adrift at the railway station. She never really left Helen, no matter how many people surrounded her now.

Paddington Station, London, 22 October 1916, 7 a.m.

Helen perched on her suitcase in a corner of the station watching the country milk being unloaded from the early train, a clank of metal canisters and harried deliverymen. Soldiers in khaki milled about, some asleep on their kitbags, many still daubed with the mud of France. A couple of Tommies had approached her but she had deterred them by keeping her eyes down and her knees primly together, handbag on her lap – respectable lady rather than girl of easy virtue. Yet she couldn't sit here much longer. The porters had noticed her and very soon someone would ask her to move along.

Her problem was that she had no idea to where she

could move. She was paralysed by indecision, frantic with terror that her identity would out. She had advanced as far as Sebastian's family home before his honour guard of relatives and friends had ejected her. No one wanted a scandalous nurse anywhere near their decorated army officer. She didn't want to be near herself either. If only it were possible, she would leave her brittle shell of a body and fly somewhere much more hospitable, like a butterfly leaving behind its cocoon.

Stupid thought.

Restlessly, she smoothed the fabric of her sensible skirt. She had little money, no job, and no friends who would want to know her now. Her only relative who would welcome her, her sister Flora, was in New York, all her attention on her baby, a little boy born a year ago. Her mother was blockaded by her U-boat father who would blast Helen out of the water if she dared venture into home waters. She had no raft to cling to, no lifeboat rowing into view.

And this was all because her friend at the front, Reg Cook, had liberated a few pills from the medical cabinet to ensure he never had to face the trenches without an emergency exit, a parachute into the next life if his suffering became unbearable.

Even struggling as she was, she understood his reasons. It didn't stop her being livid; she had no idea what she would say to him if she ever saw him again. He had not considered how his action would rebound on her. News would have reached him by now and he would be sorry, she was sure of that, but there was no way back for her even if he confessed, as the incident had brought her German mother to the attention of the authorities. She was lucky not to be interned, though it had been touch-and-go for a few minutes during that devastating interview in the matron's office. The doctors had considered it enough to pack her off to England to let the press crucify her on the front pages. Reg would be furious with himself when he discovered the chain of events his action had set running. He would want to put things right but there was precious little he could do.

Screwing her eyes shut, Helen banged her fists on her knees, squeezing tight on a knot of raw feelings – angry at Reg, at the hospital, at everyone – but there was nothing – nothing she could do. The pain reached into her numbness and wrung her out like washing through a mangle.

I have to stop or they'll lock me away as a madwoman, she thought.

Then the first glimmer of an idea came to her: Reg's family in the East End. She had their address. No one would look for her there, and his wife might welcome news from someone who had seen him recently. Going by the generosity of her spouse, Mrs Cook might well be minded to help her find work and a place to stay. It was the poorest part of London, cheap lodgings and an anonymous crowd for Helen to hide in: ideal for her needs.

A plan. A reason to keep going. Helen stood up and buttoned her coat.

'Want some company, sweetheart?' asked a sailor, tipping his cap to her.

'No thank you. I'm not that sort of girl,' she said, face fiery with embarrassment.

'Now that is a shame.' He grinned unapologetically before moving on to the next female prospect.

She really couldn't stay here a moment longer. Picking up her suitcase, she headed for the Underground.

It took Helen an hour to find the right house in the tangled streets of Poplar. They clustered around the docks beyond the Tower of London, providing cramped housing for the workers who kept the port running, ships coming and going at all hours depending on the tide. The area had one foot firmly in the urban world of pavements and bricks, the other bobbing on the Thames, ruled by the natural rhythm of ebb and flow that had made this landscape long before the city arrived. When she found the right house – Number 15, Saltwell Street – she could see that the family were at home as the front door was open, children sitting on the step in the Sunday sunshine. It was a narrow two-storey property: one door, one window. You stepped immediately into the front room, went through to the kitchen and then out the back to the yard. Blink as you walked past it and you'd miss this tiny piece of London housing.

She paused by the two children, little girls of about five and seven. 'Is your mum in?'

The eldest nodded. The younger stuck her thumb in her mouth.

'Can I speak to her?'

The elder leaned back into the house and shouted, 'Mummy, there's a lady to see you!'

A baby wailed inside and Helen could hear a woman soothing it.

'Mummy!'

'Ask her in, Maddie. I'll be down in a second or two,' a woman answered from upstairs.

A trusting place, the East End, at least on sunny mornings.

Maddie got up and gestured for Helen to follow her. The front room was tidy despite the number of children Helen knew lived here from Reg's fond tales of home. Two armchairs flanked a little fireplace. A deal table occupied most of the space, a jam jar of wild flowers on a lace doily in the centre. The table did not look as though it got much use; Helen guessed it was kept for best, like her parents' front parlour. Just inside the door, two pairs of shoes waited. The children went barefoot most of the year, but now autumn was under way the ones who attended school got to wear the hand-me-downs. It brought home to her how many rungs above true poverty she had always been in Suffolk. She was slipping right down the ladder now; below this was destitution.

The stairs creaked and a woman appeared on the steep treads, carrying a baby on her shoulder. She was a pretty blonde in her late thirties, eyes tired but with a cheerful face and sprightly manner. She looked an excellent match for her indomitable husband, who had been the life and soul of his unit.

'Can I help you?' Mrs Cook asked, tucking a stray strand of hair behind her ear.

'I'm sorry to bother you on a Sunday.' Helen felt eyes studying her from the kitchen – two little faces peered round the doorway.

'Oh, that's no trouble, I assure you. Maddie, put on the kettle for our visitor.'

The capable eldest trotted through to the kitchen, followed by her golden-haired sister still sucking her thumb.

Helen twisted her handbag strap in her fingers. 'My name is Helen Sandford. I met your husband in France.'

'*Nurse* Sandford?'

Helen nodded.

'Yes, we've heard all about you!' The woman's face broke into a genuine smile of welcome. 'Reg has mentioned you in his letters. He knows your young man, doesn't he? Lieutenant Trewby?'

Her young man no longer. Helen had just been ejected from his life and was still struggling to accept that this was the best thing for him. She already knew it was a disaster for herself. 'Yes, that's right, Mrs Cook.'

'Do call me Elsie. I feel I already know you, thanks to Reg's letters.'

'Then you must call me Helen, as he does.'

'Please, sit down. Maddie, send Joan in with the biscuit tin.'

22

The fair-haired girl entered with a tin cradled in her arms, trailed by two boys, puppies sniffing after a treat.

'Our twins,' said Elsie in explanation. 'They're two and a half.' She levered the lid off the tin to reveal a small selection of plain biscuits. The boys watched her every move. 'Please, help yourself.'

Helen hadn't had breakfast. Feeling guilty to eat in front of the hungry twins, she took a broken one. Their eyes followed every motion of hand to mouth. Maddie tottered in, balancing a cup and saucer, the family's best, in her hands. Only a little tea had slopped over the side.

Helen took it from her. 'Thank you, Maddie.'

Elsie tugged her daughter to her side. 'Well done, love. This young lady here knows your dad.' The children all perked up at that; even the baby stirred and tugged at its mother's hair. 'How's Reg?'

Last time Helen saw him, he had been desperate but by now she hoped he had a cushy job back at the hospital organizing first-aid courses; that was one of the main reasons she had kept to herself her suspicions as to his theft and shouldered the blame. She hadn't wanted to spoil his chances of escaping the inferno of the front line. Now she saw all those who depended on his survival, she felt much better about her choice.

'He's well. Fully recovered from his injuries and ended up practically running the place.'

'That's my Reg.'

'He is a credit to you, Elsie.' Helen felt a smile curve her lips, her first since France, as she recalled Reg's

23

bright-eyed, battered face with those prominent ears. He wouldn't win any prizes for beauty but he beat the competition hands down when it came to spirit. 'Everyone at the hospital thought him quite the best fixer in Flanders.'

Maddie re-entered with a chipped cup of tea for her mother and put it down with a triumphant air.

'Thank you, darling.'

'Shall I take the baby, Mum?' Maddie held out her arms for the youngest.

'Take her to visit Grandma Betts.' Maddie marched out, baby in arms, Joan trailing. 'My little helper, that one. Gets it from her father.'

'She's lovely. All your children are lovely. Reg never stops talking about them.'

'Oh, how we miss him!' Elsie sipped her tea, turning her thoughts to her visitor. 'So, are you on leave, Helen?'

'No. No, not quite. I was let go.' Helen blew on her drink, not meeting Elsie's gaze.

'They can't get rid of nurses! You're like gold dust.'

Helen gave an awkward shrug, caught unawares by the tears pooling in her eyes.

Elsie got up and shepherded the twins to the front door. 'Boys, go see Grandma Betts with your sisters.'

The twins gave a last hopeful look at their family biscuit tin, then toddled out the door together, two identical little ragamuffins. Elsie waited until they had gone, then put her hand on Helen's shoulder and gave a gentle squeeze.

'You're not just here to pass on love from Reg, are you?'

Helen shook her head, throat too choked to be able to speak.

'Does whatever it is involve Reg?'

Helen nodded.

'Is he really well or did you just say that in front of the children?'

Helen had to say something; she couldn't let Elsie worry. 'He's fine, really he is. It was just some nasty business – at the hospital.'

'What kind of nastiness?'

'He . . . I'm not sure but I think he . . . um . . . removed some morphine capsules from the nurses' store before he went back to the front. You have to understand – it's hell out there and he needs to know he can help the wounded. Only the officers have them, you see – the pills, I mean – and they aren't always around when you need them.' She neglected to mention that it was also a sure way of ending suffering when it became unendurable; Elsie didn't need to know that, though she might guess.

'Oh, Reg!' Elsie did not seem surprised to hear about her husband's light fingers. 'I take it they don't exactly allow that kind of thing?'

'No.'

'Did he get caught? Is he in trouble?'

'No.' Helen took a gulp of tea.

'So what happened?'

'He didn't mean it to go like this, but I . . . I got the blame. I was on duty, you see, and it looked bad.' As much as she loved Reg, she hated what he had done to her. She wished he were here so she could shake him, shout at him, but there was only his innocent family and she needed them.

'But you didn't have them – how could they say it was you?'

'It all got rather tangled up with something else. The matron discovered my private correspondence with my mother.' Helen gathered her courage. 'She's German.' She darted a glance at Elsie, but she did not appear appalled by the admission. 'We communicate in her language as her English is a bit shaky. They thought . . . I'm not sure what they thought, but I suppose they imagined I was working for the Kaiser, emptying bedpans with evil intent.'

'Fools. So they kicked you out.' Elsie nodded sagely. 'Why didn't Reg put in a good word for you? Take the blame? He can talk his way out of anything.'

'He had already left.'

'He's back at the front?' Elsie paled, a betraying tremor in her hands making her cup rattle.

'I'm hopeful he won't be there for long. A doctor had plans to use him for duties around the hospital. There's no point Reg owning up as the real problem was my family, not the theft.'

'That's a parcel of news, and no mistake.' The two young women sat drinking their tea in thoughtful silence. The sound of children playing outside made a comforting background. Helen thought of all the newspapers scattered around the country declaring her guilt to all and sundry. A few would doubtless make their way here too. They added to her sense of being hunted, each paperboy a beater trying to flush her from the undergrowth.

'Would you like me to leave?' Helen asked when she put down her empty cup.

'Leave?' Elsie appeared shocked by the question. 'Do you have somewhere to go then?'

That question brought on a further round of swallowing to suppress tears. 'Actually, no.'

'Then you stay here.' Elsie said it with such certainty, like it had already been discussed and agreed. 'My Reg got you in this fix, so his family will be the ones to get you out. It's what he'd expect and what I want to do.'

Helen was deeply touched by Elsie's acceptance. 'Thank you.' Old tear tracks crinkled on her cheeks as they dried. 'You don't mind me being half German?'

'What a foolish question! You're Reg's friend, Helen; who your parents are is of no matter. You'll have a home here as long as you need it.' Elsie's pale blue eyes were fierce as she announced this. 'But we'd best keep it our secret. Not everyone round these parts is as fair as they might be when it comes to nationality.'

'Who am I to be, then?' Helen mopped her face, annoyed at her tears. She was stronger than this – she had to be – but she was so very scared.

'My second cousin, come to help with the children. Helen Ford. There – that's a nice unremarkable name.

And I certainly need the help.' Elsie smiled wryly, a little chip in her front tooth adding to her mischievous charm.

It was a huge relief to have a path laid out before her when she had felt so very recently as if she was teetering on a cliff edge. 'Thank you, Elsie.'

'No need to thank me, love. You helped my Reg when he needed it, so it's only right that we do the same for you. Now, if I might be so bold, you look all in. I suggest you go and lie on my bed for a few hours, and we can discuss this afternoon what we can do to sort your situation out. We'll squeeze you in somehow.' Elsie crinkled her brow. 'With the older girls, I think.'

'That sounds like heaven. I haven't slept well since it all happened.'

'I'm not surprised. You've had a shock.' Elsie led the way upstairs to the tiny front bedroom. A baby's bed was made up in the lowest drawer of the chest. She smoothed the covers on the big mattress that took up the room. 'Use my bed for the moment. Lie down and rest. It'll all look better once you've had a chance to have a nap. You won't be disturbed.'

'I'm so grateful.' Helen kicked off her shoes.

Elsie hovered at the door. 'I hope you don't mind me asking, but what did Lieutenant Trewby say to all this? Does he know – about Reg and the pills and whatnot? Reg does admire him so and would hate to lose his good opinion.'

Helen rubbed her arms, skin stippled with goose

bumps. 'No, Sebastian doesn't know. I never got a chance to see him. He won't want to be associated with me – it would ruin him.'

Elsie frowned, a little crease forming between her brows. 'Are you sure about that?' She closed the bedroom door softly behind her.

3

Sebastian alighted from the early train from Somerset and stepped into the confusion of rush-hour Paddington. He wished he had a bloodhound's nose. Helen had been through here only a few hours before, having taken the last train up the line, but it was unlikely she was still here. The possibilities were daunting in their variety: she could have boarded another train, walked out, caught a taxi, or taken the Underground. She was now one tiny needle in London's huge haystack. He had to narrow his options somehow.

A billow of smoke and steam gulped from the train's stack, rising to mingle with the other clouds in the arched roof. The once-brilliant iron-and-glass canopy was smeared with soot, blackened to a perpetual twilight. Pigeons hobnobbed on the platform.

'Can I help you, Lieutenant?' An elderly porter wheeled his trolley over, having taken note of Sebastian's uniform, valise and his walking stick.

'I hope so.' Sebastian reached in his pocket for the portrait of Helen he had drawn only last year. 'I'm looking for a young lady who came through here late last night.'

The porter squinted at the picture, wild white eyebrows twitching. 'Well now, maybe I see her, maybe I don't. Can't be sure. So many people come through here, you understand.'

Sebastian pressed a shilling into the man's palm. 'Does that improve your memory?'

The coin disappeared into a pocket. 'That it does. She was sitting over by the ticket office. Looked a bit lost, to tell the truth, sir. Might still be there for all I know.'

Sebastian felt a surge of hope. 'Show me, please!'

The porter hefted his valise on to his trolley and led the way to the main concourse. Sebastian's officer's uniform gave him more respect than his injury – wounded men were all too common. Soldiers on leave moved out of his way. One touched his cap. Had they served together? Sebastian was in too much of a rush to check. His mind was consumed by the thought that Helen might still be here. He imagined catching her in his arms and scolding her for having had so little faith in him that she hadn't shared her troubles. Then he would kiss her, take her home and put right every little thing that had harmed her. He had no doubts that she was innocent, so all it would take would be finding out who the real thief was and clearing her name.

The porter stopped by a patch of pavement on the far side of the station. He scratched his head, dislodging his cap. His expression told Sebastian he was disappointed that he would not now get the generous tip for reuniting the lieutenant with his girl. 'That was where she was, sir, but she's gone.'

With his spirits in a sickening free fall from hope to hopelessness, Sebastian gave the man another shilling. 'Thank you. There are more like that if you can find anyone who saw her leave.'

'Very good, sir.' The man tapped the peak of his cap.

Sebastian stood beside his case, wondering what he should do next. He did his own surveillance, asking himself who might have been lingering long enough to see Helen. A couple of soldiers were sitting with their backs propped up on kitbags. They looked as though they had been there a while and were likely to have noticed a pretty girl.

'Excuse me.'

The men looked up from their cigarettes, saw the uniform and got to their feet with weary discipline. 'Sir?'

'Have you seen this girl at the station?' He handed over his precious drawing, feeling uncomfortable to have Helen's image passed from hand to hand like a banknote. 'The porter told me she rested a while by the wall, but I'm trying to find out what happened next. It would have been last night, or early this morning.'

'Sorry, sir, I was asleep,' said the first man.

The other one took a longer moment to study the picture. 'I think I might've seen her, sir, about two hours ago. Yes, I remember because she looked respectable, not the sort to sit waiting for customers. She turned away a sailor who couldn't tell his bints apart. I could've told him he was sniffing around the wrong bit of skirt –' the Tommy suddenly remembered who he was talking to – 'begging your pardon, sir.'

'And did you see where she went?'

'To the Underground. I'm sure of it – I watched her, considering if I should offer to carry her case, but decided against it. She seemed the sort to want to be alone, if you know what I mean.'

Like she did not want to flirt with a fresh lad on leave.

'Thank you, private.' No money for the men, but Sebastian offered them the pick of his cigarette case instead. 'How long are you here?'

'Our train leaves at eleven, sir.'

'Would you be so kind as to watch my case while I ask at the ticket office?'

'Of course, sir.'

Sebastian limped away, leaning heavily on his stick. He had not done so much walking since he'd been carried off the battlefield, but he guessed the soldiers would know that too, experienced as they all had become in deaths and injuries. He would be thought one of the lucky ones: invalided out of service but with all his limbs and faculties intact.

Fearing he was reaching the end of his trail before it ran cold, Sebastian waited in line and then thrust the picture at the ticket seller. 'Excuse me, sir. Have you seen this lady this morning, about two hours ago?'

The clerk gave a bored glance down at the picture, but

33

then his eyes lit up. 'I did, Lieutenant. An early customer. Very polite.'

'Do you remember where she went?'

'She was heading east, that was all she said.' The clerk's gaze went to the long queue behind him. 'If you don't mind, sir, I have to get on.'

'Yes, thank you for your time.' Sebastian drew back the picture and stepped away from the window. His gaze fell on the newspaper seller waving the latest edition for the commuters to pluck from his fingers. Helen's name was stamped on every front page, but the girl herself had vanished. Gone east.

He took some encouragement from that. 'Gone west' was slang in the trenches for death in battle; going east sounded somehow hopeful, towards the rising sun. He would find lodgings at his club, then visit her old haunts. Helen could not literally vanish. She would have to have somewhere to live, somewhere to work. He would simply keep looking until he found her.

Over German lines, France, 13 June 1917, noon

Thoughts of a quiet morning of surveillance disappeared when Sebastian scanned the skies and spotted the V-formation heading for his flight. Three aircraft, coming from the east to attack. He and another scout peeled off from the observation mission to intercept, a third plane joining them to even up the numbers. A second V appeared just behind the first. Not so good – they had stumbled upon a German patrol and they were currently over the enemy's lines. Bursts of Archie, as pilots called the anti-aircraft fire, rocked his Pup as the ground forces took a bead on the British encroachers. They hadn't yet found their range; Sebastian's plane was buffeted in the eddies of the explosions.

Now was not the time to remember that the average life expectancy of a pilot on the front was three weeks. Sebastian had already survived far beyond his allotment.

Still, his role was to counter-attack, not run. The photographers in the other two-seater planes had to get their intelligence back to headquarters. As the Germans came closer, they opened fire. Sebastian picked his target – the one in the middle – and dived at it head on, squeezing the trigger of his machine-gun as he approached. The Pup was equipped with the new synchronized mechanism that allowed him to shoot through the propeller, a huge tactical advantage on the old machines. His daring attack – a mad kind of 'chicken' game to see who would give way first – caused the middle plane to push his nose down and pass underneath, while the two on the outside fanned sideways and climbed, making Sebastian's Pup the filling in this particular German sandwich.

Not a good tactical position.

Taking a quick glance around, he saw that his two colleagues had taken on the second part of the patrol, leaving him with the front three. He couldn't let them get past him and catch up with the photography mission. Turning sharply, he came up behind the German trio, approaching in the blind spot just under their tails but not too close to get caught in their slipstream. When he had one in his sights, he fired. A lucky burst of bullets passed through the fuselage and must have hit the pilot or a vital control because the plane veered to the left, losing formation. It peeled off and turned for German lines. One down.

Now he had their notice. The two triplane Fokkers wheeled around like vultures scenting a kill, their three-tiered wings making his little Pup look hopelessly outclassed. He wasn't sticking to a collision course this time, as that meant risking two streams of machine-gun fire. He climbed, pushing his plane to the upper ceiling of its endurance, all too aware that the triplanes were superior climbers. The temperature plunged. He flexed his fingers, frozen despite his layers of silk, leather and sheepskin. A quick look behind told him he hadn't shaken the pursuit. His Vickers gun needed a new drum of ammunition, but he had too much on his hands with the manoeuvring to risk the change-over. A sudden spray of wood chips near his left shoulder told him that one pilot at least had found his range.

Then his engine spluttered, coughed, spluttered once more and fell silent. Either the fuel had run out thanks to a hole in the tank or the line had been cut. Whichever the case, he was pretty much a lame duck with no engine. There was only one defence to that with two Germans on your tail. Sebastian closed the throttle and sent his plane into a tight vertical spin. It might look to the enemy that they'd got him; the odds were they'd leave him to crash. Only a very careful opponent would follow him down this suicidal spiral. Thrown back in his seat by the G-force, Sebastian prayed his pursuers were of the careless inclination.

East End of London, 12.30 p.m.

Helen did not hear the warning. No one inside the factory did; the noise of the machines was far louder than the whistle of a policeman cycling by with a sign around his neck telling Londoners to take cover. Mrs Hopper, however, had posted a boy on the front steps and he rushed in, socks collapsed to his ankles in his hurry.

'Missus, missus, the Germans are coming!' he yelled.

The machines stopped abruptly and stools scraped on the floor as the women headed for the stairs to the basement. Helen grabbed her handbag and coat – it could be cold down there and it might be some time before they were given the all-clear. The first rumbles and thumps told them that the anti-aircraft batteries had opened up. As these were manned by half-blind rejects from the service in France, they were much mocked for their lack of success. As far as Helen knew, they had yet to bring a plane down. The most casualties they caused were from when the shells returned to earth and hit unsuspecting civilians with their shrapnel.

Helen chose a spot on the floor by the stairs and sat down, arms around her knees. In past raids, she had proved cooler under fire than most of the women. Her time in France had hardened her to the risk of shells and bombs. She knew how to judge if one would fall close by, and so far all the sounds suggested action was a mile or so away. She had worked out the odds – she would have to be monumentally unlucky to be a target. Mind you, with her recent past, it could well happen. She hoped the women wouldn't realize this and treat her like Jonah, when he got cast over the side to be swallowed by a whale.

As during other raids, some of her colleagues were so distressed that they fainted before reaching the basement, making life even more difficult for those who had to cart them down to the shelter. Nelly had a few tart things to say about Bernadette's lack of backbone as she carried her friend down the stairs with the help of Mrs Hopper. Helen felt sad for them all. They just weren't prepared for warfare. Britain's island status had bred these people to expect to be immune from direct attack, and to find they were not was a shock that was still working through the populace of the south-east.

'How about a singsong?' suggested Nelly. Helen got the impression the woman would propose a knees-up in Hell if she came face to face with the Devil. Nelly didn't wait for agreement but struck up a rousing version of 'Pack up your troubles in your old kitbag and smile, smile, smile!' Helen joined in, doing as the song said. What else could you do in the madness of some anonymous German pilot trying to kill you? There had been no time for singing at the hospital in France when the guns were firing; being kept busy there had helped keep the fear at bay. Nelly's idea of going through all the popular tunes they knew collectively had the same distracting effect even if it was absurd.

'The boy I love is up in the gallery!' crooned Nelly, changing to a music-hall favourite.

Helen's voice stumbled over the words of this one. Her boy was up, not in the gallery, but in some newfangled plane over France. She said a quick prayer for his safety. He had to be all right – had to be. She didn't think she could bear losing him; he was what made this life worth living.

Dust fell from the ceiling as vibrations rattled the earth. Buildings had not been constructed with this punishment in mind. Helen studied the cellar, trying to guess how well it had been built. She pushed away thoughts of being entombed as others had been as a result of aerial attack. Part of her preferred to take her chances out in the open, but the air would be buzzing with shrapnel so that was not a rational choice. She had to sit tight.

'The boy I love is up in the gallery, the boy I love is looking now at me,' Nelly belted out. 'There he is, can't you see, waving his handkerchief, as merry as a robin that sings on a tree.'

Helen clutched her locket and bent her head to her knees, finding her nerves were not as robust as she had thought. The pendant warmed in her palm, just the size of a robin's egg.

Sebastian stared unseeing at the sketchpad he held on his lap, pretending to be busy so no one would talk to him. He had reached the end of his strength. He had started off so full of hope; he'd even gone into a jeweller's and bought Helen a locket so he had a present to give her when he found her – a talisman with his picture in to remind her he would be on her side, no matter what. Having spent a week retracing all the places with which Helen had any connection, he had drawn a blank. The page below his pencil was empty, just like his search results. He couldn't blame her for not going back to any of the places he had visited; the reception had been universally hostile. The staff at her old hospital, Queen Charlotte's, had wanted to distance themselves from 'the German nurse', as they called her. Her former matron had acted as if Helen had purposely set out to hurt her with her lies about her provenance. Her shock wasn't fabricated: she really did feel aggrieved, and Sebastian's claim that Helen was a victim of false accusations had been brushed off. The fault was not the theft but the secrecy about Helen's real identity.

'What does that matter?' Sebastian had wanted to shout. 'She was a fine nurse and you know it!' But what was the point? The impression of betrayal had been stamped on Sister Hardwick and could not be rubbed away. Depressingly, he was unable to trace Molly Juniper, Helen's friend from training days: she was now deployed in France so would not have been able to help in any case.

Helen's old landlady in Whitechapel had been close-mouthed on the subject. The woman's surname of Glock had made her an object of suspicion, though the origin was Jewish, and she could not afford to advertise her link to the infamous nurse. Sebastian could tell Mrs Glock thought Helen a victim and he believed her when she said that she had not heard from her one-time tenant, but that was the end of the conversation, the door snapped shut in his face.

At least it hadn't been slammed, as others had been.

His last port of call was the Palace Theatre. Helen's sister Flora had been part of the chorus for a year and Helen had helped out backstage. He expected a more sympathetic audience here but got only hostile stares from the girls who knew her and flirtatious invitations from the new blood. One unbent enough to inform him that Toots Bailey, the chorus member who had been closest to Flora, had left to marry a retired general; she was living in the elderly lap of luxury somewhere in the Home Counties, just as she had always hoped. Once that gentleman passed to his Maker, there would be one very lively, wealthy widow in town.

'Thank you, ladies,' said Sebastian, bowing himself out of the dressing room, as the performance was about to start.

'Catch me after the show, handsome?' called one blonde, blowing him a kiss.

Sebastian was no longer as shy as once he had been; years in the army had cured him of that. 'A lovely offer, miss, but one, alas, I cannot take up: I'm already spoken for.'

'If it's that Helen Sandford, then she doesn't deserve you,' grumbled another, making a moue in the mirror as she touched up her lipstick.

'I assure you that it is quite the other way round.' He closed the door, relieved to be free of the perfumed and silken atmosphere.

And now he was sitting in his club, with nothing to report, no leads for him to follow. What was left? He could walk the streets looking for her, but that was futile. Where was she? He knew she would be unlikely to go home to Suffolk, not to the hammer fists of her father and cowed mother. There would be no welcome there. So how was she surviving? She had little or no money. He felt a rush of panic as he contemplated her choices. The pencil point broke under the pressure of his hand, leaving its lead buried in the paper.

Someone took the chair opposite him. Long legs crossed, settling to stay for a while. Couldn't the man see he wanted to be left in peace? Sebastian ran his finger over the broken pencil, feeling the scratch of the ragged end on the sensitive pad of his index. One of the club waiters arrived with a tray and two glasses of brandy.

'Your drinks, sir.'

The man gestured for them to be left on the table between them.

'Will that be all?'

'Yes. Thank you.'

Sebastian looked up and met his father's kind grey eyes, his tawny hair swept back from his forehead. Long-limbed like his son, he did not fit well on most chairs, this one no exception. His hands were folded together, fingers tapping in thought. He nodded to the brandy.

'For you. It looks like you need it.'

'Thanks.' Why was he here? Come to fetch the errant son home?

'How are you?'

'Leg's much better, thank you. I've been too busy to think much about my injury and have managed well with the cane you gave me.'

'I wasn't asking about your leg, though I'm pleased to hear that.'

'Do you know what I'm doing in London?' Sebastian wondered how much the ones who had confronted Helen at the ball had told his father.

'Your Aunt Gertrude told me some nonsense about your young lady being mixed up with a theft and spying for Germany. Utter rot. I assume you hared off to London to offer her your help?'

Sebastian took a sip of the brandy, conscious of his maimed hand curled around the glass. His little finger on the left was missing thanks to his experience on the battle-field of the Somme. 'Something like that. I can't find her.'

'Well, it is only human nature that she will have wanted to vanish. Lick her wounds somewhere in private.'

'I could help her.'

'Could you? She stands accused of things she cannot

defend herself against. She probably fled to spare you the mud-slinging that has come her way.'

'I'm sure she did.'

Theodore Trewby cleared his throat. 'I'm sorry to say that Jilly Glanville and your aunt were not kind to her; neither was your grandfather's butler. I took them to task for it but they admitted they had been cruel, thinking her a traitor. You mustn't blame her for running.'

Sebastian closed his eyes. 'I don't blame Helen. I blame this blasted war.'

'What are you going to do?'

Sebastian shrugged, his throat tight with emotion. 'I've looked everywhere I know to search. She would have had no welcome anywhere; every door would have been closed to her.'

'Do you think she will contact you?'

'I fear she's being the martyr – sacrificing herself for what she thinks is my benefit – but she doesn't know me very well if she expects me to let her get away with that.' It hurt that she hadn't wanted to trust him with her pain. He had thought their relationship had gone deeper than that, to a point where she knew she could bring any trouble to him and he would help her shoulder the burden.

'You can't stay here though.'

'No.'

Theo lit a cigar, the ritual buying Sebastian time to regain control of his emotions. 'Look, Seb, I know a few useful men, former Scotland Yard detectives. I've used them to track down a client or two who have tried to run out on their responsibilities. Why don't you employ them to search for you?'

He liked the idea of the lines of enquiry spreading from his single effort to a network. 'That's a good notion. Yes, I'll do that. They mustn't scare her away, though, if they find her.'

'Naturally. Trust me: they have more discretion than that.'

Sebastian's gloom lifted a little now he had a plan. 'I'll come back with you but I think I should warn you, I've decided I'm going to return to active duty.'

Theo looked grim but resigned. 'Can't say I'm surprised. This isn't a time when young men can sit at home.'

'I'm thinking of signing on for pilot training with the Royal Flying Corps if they'll have me. This leg will slow me down in the army.'

'I can't tempt you with a back-room position, something in Whitehall perhaps?'

Sebastian shook his head. 'We have to end this thing. It isn't going to be settled by people sitting at desks.' And, he added silently, only once peace had been declared would Helen be really safe and able to come out of hiding. Whatever the personal cost, he wanted a world where she could live openly.

Theo sighed. 'What about taking on an observer's role, doing the surveillance and photography?'

His father had been dropping hints in this direction for

some time but it was no good. Nothing in war was really safe. 'I thought about it when you mentioned it the first time, but I think I'd prefer to be the one in charge of the controls. Depending on another man's skill was what got me shot.' He took a sip of brandy. 'And besides, flying a plane sounds like a challenge I'd enjoy.'

'I can understand that. It's a glamorous profession, though it gives me nothing but more grey hairs to contemplate it. I'm proud of you for being willing to do your duty when you have an excuse not to.'

'Thank you, Pa.' Theodore Trewby always supported his sons even when he would prefer another course.

'Just make sure you do your very best to survive this insanity. The war's taken Neil – that's more than enough for your mother and me to bear.'

Throat tightening again, Sebastian remembered his older brother, lost at sea. He rubbed his neck to loosen the chokehold. 'I'll try my damnedest, sir.'

They spent the rest of the hour sipping the last of the club's stock of pre-war brandy, steering clear of topics to do with the conflict that raged beyond the doors of the hushed library.

4

'Elsie, Elsie love!'

Helen rolled over, burying her head in the pillow. Joan's sharp elbows were digging in her ribs and Maddie's cold feet were chilling her legs. Sharing a bed with two little girls did not make for a quiet night and she could do without the early-morning interruption.

'Come on, love, let me in! I'm freezing me walnuts off out 'ere.' Now Helen recognized that voice: Reg. Unwelcome like a lump of coal from Saint Nicholas, she didn't want to see him. She didn't trust herself to keep a hold on her temper.

There was an excited squeal from the front bedroom where Elsie slept with the baby. The two twins slept on a truckle-bed by the kitchen fire, like two puppies rolled together in a blanket. Helen could hear them thumping on the door as they jumped in vain for the handle.

Joan and Maddie were awake now too. No point asking children to go back to sleep on Christmas morning. They knew full well that knobbly stockings of treats were waiting for them downstairs.

'What is it?' asked Maddie with a yawn. 'Who's outside?'

The front window was thrown open with a rattle of wood in the frame. 'Reg! Reg! Is that you?' Elsie had to be hanging out of the casement in her excitement.

'Now there's a real Christmas present for this lucky fellow!'

Trust her old comrade to wangle leave at Christmas when such a thing was as rare as a decent bit of meat at the butcher's. Helen hurried the girls from the bed.

'Quickly, sweethearts, your daddy's downstairs; go give him a hug.'

The two girls leapt from the covers and raced their mother to the door, bare feet flashing on the cold lino. Helen lay on her back and gazed at the ceiling as she listened to the excited chatter. The little boys joined in, giggling and chirping as their dad produced the marvel of sweets from one of his pockets.

The joy downstairs emphasized her loneliness. Taking her time, she got up and dressed. If she had her way, she would avoid seeing Reg entirely. But the baby had other ideas. The little one woke up and discovered she had been left out of the party. Her wails built in strength.

Helen picked her up out of her drawer bed and settled her on her shoulder.

'There, there, angel. Let's take you to see your daddy.'

Familiar now with Helen's touch, the baby snuggled into her neck and allowed herself to be carried down.

Reg was already ensconced in his seat in the kitchen

by the stove, boots off, socks confiscated for the wash, toes wriggling in the warmth. His four children were gathered around him, listening to his tales of the war, heavily edited for their benefit. He was telling them about a dog the hospital had adopted who had an uncanny knack of predicting enemy attacks. Elsie was bustling about, getting breakfast ready. She kept casting wondering looks at her husband as if she could hardly believe that he was here.

The baby gave Helen's presence away with a proud 'Da-Da'. Reg looked up and reached out to take the child. 'Here's my clever girl! Speaking already!' he exclaimed and jiggled the baby on his lap. He wasn't meeting Helen's gaze. 'And Miss Helen. How are you, love? Elsie says you've been a godsend, helping out with the little ones. She doesn't know how she managed before you came.'

'She's been wonderful,' Elsie said breezily, not wanting the awkwardness between Helen and her husband to spoil the moment.

'I'm well, thank you, Mr Cook,' Helen said stiffly. 'Your family have been very kind to me.'

'It's Reg, love, as well you know.' He waved the baby's fist at her in mock reprimand.

The children didn't want their father's attention taken up by the outsider in their midst.

'Daddy, Daddy, tell me about the tanks: have you seen one?' asked Maddie.

Reg turned to his eldest and tweaked her nose. 'Why,

49

yes I have. Lots and lots of 'em. Miss Helen has too. We saw our first one together.'

Helen shook her head slightly. She had not told the children anything of her time in France in case they said too much to one of the neighbours.

Reg, sensing his mistake, quickly ploughed on. 'They're great big things, like a tug on the river, but these beasties go on land. They have tracks instead of wheels, if you can imagine it! Anything that gets in the way is squashed flat as a pancake.' He slapped his thigh, making the baby giggle.

Helen moved over to where Elsie was laying the table. 'I think I'll go for a little walk,' she told her. 'Leave you in peace.'

'There's no need. Have some breakfast.' Elsie's hand fluttered on Helen's forearm, an uncertain gesture pleading for a truce.

Helen covered Elsie's fingers with her own and squeezed her reassurance. 'It's fine, Elsie, really it is. I'll be back in an hour. You only have him for a few days. I'm just in the way.'

Wrapping up in her scarf and second-hand winter coat, Helen stepped out on to the street. No picturesque snow had fallen to make this a proper Christmas scene, but at least the rooftops were glittering with frost. Windows had been etched with feathers of rime. Breath puffing like smoke from a steam engine, Helen made her way down to the riverside. She passed noisy houses full of children shouting with excitement, quiet ones where the owners were taking a chance to sleep in. A few had no homemade decorations – news of the death of a loved one having sucked all Christmas cheer from them. The whispers were constant up and down the streets in this part of London.

'Have you heard, Johnny Baitman's gone? . . . Mrs Eastman's son's missing . . . The carpenter's boy, he's died of his wounds, they say.' Gossip, once a chief amusement over the fences and on street corners, was now a grim litany of loss.

She had to walk some way to find a place where she could see the river. Most of the riverbank was fenced off as part of the huge dockyards. Taking a route west, she came out by the Tower of London and had as her reward one of the prettiest views of the Thames, framed by the magnificent bridge. For the only time in the year, the river itself was quiet, no craft making journeys this early on a Christmas morning. She had the bank to herself, apart from a companionable raven that had somehow escaped from the Tower to pick at the crumbs left on the embankment.

She looked across the green rise to the stone walls of the old fortress. 'You'd better get back in there,' she told the raven, 'or the Tower might fall.'

The raven was uninterested in his legendary duties and strutted onwards with huge self-importance. Perhaps he knew something she didn't about the state of the war. It was no longer unthinkable that something as solid as the Tower might collapse, the way the conflict was developing.

The gravel crunched under boots.

'Elsie told me I'd find you here.' Reg came to stand beside her. Somehow she wasn't surprised to see him.

'It's my favourite place round these parts.'

'Mine too. Used to pick pockets over there when I was a nipper.' He pointed to the gate where the tourists lined up to enter the Tower. 'Reformed character now, I hasten to add.'

She wasn't so sure about that. 'What are you doing here now, Reg? You should be with your family, not running after me.'

'I can't sit with them, knowing I've an apology to make to you.'

'An apology? Is that what you think I want?' Her voice cracked as her control slipped.

Reg took out a cigarette, fingers trembling as he lit the end. 'I dunno, love. I cocked up, didn't I? Hurt you by mistake.'

Helen tugged at the frayed ends of her red knitted scarf, a substitute for strangling him. Having battened down her emotions for so long, they were on the point of erupting from her in a scalding lava of blame. 'A mistake, was that what you call it?'

'Yeah, of course. I didn't mean you to get caught.' He puffed a little plume of smoke like a sigh of regret. He didn't see it — just didn't grasp how completely he had destroyed her life.

She began to laugh, but the feeling inside was perilously close to tears. 'Reg, your "mistake" has cost me everything. My nursing, my name, my future. It's not something that an apology can mend.'

He opened his mouth to speak but she cut him off.

'I can't say "I forgive you" and then everything'll be all right again because it won't. It really won't. And I find myself wanting to hate you for that.' She blinked back the tears, knotting her fingers in the scarf. The river swirled round the buttresses of the bridge, a muddy brown on this overcast winter's morning. Traitors' Gate, the waterside entrance to the Tower, was half-drowned by the tide. She couldn't look at Reg – couldn't bring herself to face the man who had been her undoing. 'God, if only I could.'

Reg ground his cigarette out under his boot. 'Jesus Christ, love, I'm so sorry. Please hate me if it'd make you feel better.' He took one of her hands and used it to hit his chest. 'Go on: make a fist, take a shot at me! I deserve it. I dunno what to do, how to make it right.'

She let her hand drop when he released it. 'That's the thing, Reg: this isn't something you can fix. It's torn me apart. I'm beyond mending.'

'Let me try –'

'No!' She couldn't bear it if he offered her hope he couldn't deliver.

They stood in silence for a minute, Helen battling despair and fury, Reg racked with guilt. Then the tears came, despite her best efforts to stop them.

'Oh, Reg.'

He pulled her to his chest and hugged her tightly. 'Go

on, love, cry. If anyone needs a good weep, it's you. You've been so brave.' Her shoulders heaved and she could feel that she was getting his shirt wet, but he kept on talking and stroking her back, patiently waiting for the storm to pass. 'When I heard what had happened, I was ashamed. I wanted to confess but you'd gone. The doctors said you were German or some such nonsense. Do you still want me to put 'em right?'

That bridge had been well and truly burnt behind her; there was no way back to the nursing service.

'I will. I'll set those doctors straight – demand they prosecute me instead. I can't bear you taking the blame for me.'

He would as well; this was no empty offer.

'There's no point, Reg. I didn't tell because I didn't want you to lose your chance of a safer job.' Helen pushed away from his chest. The sensation inside was like when her father had punched her in the stomach: winded with a dull, lingering pain, but crying had helped a little.

He reluctantly let her go. 'I got the job, thanks to you. But it don't seem fair, what with you being kicked out, blamed for my mistake.'

'Nothing about this war is fair.' Helen leant on the parapet, flicking a stick that had fallen there into the river, sending some of her anger with it. She watched it bob away, battered by little waves. 'My mother is German, you know. They were right about that.'

Reg threw a second twig. His went twice as far into

the main channel, where it was swept rapidly away. 'Who cares?'

'Quite a lot of people, it seems.'

'Elsie and me don't give a fiddler's jig for that. What did your lieutenant say about it all?'

Helen toyed with a leaf, brown and brittle. 'I don't know. I thought it best to . . . well, what could he do?'

Reg did not look pleased by her answer. 'He could've stood by you, that's what he could've done.'

'He would've, but my reputation has been ruined; I didn't want his destroyed as well.'

'Wasn't that for him to decide?'

'I did what I thought right at the time.'

He scowled. 'That's not right and you know it – not right you should face this alone.'

'Reg, there's nothing anyone can do.' She scrunched up the leaf, letting the dust fall from her gloves into the water, then brushed her hands clean. She was used to being alone.

'If you won't let me fix that, then at least let me make some amends now.' Reg offered her his arm. 'How about a bit of breakfast, eh? Spend the day with Elsie, the little ones and me? Let us help find you a silver lining, if we can.'

The rush of anger had passed, leaving her exhausted. Reg had said he was sorry; making him feel worse by refusing his kindness achieved nothing. 'I can do that.' She slipped her hand through the crook of his elbow. Turning their back on Traitors' Gate, they headed home.

Sebastian had become used to the fact that the greatest part of training for a pilot was spent waiting. If the weather wasn't favourable, or the planes were not ready, some other chap was first in the queue, or the trainee feeling under par, the answer was the same: back to the mess to wait. Not that he was complaining: he'd rather sit it out in a warm room on Salisbury Plain than in the mud of France.

Holly and ivy wound round the door frames and the pillars of the long, low-ceilinged room, chief apartment in the old house the Royal Flying Corps had requisitioned. Over at the piano, Charlie Cordel, a golden-haired, brown-eyed innocent of a lieutenant, was banging out a selection of Christmas carols. Two other men were playing ping-pong on a dining-room table, a row of books serving as the net. The buzz of conversation and laughter made it a pleasant place to wait.

The reason why they were all sitting by the fire today and not learning the rather pressing task of how to defeat Germans in the air was that the cloud was too low. Too many pilots lost lives and valuable equipment in training accidents to risk sending the new ones up in anything short of fair conditions. Sebastian therefore had plenty of time to leaf through his correspondence. He was studying the most recent report from the private detective agency his father had recommended. They had dispatched one of their most trusted people, a Miss

Kenley – 'she comes with impeccable references' – to Haverhill to investigate if Helen had returned to her family. Her report made disturbing reading. There had been no sign of Helen, but it appeared Mr and Mrs Sandford had parted due to the lady's shockingly guilty state of having been born German. When he had come across that sentence, Sebastian had wanted to lob something at Mr Sandford for his lack of loyalty to his wife of many years. However, the wryly phrased Miss Kenley reported that Mrs Sandford appeared to be happy, having been taken in by a distant cousin of her husband who did not worry about such ridiculous accidents of birth. The authorities had not interned her as she was living so quietly, there seemed no point. Mrs Sandford had confided to Miss Kenley that she was anxious for her daughters, however, having not heard from either of them for many months. Sebastian knew how that felt.

'Close the lid on the piano, Cordel, old boy!' called Tufty Burton, one of the most qualified pilots among them. 'I've got a new disc for the gramophone.'

When Charlie didn't move quickly enough, another trainee did it for him, nipping his fingers in the lid.

'Ouch!' Charlie blew on his nails. 'You've just ruined a promising musical career!'

'Hardly. Spared our ear-drums, rather!' Tufty reverently slipped the disc from its cardboard case and put it on the turntable like a priest making an offering. Winding the handle, he dropped the needle in the groove. With some preliminary crackles, the familiar strains of 'Eine kleine Nachtmusik' wound from the horn as if there was a tiny orchestra hidden in the wooden box under the disc, a little modern miracle.

'Don't you have something we can dance to?' complained Charlie. He always moaned when anyone put on classical music, preferring tunes that were all the rage in London. 'Haven't you got something sung by Lily Elsie?'

'If only she were here!' sighed Tufty dramatically. The actress was the mess's favourite muse; all had been on pilgrimages to see her in the West End hit, *The Admirable Crichton*. He picked up a cushion for a partner and did an impromptu quickstep to Mozart, to the howls of his audience, concluding with a passionate smack on the lips (or decorative button in the case of the pillow). 'No, you're right, Miss Lily, it is no good for dancing.' He cast the pillow back on the chair and lifted the needle.

'How about something to sing to?' He put on the mess's favourite record, Ivor Novello's 'Keep the Home-Fires Burning'. 'Come on, lads, up and at it!' He conducted his fellow pilots as they joined in the words. Distracted by Tufty's antics and enjoying the tune, Sebastian forgot to keep his contribution muted, letting his rich tenor swell.

The cushion sailed towards Sebastian and hit him on the back of the head, scattering his letters to the floor. 'Hello, Trewby, that's quite a voice you've got there,' said Tufty. 'Lily wants an introduction. Choirboy, were you?'

Sebastian chucked Lily-the-pillow back. 'Never had that pleasure.'

'You should've been.'

Charlie leapt on a chair. 'A solo from Trewby! A solo!'

Sebastian shook his head and bent to gather his papers.

'No shirkers. Up with you, Trewby.' Tufty was giving it his best sergeant-major voice. 'What have you got to lose?'

'My pride?' Sebastian retorted.

'Rubbish. How can you hope to face the Hun if you can't face your friends?'

'*They* don't ask me to sing.'

'Come on, "There's a silver lining, Through the dark clouds shining" – that's a line for a pilot if ever there was one!'

'Trew-by! Trew-by!' chanted the other men, refusing to let him wriggle from the hook.

'All right, play the damned record again.' The quickest way out of this was to sing a verse. He refused the chair Charlie wanted him to stand on but stood firmly on his own feet. Once he set out on the first verse, he found the lyrics difficult to sing. 'Till the boys come home' – so few of his friends had. He forged on, the others joining in at the chorus. Sentiment was not welcome in the mess. The empty chair of a fallen comrade was nodded to once, then throats were cleared and life attacked once more. He finished to a nice round of applause, so he bowed with operatic flourish.

The needle lifted from the disc with a pop. Their instructor, Captain Ward, had come to put an end to the party. 'All right, men, clouds have cleared. Report to the sheds.'

'Yes, sir!'

It was late in the day to begin flying again, but no one wanted to miss the chance. Putting in sufficient practice hours was the only way you could hope to be prepared for deployment. Too many pilots had gone out with too few hours on their record sheet. Sebastian bundled his letters together, noticing the unfamiliar writing on one envelope he hadn't yet opened. It had been sent first to his home and then forwarded to him by his parents, so was a good few days late in being delivered. As he jogged to his billet to fetch his helmet and gloves, he broke it open. A letter from Reg Cook, his old servant in the trenches. The writing was carefully formed; the correspondent was a man not used to using his pen to get his way, relying on his wits instead. Sebastian chuckled to himself, fond memories of Cook rushing back.

> *Dear Lieutenant Trewby,*
>
> *I hope this finds you well. I have been given ten days' leave and wondered if you would meet me in London before I head back to France. I have news of a certain young lady of our acquaintance that I want to share with you.*
>
> *Yours sincerely*
> *Reginald Cook (Lance-Corporal)*

The laughter caught in Sebastian's throat as surprise took over. Finally – someone who knew something about

Helen! This was the break in the clouds he had been waiting for. He hadn't dreamt that she would go to Cook rather than to him; he had underestimated how close they had become over the summer when they served together in the field hospital. Cook was just the sort of capable, paternal chap to take a young girl under his wing; he should have considered the possibility Cook had stepped into the slot abandoned by Helen's real father. Worried he was too late to catch the soldier on leave, Sebastian checked the date – it had been written on Christmas Day. If he sent a telegram immediately, he might be able to reach Cook before he went back to his regiment.

But the clouds had cleared and duty came first. Cursing all the way to the sheds where his antiquated BE2b awaited him, he prayed his message would arrive before Cook's troop train left for Dover.

Piccadilly, London, 2 January 1917, 12.05 p.m.

Helen ran her fingers down the spines of the books shelved in the History section of Hatchard's bookshop. Many were pre-war publications, no stinting on leather binding and paper quality, far beyond her budget if she had been here to purchase one. Would they ever be read or was their purpose to be bought for show in some old buffer's library? She could feel the eyes of the assistant following her, the woman's instincts correctly warning that Helen was not a proper customer. Helen gave the lady a weak smile, part apology, part attempt to pre-empt any move to have her ushered out. She couldn't leave yet, as she had promised to be here.

Reg had departed that morning with brave cheerios and cuddles for each of his children, his leave over far too soon for everyone's wishes. He had asked Helen to accompany him to Victoria and – as her next shift was not until the following day and Elsie was nursing the baby, who had a bad cold – she had of course agreed. Then the infuriating man had remembered he had promised a chum that he would meet him in Hatchard's that lunchtime, having miscalculated how long it would take him to return to the military hospital. He asked Helen to take a message, explaining to his friend that he would not be able to make their appointment.

'Hatchard's, Reg? I didn't think you were the reading sort,' teased Helen.

'I'm not. My mate is. History section, don't forget.'

'What's your friend like?'

Reg grinned and tugged his cap straight. 'Oh, he's a little wisp of a fellow – straw-blond hair, spots, short-sighted. No risk to a lady, I promise you.'

Helen felt rather sorry for this poor specimen of manhood; she couldn't add to his woes and leave him languishing in a bookshop. 'All right, I'll run your message. It's fortunate for you that I like browsing in Hatchard's.'

'Noon sharp. Don't make him wait.'

'I won't. What's his name?'

Reg's expression went blank for a second. 'Private Albert . . . um . . . Jones.'

Something wasn't quite right about this. 'Albert Um Jones?'

'Yeah. Known as Jonesy to his friends. Plays the mouth-organ like a champ and keeps whippets.' Reg was looking decidedly shifty.

'So I'm waiting for a skinny, pimpled fellow called Albert, dog lover with the dubious skill of serenading us on a mouth-organ? You do give me the most glamorous assignments, Reg.'

The whistle on the steam train, warning that it was ready to depart, cut off her words.

He winked and shook her hand. 'Don't I just. Tell Elsie I'll write as soon as I can.' He shouldered his kitbag and went through the gate to the train. 'Thanks for seeing me off.'

Standing with the other women who had come to bid their men farewell, Helen waved until she could no longer spot Reg's cap in the sea of khaki. She refused any morbid thoughts that this could be the last time she saw him. He would be returning to a safer post than many in that crowd. Reg was nothing if not one of life's survivors.

And now she was waiting in Hatchard's on his behalf, preparing a little speech for this spotty Private Jones. She hoped he did not expect her to take Reg's place at luncheon. She had her excuses all ready, just in case he summoned up the nerve to ask her, and reminded herself not to let the fact that she felt sorry for him undermine her good judgement.

The bell over the shop door jangled.

The assistant perked up. 'How can I help you, sir?'

'History section, please.'

Helen knew that voice and realized she had been well and truly set up by Reg Cook. She couldn't bear it – absolutely couldn't face Sebastian, even though in her heart she was longing to do just that. Scared of rejection, afraid of acceptance, embarrassed that she had fled: she knew she was in such a mess that all she could think of was hiding, delaying the confrontation. She searched for an escape but the shelving hemmed her in a cul-de-sac of books; she had been left without a bolt-hole. Her only hope was that Sebastian would not see that she was there. She turned her back and buried her nose in the nearest book. She could hear Sebastian walking around the little area, a tap accompanying every other step. He still used a stick, then. She was desperate to see how he was, but daren't look up.

There was a rustle of clothing and a sigh. From the click, she guessed he had checked his pocket watch.

'Excuse me, miss, but did you see a soldier waiting in here a few minutes ago? I am a little late for an appointment.'

His voice was like the tickle of silk across the skin at the nape of her neck. She shook her head, eyes down, praying that her small brimmed blue straw hat would hide her features.

Silence. Then . . .

'Helen?'

She closed the book and slid it back on to the shelf, refusing to turn round.

A warm hand closed around her elbow. 'Thank God! It is you. Reg told me to meet him for news of you but this is a hundred times better!'

She could feel his body standing directly behind her, the warmth of his breath on the side of her face as he bent to catch a glimpse of her features. 'Aren't you talking to me?'

She shook her head again, panic swamping her. All her sacrifice would count for nothing if she spoke – the distance she had forced between them would collapse and he would be caught up in her scandal.

'Then I'll do the talking. I am guessing Cook engineered this meeting?'

She nodded.

'I'll have to write and thank that brilliant schemer.' A thumb brushed against the sensitive skin of her inner arm where her kid gloves met her sleeve. 'I'm mad at you, you know. You should have come to me.'

Her fingers were trembling when she rested them back on the shelf.

'I know you tried to speak to me but were turned away. I'm sorry about that. But if you'd just left a letter, told me where to find you, I would've been with you months ago.' He couldn't hide his exasperation with her. She wouldn't have liked it either, had the situation been the other way round: him hiding from her.

'Excuse me, sir, are you importuning that young lady?' The efficient assistant had noticed all was not well near Tudor history.

Here was her chance to escape. 'Thank you, miss, but it's nothing. I have to go.' Helen pulled her arm from Sebastian's grasp and ran for the door.

'Helen!'

'Now really, sir, you cannot treat respectable ladies like that! I'll have to call the manager.'

Helen didn't hear his reply as the door tinkled shut behind her. But where to run? Thoughts scattered like beads from a broken string; she couldn't make a decision. Blindly, she headed towards the nearest station.

'Helen, Helen, wait!' Sebastian had got past the book-shop woman. 'Wait!'

She doubled her pace, barging past shoppers in her flight.

'Stop her – stop, thief!'

Helen swung round, startled. Sebastian was gaining on her. A cabbie in a grey overcoat grabbed her elbow. 'Is this the one, sir?'

'That's her.' Sebastian took hold of her other hand.

'What's she stolen?' The cabbie looked set to search her pockets. 'Shall I fetch a bobby?'

'I haven't stolen anything!' exclaimed Helen.

'Yes, you did. You stole my heart,' said Sebastian sombrely.

The cabbie gave a snort of disgust and let go of her arm. 'Like that, is it? Sorry, miss. I was only trying to help the officer.' He disappeared back into the crowd, muttering something about 'damn foolish lovers'.

'Sebastian, please. You've got to let me go.' Helen's eyes were devouring him, charting every tiny change, every inch of his beloved face. She felt like a beggar with her nose pressed against the baker's window: all that she wanted before her but out of reach. She struggled to remember why she could not give in to the temptation.

'Not in this lifetime. Do you know how long I've been looking for you? You've cost me endless sleepless nights, Miss Sandford.'

She closed her eyes against the force of his earnest gaze. 'I couldn't. You mustn't.' She wished she could make an argument, but all she could summon were disjointed sentences.

'You couldn't what? Share your trouble with me? Don't you think me strong enough to bear it with you? Do you have me down as some kind of weak cripple unable to support you?' He sounded fierce with self-loathing.

'No.' She gulped. It all made so much more sense when she was on her own, when she didn't have him standing right in front of her. 'But you were hurt and I didn't want to make things worse for you. I wanted to save you from my disgrace.'

'But I didn't want to be saved!' He was bellowing now, attracting stares from the people passing by. 'I wanted to cry with you – fight for you – but no, you wouldn't let poor crippled Lieutenant Trewby be the one who stood by you. You took the decision for me and it should've been my choice.' He thumped his chest. 'Mine.'

'It wasn't because you were . . . were crippled.' She hated the word.

'Wasn't it? You came as far as the door of the ballroom, saw me, scars and all, then ran for the hills. What was I to think?'

Helen didn't know what she had been thinking; that whole night had been confused and shaming: those beautiful perfect women surrounding him, the war hero, and her arriving, trailing in disgrace and infamy. She hadn't wanted to run from him; she'd wanted to run from herself. 'I was afraid.' There: finally she had admitted the truth.

'Afraid of what I had become?' He was still thinking this was about his injuries. He couldn't be more wrong.

'No.' She shook her head. 'Never that.' She reached up and traced the scar down the side of his face. 'No, you are as you have always been to me: the most wonderful man alive. I was scared that I wouldn't have the strength to keep you from going down with me in the scandal. I knew if I reached you, I would cling and we would both drown.'

His grip softened and he pulled her to his chest. 'But, darling, didn't it occur to you that I might help you float?'

It felt so good being held in his arms, better than any lifebuoy thrown to a castaway. She let her head fall to his shoulder, marvelling that she was here in her favourite place and that he was letting her get close, after all she had done to push him away. 'Sebastian,' she whispered.

'My love.' He kissed the top of her head. 'You talk about being scared but I was terrified when you left me. I can bear anything, any scandal, any harsh words, as long as you are with me. Don't leave me again. Please, I can't bear it.'

'I . . .' She could no longer find the strength to keep away. 'I won't.'

'Promise?'

She nodded.

Easing her head away from his chest, Sebastian looked down into her face and thumbed her tears from her cheeks. 'Then that's settled.'

She gave him a watery smile, happy despite the whisperings from her conscience that she was making a selfish mistake. 'What's settled?'

'We're getting married.'

'What! Am I not supposed to have a proposal first?'

'In this case, I think not.' He gave her one of his tender smiles that made her heart skip. 'You don't make sensible decisions when it comes to us, so I've decided I have to step in and put everything back on track. We had an understanding in France and now we have an engagement in London. Next we will have a wedding and will live happily ever after, if the war allows.'

She wanted to laugh at his matter-of-fact statement of their life plan but he sounded serious. 'You are quite mad.'

'Quite possibly.' He began towing her up Bond Street, threading through the lunchtime crowds.

'What's the hurry?'

'Oh, nothing, except I might be shot down next month and I wouldn't want to tumble from the sky knowing I hadn't got my ring on your finger and my lips on yours one more time.'

This time she did manage to stop him. 'Shot down? What do you mean?'

He turned to face her, letting the other pedestrians flow past them, their conversation a little rock in the stream of humanity. 'I've joined the Royal Flying Corps. You're somewhat behind on the news – your own fault, of course. I'm back on active duty, earning my wings.' He cupped her cheek. Behind him, Cupid, frozen in the act of shooting his arrow across Piccadilly Circus, had his pinions spread ready to take off. 'I have forty-eight hours' leave. Let's not waste it.' Her gaze dropped to his lips and he smiled. 'My thoughts exactly.'

'Where are you taking me?' asked Helen, unsuccessfully covering for the fact that she was blushing.

'Asprey's. I'm going to spend a ridiculous amount of money on a ring and make the salesman's day. After that, we are going to have lunch together and talk. You are going to apologize very prettily for ignoring me for the last few months and I'm going to tell you what I've been doing. Now, does that sound like a plan?'

She nodded shyly.

'Then, let's not stand here getting cold.' A flake of snow fell from the sky as if to prove his point. More joined it, tumbling to melt on his leather coat.

'Sebastian?'

'Yes, darling?'

'I'm sorry.' She meant it as an apology for the trouble she would bring him but he chose to misunderstand her, applying it to the past.

'Apology accepted. I can't tell you how much I have missed you — how empty my arms have felt not being able to do this.' He brought her closer and bent down to kiss her. Helen's whole body sighed with relief. Yes, this was right. How had she survived without this closeness in her life? She hadn't — not really. She had been frozen, waiting for spring.

'I've missed you so much, Sebastian.' Her fingers spread on his chest, savouring the solid fact of him under her palms. 'How long can you stay?'

'Not long, I'm afraid, but I'm going to make use of every moment.'

'You understand why I did it, don't you? It wasn't because I felt any less for you or didn't trust you. I did it —'

He put his finger on her lips. 'Because you were trying to protect me.'

He did understand, even if he hadn't quite forgiven her yet. 'I'm sorry to spoil your leave, making you run around looking for me. I know how precious your time is.'

'On the contrary, darling, I think my leave is going very well indeed, thanks to one enterprising friend of ours.'

5

Sebastian pulled his plane out of its spin. There was no sign of his pursuers, but the ground was fast approaching and, with no engines, he did not have enough altitude to glide back to the aerodrome. Arcs of shellfire reached his level like bullet-nosed dolphins leaping from an ocean of smoke, alerting him to the fact that from his cool heights he was about to enter the storm of war. He had no choice but to put down on the nearest patch of relatively smooth ground. Trouble was, he was pretty much over the battle-field, the earth churned by repeated shelling, snarled with barbed wire. Smooth was not possible.

Trying to reach the British lines, he spotted a likely place between two water-filled holes. This wasn't going to be pretty: he was coming in too slow, without engines to give the final boost. Gravity always won – that was the message his instructor had drummed home into each of his pupils. His flight commander was not going to be pleased with what this was going to do to his plane.

With a quick prayer, he got the three points down,

front and rear wheels, as he had been taught on the level grass of Salisbury Plain – but the copybook landing soon went to hell as the undercarriage caught on a metal fragment. Landing-gear sheared off, flipping the plane over. Held in his seat by his belt, Sebastian could do nothing but hang on as he was thrown from side to side, harness cutting across his chest and thighs. He finally came to a halt upside-down, fuselage miraculously intact around him, one wing crumpled. Suspended like a side of beef on a butcher's hook, the blood rushed to his head. He could predict the next move: he had just presented German artillery with a nice big target to practise their aim on – there were even the RFC bull's-eye roundels painted on the wings and fuselage. Slapping the seat-belt release, he fell from the cockpit, landing on one shoulder. Scrambling on hands and feet, he slid over the lip of one of the shell holes, right back in the place he had spent the last few months trying to escape: no man's land. He was an Icarus who had survived the fall from heaven, but now was in the same danger as the worms under the ploughshare. Ironic, that.

Hot and thirsty, Sebastian leant back against the wall of the pit to take stock of his position. Flying-gear was far too warm and ungainly for land. He unbuckled his helmet, feeling a trickle running down his neck. Brushing it away, he discovered he had blood, not sweat, seeping from his hairline. One of those bullets must have creased his scalp in the spin and he hadn't even noticed till now. No time to feel pain; he had to get out of a place in which he had no business. The key thing was to make the right decision about which way to head. In his disorientation he did not want to stumble the wrong way and into a hail of bullets or a German prison camp. He patted his pocket for the little compass Helen had given him the day he had bought her the ring. She had spent the entire contents of her purse on it, as the shops in Bond Street didn't run to anything modest. The casing was etched with their initials and a message for him inside. Neither of them had known how true those words would prove. The needle spun, pointing north. With a little imagination, he could imagine it pointing towards her. So what could it tell him? Interesting: west lay to the other side of his plane; he had started by going the wrong way. Still, better to realize that now than when it was too late and Fritz was frogmarching him to an interrogation or shooting him to bits.

Now he had his bearings and hadn't been instantly annihilated by shells, he began to feel a little more optimistic. If his luck held, he could get back without being picked off by a sniper and maybe, under the cover of dark, the mechanics could venture out and retrieve what was left of his Pup. It looked more of a wreck than it was in truth – controls and engine were still fully functional – so he could report that it would be worth the salvage trip.

But that was not his problem now. It was high time he got out of no man's land.

The last explosion had been some half an hour ago but still the women waited. The Germans had been known to leave a plane straggling, emptying its last bomb long after the others had turned to go back to base. Eggs, Sebastian and other airmen called the bombs: horrible, death-bringing missiles that hatched in flame. The ringing of fire-engine bells as they rushed along the roads told their own tale of others not so lucky as their factory. Finally, the same policeman cycling down the street, blowing his whistle, sounded the All Clear. A few of the women ventured outside to see how much the world had changed since they went down into the cellar. None of the buildings around them looked any different; the shadow of death had passed over without plucking lives from among them, like the Israelites with the blood of the lamb on their lintels before the escape from Egypt.

'Good riddance,' said Nelly, shaking her fist at the empty sky. Smoke rose up from the direction of Poplar. Helen worried for the little Cook family, scattered across Poplar in their school or at home. She hoped none of them had fallen under the shadow.

'Looks like the docks were hit.' Nelly pointed to the spreading canopy of smoke.

'I live near there,' Helen said quietly.

Nelly gave her a sympathetic look. 'Nowhere is safe, love.'

Mrs Hopper clapped her hands. 'Back to work, ladies. We can't do anything about those devils in the sky, but we can do our bit by working twice as hard to catch up on the time we have been forced to miss.'

Helen sat back down at her machine and finished the uniform shirt she had been working on. It was comforting to have something practical to do – better than imagining the horrors a few streets away. She did not envy the firemen and police their task of helping the victims, though it seemed a crying shame for her to be sewing seams when she could be using her nursing skills to save lives.

The telephone rang in the manager's office. Mrs Hopper went to answer it, visible through the glass partition. She had her back to the women but everyone was keeping an eye on her; phone calls usually meant more work or bad news. Of the two, they much preferred the first. Mrs Hopper replaced the handset on its hook and then took a moment, head bent, arms resting on the desk. Bad news then.

She came out and flicked the switch to cut the power to the machines.

Very bad news.

'Ladies, one of the local schools has been hit. Upper North Street. Please, if you have children there, you are asked to collect them immediately.'

There was an ugly silence. Two women at the far end of the room rose to their feet and ran out.

Joan.

Helen got up.

'Miss Ford, I don't believe you have children,' Mrs Hopper said severely.

'My landlady's girl – I take Joan to school every day. Upper North Street. She's only five.' Her wits were scattered; she barely knew what she was saying. 'Oh God, please, please let me go. I can help. I was a nurse. I mean, I know how to nurse.'

Mrs Hopper's face softened. 'Yes, go. Go, do what you can.'

Snatching up her handbag, Helen ran for the door.

Nothing could have prepared Helen for the scene that greeted her when she arrived at the school. Women crowded at the gates, crying hysterically, held back by policemen who were having huge difficulty keeping them from swarming into the bombsite and hampering the rescuers. Children were being helped out, scooped up by their parents and hurried away. None of them had escaped without at least cuts and bruises.

'What happened?' asked Helen, grabbing the arm of the nearest woman.

'A direct hit. Passed straight through the school roof. They say it exploded in the basement.'

'Dear God.' The basement was where the infants were gathered. 'How many dead?'

'I don't know. I don't know. I can't see my Dora. Why won't they let us search?' The woman clawed the back of Helen's hand in her distress, quite unaware of what she was doing.

Helen pulled away. She had spotted the casualties being loaded on to horse-drawn carts to be taken to hospital. That was where she needed to be. Pushing through the crowd, she reached the police cordon around the evacuation zone.

'Let me through. I'm a nurse.'

'Really, miss?' The young policeman showed signs of shock, weaving on his feet as he directed the drivers to carry their charges away. The little bodies were horribly stained with yellow TNT powder from the blast.

'Yes. I served a year in France.' Helen stripped off her gloves and rolled up her sleeves, already taking note of the injuries. 'That boy there has a punctured lung. I can help stabilize him.'

'Right you are, miss. Come on through.' He seemed relieved to have some expert help.

'You there, rip up some material for bandages!' snapped Helen to the nearest bystander. The woman yanked off her petticoat and set to work, joined by others when they saw what was needed. 'Someone fetch some water! Blankets for shock too.' What else did she need? 'Smooth sticks for splints. All the dressings you can find.' She knelt by the boy and checked his vital signs. He didn't have long. She needed a system to make sure the hospital knew which casualties to prioritize. A textbook flapped by. She caught it and tore out a page.

'Pencil?'

A stubby end of one was found for her. She wrote a quick summary, as she would have done at the military hospital. 'This one can't wait. Someone carry him!' A dockyard worker shouldered through the press and picked up the limp figure of the boy; Helen stuffed the note in the boy's shirt. 'Hurry, please!'

It was only when she turned to the next casualty that she realized the boy had been the same one as had leapfrogged in the playground that morning – the Morris lad. His chances of survival weren't good.

No time to mourn or scream as others were doing. Trained in the theatre of war, Helen kept her head down, dealing with each child and the few adult casualties one by one. Some were lucky – a broken bone or a few cuts. These she sent off as walking wounded. It was a horrible fact that by far the worst impact had been felt by the very youngest. Too many little bodies were loaded on to the carts with horrible burns, some unlikely to make the journey. None of them so far had been Joan.

'Nurse, nurse, over here!' The policeman ran to fetch her. One of the fathers, the school caretaker, had picked his way through the rubble and found a hand. 'He says it's his boy.'

From a glance at the limp fingers, Helen knew it was hopeless, but she went over as requested. The man was frantically digging, clearing away the bricks. She felt for a pulse. 'I'm sorry. He's gone.'

The caretaker collapsed to his knees, mouth open in a wordless howl.

'Here's another one!' Someone summoned her from the other side of the bomb crater. Helen picked her way across the masonry mixed with glass, slate and books. In the very centre fluttered a perfect paper lantern, that morning's school project for the little ones.

The rescue worker was holding a tiny body in his arms, having dragged her out from under the remains of a desk. Bloodstained gold hair draped over his sleeve.

'Joanie!' Helen reached out to check for a heartbeat. Joan was barely recognizable, having been burned down one side. 'She's alive. Sweet Jesus, she's alive.' Helen's knees trembled, threatening to give out from under her. *Think like a nurse*, she told herself. *Joan needs you to hold it together*. Fighting back her hopeless, helpless rage that the little girl had been hurt, Helen quickly checked for breaks or major injuries. No sign of any, but the burns in their severity were life threatening. 'Get her to hospital quickly. They'll want to do a No. 7 Paraffin treatment to stop infection if they've got it.' She scribbled another note, identifying the patient and recommending the treatment. She tucked the note in Joan's waistband, tears dripping down her cheeks to fall unheeded on the little girl's dress. 'Make sure they know that.' Her voice caught in her throat. 'It gets good results on the battlefield.'

With a curious glance at her for this unexpected knowledge, the man hurried off, his burden barely slowing him down. Helen felt like he was taking part of her with him, a cord tying her to the little girl stretched to breaking point. She was desperate to go with Joan, but knew she should stay and save lives here rather than get in the way at the hospital where she had no place, no duties. She could not turn her back on the cries of the little ones who needed her.

Helen worked on until there were no more survivors to be found. She wiped her bloody hands on her skirt, swallowing against bile. The scene was unutterably awful – the ordinary things of the school reduced to heaped-up tombs, bodies among the stones if you looked carefully.

The young policeman found her again and handed her a mug of tea provided for the rescuers by the local pub. 'Here you go, love. You've earned it.'

'It's not fair. Why them?'

'No rhyme or reason to it.' His voice was hoarse from shouting instructions for the last few hours. 'Massacre of the innocents, I call it. You've done your bit, miss: take some comfort from that. Might I have your name, in case anyone has any questions later?'

'Helen Ford.' She gave her address. 'I have to go. One of my landlady's children was among the injured.'

The policeman nodded gravely. 'I don't think there's anything else you can do here. It's down to the undertaker now.'

'How many?'

He knew what she meant. 'At least fifteen unaccounted for. There was six hundred here this morning, so I suppose we should be grateful not more were killed. The bomb passed through two floors before exploding, blast contained down here.' He nodded to the crater.

'That's not the kind of thing I can feel grateful for.'

Fury at the senseless waste of war boiled through Helen. Screaming at the skies would not help here. 'Where were the injured taken, do you know?'

'Poplar Hospital.' He pointed out the direction. 'Thank you for all you've done, miss.'

Helen handed back the cup. 'It wasn't enough, though, was it?'

PART TWO

Banknote

6

Sebastian staggered over the last stretch of open ground, keeping low. He was carrying his coat and helmet slung over his shoulder – both too expensive to dump in the mud – so he felt like one of the Chinese coolies who carried the heavy loads around the aerodrome, strange little chaps in the same blue uniform with a twittering language no one understood. He often wondered what on earth the Chinese were doing in France, in this battle between nations totally foreign to them. Something to do with the empire, he guessed. Not a mystery he had the leisure to solve today.

Nearing the Allied lines, he held up his hands in a gesture of surrender. 'Lieutenant Trewby. British. I'm coming in!' he warned.

His luck held: no bullet greeted his arrival this time. The daylight revealed him to be an English airman rather than an enemy soldier, thank God.

A grubby hand appeared over the lip of the trench and relieved him of his burden. 'There you go, sir.'

Sebastian slid down the side of the ditch and on to the

duckboards. The tension in his body unknotted as the anxiety of expecting a bullet between the shoulder blades finally subsided.

'We saw you land – beautiful bit of flying, that was,' said the private who had hold of his stuff.

'Until he hit that bit of the old tank. Could've told you it were there if you'd asked,' grinned a second man, showing a rare collection of blackened teeth.

Both had the hardened look of veterans of the front line: dirt engrained in their skin, brittle humour, wary stance like foxes hearing the hunt in the distance.

'Well I never: you should've said something!' Sebastian said wryly as he accepted the canteen of water and glugged down a healthy amount. 'I wouldn't have dropped in for tea if I'd known. I need to phone my base: have you got a line?'

The first Tommy jerked his thumb over his shoulder. 'With the captain that way. Signals have kept us in touch despite the chewing-over by the battery last night. But then you Fly Boys wouldn't know about that, would you?'

True. Back at the aerodrome, the heaviest onslaught was only a rumble in the distance. It made for some friction between the ordinary soldiers and the pilots.

'Afraid I was sleeping like a baby.' Sebastian took back his coat with its sheepskin lining and began to limp away.

'You injured, sir?'

'I was. First day of the Somme.'

The Tommies exchanged a glance. Everyone knew what that meant: the single day that produced the highest casualties so far in the war.

'Let me carry that for you.' The first Tommy was ready to be kind, now he knew Sebastian had earned his wound stripes in the mud like them.

'Thanks.'

'You'll need your head examining,' said the other, pointing to the cut on Sebastian's scalp.

'Don't we all – for still being here,' he quipped.

They laughed at that.

The captain, in his command post dug out a little back from the first line of the trenches, was most obliging, letting Sebastian report his arrival and arrange for a tender to be driven out to collect him.

'Should be a good night to salvage your craft,' Captain Morton added. 'The Germans have been noisy for a bit, so we're due for a spot of P and Q.'

Peace and Quiet. The trenches bred an ironic sort of man.

'How did you get to be there?'

'A Fokker triplane shot through my fuel line. Ended up with no power and two on my tail.'

'Lovely craft, those.' Morton waved up in the direction of an imagined enemy squadron.

All the pilots admired the German planes, even though they were murderous. 'You're right there – the three wings give them an amazing rate of climb. Quite outclass us. All the same, I think I bagged one – at least disabled him. Did you see any come down?' His commander would be slow to allow it as a 'kill' if there was no proof.

'No, lieutenant. All we saw was your rather spectacular entrance.'

'It probably happened a few miles away. I rather lost my bearings in the spin. Where are we exactly?'

'You're near Fricourt.'

'Good Lord, is that so? I was up the line only a few miles when I served in the First Somerset Light Infantry. So we're near the hospital at Albert?'

'Just over the rise.'

'I've a friend on the staff.'

The captain beckoned to his lance-corporal. 'Kingston, take Lieutenant Trewby to the hospital to get his cut seen to. I'll send a message for your people to collect you from there.'

'That's very decent of you.'

'No trouble at all. Gets you out of my hair, doesn't it?' Morton smiled and walked off to make an inspection of his men. It was a strange thing: a quiet day on the front. No one quite knew what to make of it; the worry was, it always heralded some concerted push by one side or the other.

Sebastian found himself the passenger on Lance-Corporal Kingston's motorbike for the short journey to the military hospital. The jolting ride over the potholed road gave him time to consider his mixed feelings about his impulse to go there: he expected to find Cook knocking about the place, but it was also packed with the very people who had hounded Helen out of France. He had a score to settle with them. Helen had never exactly explained how the pills had gone missing and, in any case, that was hardly the point: the doctors had taken her parentage against her, with no proof that her loyalties were suspect. They should have known her better. On that kind of mutton-headed reasoning, the Royal Family should be locked up, as the King was cousin to the Kaiser himself.

'Here you are, sir.' Kingston slowed to a stop outside the hospital doors. Sebastian had come through here last year with far worse injuries and had not been lucid; nothing looked familiar.

'Thanks for the lift.' He swung off the back of the bike.

The corporal touched his cap and headed back to his post.

Sebastian stamped the mud from his boots and entered the long, low building, hastily put up on the site of what had once been a farm. The room was quiet: only a few patients waited for treatment. He was fortunate not to have arrived during one of the many waves of casualties that had passed through here. A nurse at a desk looked up, serious face framed by her white scarf.

'Can I help you?'

What a civilized question. Last time he had been prodded, poked and stabilized with no thought of conversation.

'Ah, I see, head wound. Any other injury that you know of?' She was already on her feet.

'No, Sister. I came out of the crash with surprisingly few problems.' He touched his scalp. 'This is courtesy of a German machine-gun.'

'Don't fiddle with it. Let's get you cleaned up. I don't think we need bother a doctor.' She gestured for him to take a seat as she set out her dressings. 'Pilot, are you?'

'Yes. I was here before, though, as a casualty. In May last year.'

The nurse gave a vague smile as she concentrated on cleansing his cut. 'Liked us so much that you came back for more, did you? I might have treated you then too. I'm Nurse Henderson.'

The name was very familiar. 'Then you know my fiancée, Helen Sandford.'

The woman's hand stilled for a moment, then carried on with her task. 'I do indeed. How is she? It was a terrible thing what they did to her.'

'She's as well as can be expected. She misses nursing.' He hissed as she splashed some iodine on the wound. 'What happened that day? She won't talk about it.'

'I'm not surprised. The accusations came out of the blue – took us all by surprise. Someone had been in the stores and taken just a few pills, nothing really worth mentioning, but the sister-in-charge was a martinet for such things and went after the thief. Unfortunately, they leapt to the conclusion it was Helen, found letters in German in her possession and ran rabid with suspicion.'

He appreciated her concise summary of events – it cleared the fog a little. 'Who did take the pills?'

'There: all sorted. You'll have a scar, I'm afraid, but your hair will hide it when it grows back.'

Her attempt to change the subject worked, as Sebastian felt his scalp and discovered he'd lost a clump on the right-hand side. 'I must look like a dog with mange.'

'Hardly.' Nurse Henderson packed away her first-aid supplies.

'Is Corporal Cook around?'

Her shoulders stiffened. 'Why do you ask for him?'

Interesting. He should have thought about this before. Helen and Reg Cook in the same place; missing medicine: of the two, who was more likely to take it?

'We served together.' Anger brewed inside, but he managed to keep a charming smile pinned to his lips.

Her tension melted. 'Yes, he's probably in the doctors' office along there. They're going over supplies.'

I bet they are. 'Thank you. I'll tell Helen you asked after her.'

'You can do better than that. Tell her to write to me. I'd like to see her when I'm next home on leave.'

Sebastian knew that Helen's greatest fear was being exposed for who she was in England, removing her safe anonymity. He had to test Nurse Henderson had no ill intent. 'You're not afraid to be associated with her?'

'Fiddlesticks!' Nurse Henderson snapped her fingers. 'It was idiocy from start to finish. I didn't for one moment think her guilty and I'll be blowed if I'll let that come between us. She was – is – my friend. You tell her that.'

'I will.' Sebastian shook her hand, convinced he had

found a sound one among the many faulty people at the hospital. 'She has more friends than she realizes.'

'It's just a shame I couldn't do more for her. We were outgunned by the doctors.'

Leaving his flying-gear with Nurse Henderson, Sebastian made his way to the doctors' office. He could hear the murmur of voices inside.

'. . . running out of silk thread. See what you can do, Cook. Some more paraffin wouldn't go amiss either.'

'Right you are, Dr Cameron. Anything else?'

'Not for the moment. That'll be all.'

There was a shuffle and scrape of a chair. Cook emerged from the office, a pencil tucked behind his ear, a list in hand. Sebastian wrestled with the conflicting impulses of wanting to strangle the larcenous cockney and hug him for returning Helen to his arms.

'Hello, Cook.' He folded his arms to keep both impulses in check.

Cook clapped a hand to his chest. 'Blimey, Lieutenant Trewby! Where did you spring from?'

'Fell from the skies. It's been quite an eventful day.'

Cook grinned and scratched his head. 'Fancy a cuppa?'

His familiar question took Sebastian right back to the dugout they had shared as officer and servant. A cup of tea would serve nicely for the settling of accounts. 'Don't mind if I do.'

Sebastian watched Cook as he headed off down the corridor, completely oblivious to the fact that he had been rumbled.

'Follow me, sir.' Cook beckoned over his head. 'How long you got?'

Sebastian wasn't sure what he was going to do with his newfound knowledge. Kicking Cook from here to Calais was a favourite.

'My people are coming to fetch me, but I'm a fair way from home. I'd say I have a couple of hours yet.'

'Good. Come make yourself cosy in my office.'

'You have an office?'

'Cupboard – but everyone calls it my office.' Reg opened the door on a store-room he had clearly arranged to his convenience. Two little armchairs were squeezed in – Lord knew where they came from – and a bedding roll lay on the floor.

'You sleep here?'

'As comfortable as at the Ritz, I tell you. It's quiet, no snoring, no lice, rats or flies – heaven. Make yourself at home. I'll just fetch your tea.'

He vanished down the corridor. Sebastian took him at his word and settled in one of the chairs. He rested his head on the back, reliving in his mind the sickening sensation of landing on a battlefield. He was extraordinarily fortunate to have survived that experience; many better pilots had died in crashes as a result of less extreme landings. What made the difference between the ones that came through and the ones that were lost? Not skill. The British hero, Albert Ball, bane of many a German pilot, had come down in a field just the month before. He met his end in the arms of a young woman from the village, an almost operatic end for England's flying ace. Lesser men had lived on, avoiding death by a whisker.

He studied Reg's cosy arrangements, proof that the ones who knew how to work the system stood a better chance in this war than those who played strictly by the rules. The top brass denied that, of course, claiming God was on the side of righteous Englishmen and their allies. It was hard to believe there was any benign god watching over their fate; fairness was no part of the real picture. Perhaps if the promise of Heaven was true – and Sebastian was tempted to trust more in Cook's kind of earthly heaven than a celestial one – the rewards somehow evened out in an eternal afterlife. How hard it was to keep up that belief when the evidence pointed to nothing making sense, youth being wasted for little or no reason.

Cook came back with a mug. 'I added some sugar. You look like you could use it, sir.'

Sebastian murmured his thanks and took the drink. 'So, Cook, you've fallen on your feet here.'

'Yes, thanks to Dr Cameron.' Cook gave a sheepish grin and dropped down in the other chair, thumbs hooked into the braces over his slight chest. 'See, in here, I'm lord of all I survey. A useful person. I can make a difference to how the hospital runs.'

His cheerfulness seemed to mock Helen's dire predicament. 'I bet you do. I bet you know how to lay your hands on supplies others can't find.' Cook's face dimmed as he heard the anger in Sebastian's voice. 'I mean, if there were a shortage in the medicine cupboard, I imagine you'd know where it went and how to replace it, wouldn't you?'

'Ah.' Cook sat up. 'You know about that, do you?'

'Not that anyone has given you away, you damned fool, you!'

'How do you know then?'

'I'd say you just confirmed it yourself. My suspicions are correct then? You saved your own skin at the expense of Helen's?'

Cook ran a hand over his face, scrubbing at the frown lines. 'Yeah, yeah, I did. I'm not proud of it. Here.' He cocked his head to one side, exposing his jaw. 'Go on: hit me there. Hard.'

Cook had a way of beating you to the punch – literally. Sebastian shook his head. 'I'm not going to hit you, Cook.'

'I wish you would. She was so bloomin' brave about it all – said I wasn't to do anything, that the harm had been done. I been feeling like the worst sort of villain ever since.'

'So you should. You've stopped her life in its tracks. She's in hiding, unable to use her skills.'

'I know it. Elsie knows the truth too. We think of Helen like a daughter. Neither of us wanted anything like this to happen. If I have to spend the rest of my life making it up to her, I will.'

'You might just have to do that. Despite your reputation for working miracles, it's not easily fixed.'

Cook sighed and stretched out his legs, grinding the

heels of his boots into the floor. 'At least she's safe with my family – no harm will come to her there. No one knows who she is – nothing about her nursing background. We put it about that she's a cousin helping out with the nippers.'

Cook was right: Helen was in the safest place they could think of, hidden unremarked in a large family. The flame of Sebastian's anger fizzled and spat, then went out. As Helen had once observed, no one could stay angry with Reg for long. 'How are your little ones and Elsie?'

Taking out a photograph from his breast pocket, Cook displayed his brood proudly. Elsie was sitting in the middle with the baby on her knee, Helen had the two boys by the hand as the older girls stood between them. 'They had this taken for me last month. Elsie said the boys were a nightmare at the photographer's studio.'

'They look angelic – all of them.'

Cook chuckled and stroked the faces of his children. 'Misleading for the boys but right on the button for my lovely girls.'

'You are a lucky man.'

'Yeah, I count my blessings each day. One, two, three, four, five and six' – he tapped each face in turn. 'And Miss Helen makes seven: she's a blessing to Elsie, she is. So, you and she are courting again?'

'More than courting: engaged. The very day you set us up at Hatchard's – so I can't really be angry with you for long, can I?'

'That was quick work, sir. I wonder why she didn't tell Elsie?'

Sebastian laced his hands behind his head. 'This is Helen we are talking about. I bought her a ring but I don't think she often wears it openly. She is leaving me so many escape routes from our relationship in case I change my mind that it feels pretty breezy.'

'I thought she might not say "yes".'

Sebastian smiled down at his tea and took a sip. 'She didn't.'

'Sorry, sir: I'm not following you.'

'I didn't make the mistake of giving her a choice. Marched her up Bond Street and got her the ring: deal done; signed, sealed and delivered express.'

Cook toasted him in tea. 'Good work, lieutenant. You are exactly what she needs.'

'What? An overbearing commanding officer? I don't think she'll put up with me for long. She only fell in with my plan because she wanted to say yes but felt she shouldn't.'

'Got the right result though, didn't it?'

'There is that.'

They grinned at each other.

7

Bond Street, London, 2 January 1917, 1 p.m.

Sebastian steered Helen through the doors of Asprey's, the West End's most exclusive jeweller's shop. Even though there was a war on, the showroom managed to project an air of unchanging calm. Kingdoms came and went, men rose and fell, but gold and diamonds continued to hold their place in the hearts of humanity.

'Are you sure about this?' asked Helen. The plush velvet curtains, the shining glass counters and priceless contents – not to mention the severe assistants who guarded the treasure with the judgemental gaze of those who could measure a person's worth in five seconds – unnerved her. They were assessing the pair of them even now, withholding their verdict.

'Of course I'm sure, you goose.' Sebastian rubbed his thumb over the back of her hand, letting the material of her glove slide to and fro. That little touch sent tingles up her arm, distracting her from her misgivings. He led her to the nearest counter and set his walking stick to rest, hooked on the edge.

'May I help you, sir?' the elderly assistant asked in

a tone usually employed only by disapproving butlers of the highest calibre.

'I wish to see your selection of engagement rings.'

The gentleman swept his eyes over Helen, then back to Sebastian. Uniforms were hard to gauge: they could contain a prince as well as a pauper, though Sebastian's showed signs of having been tailored to fit him. 'Of course, sir. Would sir and the young lady like to follow me?'

He led them to a velvet-draped cubicle with padded chairs for them to rest on. 'Might I enquire, sir, what range you would like to see?' This was a delicate way of asking if they could afford the more expensive jewellery.

'Your best, naturally.'

'And does sir have an account with us?' The refined probing amused Helen. Now he was getting down to the nitty-gritty, as good as asking to see the money before he unlocked his display counters.

'My family has an account with you. My father is Theodore Trewby of Trewby Holdings.'

The assistant relaxed his guard. 'The financier. Oh yes, we know Mr Trewby. That would make you the grandson of the Earl of Bessick?'

'Exactly.' If Sebastian was annoyed by the man's ferreting out of his background, he gave no sign. Helen would have been walking out by now if it were left to her.

The assistant rang a little bell on the counter, a high-toned alarm alerting all in hearing to the presence of someone to whom it was worth paying attention. A young woman dressed in severest black responded instantly. 'Yes, Mr Handler?'

'Tea and biscuits, please, for our distinguished clients. And inform Mr Parker that we require the engagement tray from the safe.'

'Yes, sir.'

Helen was struck by an irreverent mood: all this bowing and scraping now they knew who Sebastian was, whereas before they were being regarded with disdain. Taking advantage of Mr Handler's turned back, she whispered:

'And if they only knew who *I* was, would it be bread and water in the cellar?'

Sebastian's mouth quirked at the corners. 'Hush, love.'

'Of course not: I'd be out the door. Thank goodness I have the grandson of an earl at my side.'

'We have our uses.'

'I'm determined to make them sell me something.' She furrowed her brow, wondering what in this Aladdin's cave she could buy. There were no battered lamps with genies inside as far as she could tell. 'Do you have any small tokens suitable for a military officer, sir?'

Mr Handler looked up from his arranging of the first tray of rings in front of Sebastian. 'I beg your pardon, miss?'

'I wish to buy my . . . my fiancé a gift.'

Sebastian grinned at her, more for the acknowledgement of their engagement than the promise of a present.

The assistant's face broke into a smile. 'Ah, but of

course. A diamond tie-pin perhaps? Or a silver cigarette case?'

'Something a little more modest,' Sebastian said swiftly. 'I have very unflashy tastes. A practical gift.'

'Hip flask? Silver-tipped shooting-stick? Compass?'

'Yes, a compass. That's just the ticket. Something plain and serviceable. But let us choose a ring first, darling. My needs can wait.' He repositioned the tray so it was in front of her. 'Do any of these take your fancy?'

Helen ran her finger down the lines of rings: all of them were gorgeous and all of them far too expensive for her. Diamonds, filigree white gold, aquamarine, Ceylon sapphires, blood-red rubies. 'Perhaps this one?' She pointed to the smallest diamond in the tray.

Sebastian smiled into her eyes and purposely plucked out the one next to it, which had the largest round brilliant cut stone, slightly yellow in hue like the palest flush of a primrose. 'Excellent choice, darling.' He slid it on to her finger. 'Yes, you are right: it does seem made for you. The size is good too. What do you think, Mr Handler?'

'Oh I do agree, sir, a lovely piece. Note the adjacent duos of diamond-studded, heart-shaped motifs, holding the central stone in place. Perhaps you would like to inspect the gemstone, sir?' He offered his eyeglass. 'I think you will find it has first-rate clarity and is highly reflective. The young lady has exceptional taste.' He played along with Sebastian, both men knowing full well she had chosen the ring next to it.

'But Sebastian —'

'Yes, I agree: this is the one. Perhaps Mr Handler can have it checked for size? I would like to take it with us.'

'Of course, sir.' He slid the band up and down her ring finger, checking the fit over her knuckle. 'A little loose. I'll send it upstairs at once. Perhaps the young lady would like to choose her gift for you while we settle the paperwork?' The assistant was back with the tea-tray. 'Miss Tate will look after you.'

'My pleasure, sir,' said Miss Tate on cue.

Sebastian whisked the ring from Helen's finger before she could object. 'I'll be back in a tick.' Seeing her doubtful face, he chuckled. 'It's the perfect ring for you, darling, and I can well afford it.'

'But . . .'

'Oh, you want to buy a wedding ring too? We could, you know – get a special licence and have the business over and done with tomorrow.'

She laughed and shook her head at him. 'You, sir, have taken your flying training to heart. You are determined to sweep me off my feet!'

'That's the idea. Us pilots are all dashing fellows, don't you know?' He struck a heroic pose.

'I'm sure you are, but I'm more of a stumbling-along girl. The engagement ring is enough for now – and you really don't have to spend all that on me.'

'You deserve it – and I refuse to argue. I am not leaving my fiancée with a shabby ring; only the best will do for her.' He kissed her hand where the ring had rested but briefly.

He disappeared off with Mr Handler to talk money at the cash desk. Of course, it would all be hidden behind the fussy language of accounts and sums to be drawn on bank accounts, but it all came to the same thing: Asprey's was checking Sebastian was good for the huge amount the ring was going to cost him.

The female assistant came back with a tray of compasses and set them before Helen. 'Is there anything here that Miss thinks appropriate?'

She silently totted up the amount in her purse. In for a penny, in for a pound, so to speak. 'I have to be frank with you, Miss Tate, I only have a little to spend.' She emptied her coins on to the counter. 'Is there anything – anything at all I can afford here?'

'Miss?'

'I work for a living like you.' The girl glanced out to where Sebastian was settling his bill. Helen shook her head. 'It's my fiancé with the connections, not me.'

Giving her a swift smile, Miss Tate bent over the tray conspiratorially. 'If I let you have it at my staff discount, you can just about afford this one.' She pointed to a small silver compass. 'I think I might even be able to get it engraved for you for free.'

'Would you? Thank you.'

Miss Tate quickly scooped up the coins before Mr Handler returned. 'Us working girls have to stick together, don't we? Just write your message there and I'll send it upstairs. It should be ready by the end of the day at the same time as your ring.'

'That would be perfect.' She paused, wondering what she should have engraved on it. It came to her that the message of her heart was obvious.

So you can always find your way home.

Helen found Elsie by Joan's bedside in the hospital. News had spread fast through the streets of Poplar; half the families with young children appeared to have ended up on the ward. The little girl was lost under a swathe of bandages like a fancy-dress costume of an Egyptian mummy – if only it were something so frivolous.

'How is she?' Helen tried to hide her desperation for Elsie's sake but she feared the worst.

Elsie held out a hand to Helen and clung, a mother's anguish carved in her face. 'Please do something for her – please help her.'

Helen bent over the child, checking what had been done already. Her burns had been treated with the paraffin preparation – she could smell it on her skin. That was the best-known method for dealing with such serious burns, rigorously tested in the field. 'What have they given her for the pain?'

Elsie shook her head. 'I don't know. The doctors come and go and say nothing to me.'

Helen was used to the arrogance of doctors who thought working-class patients below their notice, and Elsie wasn't the sort to demand answers. She checked the chart at the end of the bed. Morphine. Probably very like the pills Reg had taken, cut down to a child's dose. The doctors' attitude might be wrong, but they were competent at least. 'They're doing all they can for her, Elsie.'

'Will she . . . ?' Elsie didn't want to speak the words in case Joan was listening somewhere under the bandages.

In truth the odds were stacked against her. 'She's safe now, got the best of care. She had every chance. Joan, we will help you get better, sweetheart.'

The little girl didn't move, her eyes tightly shut. Helen couldn't blame her: why open them on a world that had treated you this way at five?

'Are the other children all right?'

'Grandma Betts has them. Thank the Lord, Maddie was home with me helping with the baby, otherwise she'd have been at school. It's not safe in London – we'll have to move. But where can we go? How can we afford to live? Oh God, someone has to tell Reg.' Elsie was spinning with panic, mind flitting from one thing to the next.

'I'll send a telegram. You can decide the other things tomorrow – now all you have to do is be here for Joan.'

'Yes, yes, you're right.' Elsie pressed the heels of her hands to her eyes. 'I'm sorry. I can't think straight. She's going to be badly scarred if she does survive, isn't she?'

Yes. 'One step at a time, Elsie. She's survived the first few hours; now we have to help her live through the rest.' She put her arm around her friend's shoulder, knowing she could not do that for Joan without making the pain worse.

Elsie rested her head against Helen's side. She sniffed

her clothes, heavy with the smell of smoke and brick dust. 'You've been at the school?'

Horrific images flashed before her mind's eye. Helen took a breath to calm herself. 'I did first aid at the site. I saw them pull Joan out. It is a miracle she lived.'

'Her friend Kitty's gone. I saw her poor mother.'

'It would have been instant. The children wouldn't have known anything about it.' That was what she had told herself as she'd worked.

'One small mercy, that.' Elsie gulped. 'I hope those bomber pilots roast in Hell for doing that to my little girl.'

Helen stroked Elsie's arm. Fair enough to think that way as a parent at the bedside of your injured child. The horrid truth was that to the German airman it had been just a job, a target; he had been following orders. The only thing stopping British pilots doing the same to German cities was the lack of long-range planes. No doubt the military were busy making up for this gap in their capability even now; pilots like Sebastian would be asked to fly them.

'I'll go send the telegram before the post office closes.'

Elsie nodded. 'Then you'll go home – look after the others for me? Grandma Betts can't keep them overnight and I want to stay here.'

'Of course.'

'Thank you, Helen. I don't know what I'd do without you.'

'I'll be back tomorrow. Send a message if you need me before that.' She didn't want to mention that the next twelve hours would be touch-and-go for Joan. Elsie was no fool; she probably knew that already.

'I will. Hurry now. Reg has to know.'

There was a queue at the post office – so much bad news to be shared across the country and to those serving abroad. Helen waited patiently in line, her thoughts blank as she absorbed the shock of the day. Poor sweet little Joanie.

A man behind her in the queue tapped her arm. 'Miss?'

Wiping a wrist across her eyes, she turned. 'Yes?'

'I just want to say thank you. I saw you there. You helped my Lenny. He's going to be all right.'

'Lenny?' There had been so many, Helen had lost track.

'Little lad with carrot hair. Broken wrist and a couple of burns on his legs.'

She remembered him now. He'd been so brave. 'I'm glad.'

'Proper good nurse you are. Everyone is saying so who saw you at work.' The man folded his arms across his barrel chest. He had the blackened hands of a coal deliveryman. 'You work at the hospital?'

'No, I, er, no, I don't.'

'You should, you know. They need girls like you.'

She gave him a smile. 'Thank you.'

She reached the head of the queue and sent her telegram to Reg. As the clerk tapped out the message, she closed her eyes, sending a brief prayer that he would not be alone when he received the terrible news. She hoped he would have a friend to stand beside him.

The tender drove up to the hospital doors and honked.

'That's my signal to go.' Sebastian brushed the crumbs from his lap.

Reg accompanied him outside. 'Got all your stuff, sir?'

Sebastian threw his flying jacket and helmet in the back of the tender.

'What, no parachute?' Reg sniffed in disapproval. 'The lookouts on the air balloons have them. I know where I can get you one.'

'It's against regulations. Our commanders think it would cultivate a cowardly pilot who will bale rather than fight.' Sebastian felt the familiar tired sense of insult that their leaders saw fit not to trust them.

Reg spat at the ground. 'I've never heard anything so stupid! The brass hats should try going up in one of those contraptions and then say if they fancy a parachute to get 'em out of trouble.'

'Ready to go, sir?' asked the mechanic who'd come out to fetch him, a Scotsman with a genius for fixing engines.

'Yes, Gordon. I'm afraid I've left you with a bit of a problem with my Pup.'

'All in hand, sir. Team going out at dusk to salvage. I dropped them off earlier.'

'Let me guess: I'm not a favourite with the Ack Emmas today?'

Air mechanics, or Ack Emmas as the pilots called them,

were scathing about any airman who didn't return his craft in reasonable shape. 'I couldn't say, sir.' That meant he was indeed in the doghouse with them.

Nurse Henderson came running out of the hospital building, white wings of her scarf flapping, a slip of paper clutched in her hand. 'Cook, wait! Oh Cook!'

Reg turned to her. 'What's the matter, nurse?'

Panting from her dash across the hospital, she thrust the message at him. 'This came for you. I'm so sorry!'

The three men fell silent. Telegrams always came trailing death. Hands shaking, Reg unfolded the slip. Then, like a horse taking a bullet to the brain, his knees gave out under him and he sank to the mud, paper scrunched in his fingers.

'What's happened?' Sebastian tugged the note from him. Reg let him have it as his shoulders began to heave with grief.

School hit. Joan alive but in hospital with serious burns. Many killed. Rest of family safe. Helen

'Sir?' asked the mechanic, still awaiting instructions.

'Can you give me a minute, Gordon? His little girl was caught in an air raid.'

'Of course, sir.'

Sebastian put his arm around Reg and gently brought him to his feet. 'I'll take Cook to his room. Tell the doctor in charge, please, what's happened and see if they'll allow him leave.'

Nurse Henderson touched Cook's hand briefly and ran in the direction of the doctor's office.

'Come, Cook. Let's get you comfortable. Then you can work out what you are going to do to help your girl.'

'I've got to get to my family, help Elsie.' Reg's voice was distant.

'That's right. First, you need to give yourself a moment to get over the shock.'

In Reg's cupboard, Sebastian sat him in a chair and wrapped a blanket round his shoulders. Spotting a flask of Dutch courage, he handed it to Reg. 'Here – a sip of brandy to take off the edge.'

'What's the point of fighting this war if I can't even keep my own family safe?'

'It's not a war like any we've known before.' Sebastian crouched on his haunches at his friend's side.

'I should've been there! My little girl! She didn't do nothing to deserve this!'

'No one does.'

Nurse Henderson came back. 'Dr Cameron says he can go on the next hospital train. It's due in two hours.'

Sebastian did not like the vague look in Reg's eyes. 'You hear that, Cook?' He slapped Reg's shoulders. 'You need to pull yourself together, man, and go home. Elsie will need you.'

'What?'

'You are leaving – on the train. You'll be able to be there for Joan.'

Something snapped into place. 'Yes. Joan.' Reg got to his feet and picked up his kitbag. 'I'm going home.'

Sebastian turned to Nurse Henderson. 'How long has he got leave?'

'A week. Unless, you know . . .' The nurse gave a delicate shrug, indicating extended leave to bury a child.

'You mustn't waste a moment.' Sebastian broke with years of upbringing and gave Cook a bracing hug. 'Be strong, Cook.'

'Yes, sir. Oh God, sir.' He was collapsing again. The embrace had been a mistake; men did better with no one allowing them to air their emotions. How else could they fight a war? Sebastian released his hold.

'Try not to think too much about it. Do the next thing you need to do.'

Taking a deep breath, Reg firmed his shoulders. 'Yes, yes, you're right. I need . . . I need to get packed and get to the train.'

'Let me know how everyone is, won't you?'

Reg saluted, using military discipline to keep him moving. 'Yes, sir.'

Sebastian wished he could stay but he couldn't keep the driver waiting any longer. 'I send my love and best wishes to everyone.'

'I'll tell her, sir.'

Reg knew he had meant Helen. 'And I hope you find Joan on the mend.'

'So do I. Oh please God, so do I.'

8

After a winter of courting while Sebastian trained at Upavon, this was their last chance to be together before he joined his squadron in France. In honour of this fact, Helen had given him carte blanche to choose their outing. The huge palace of paintings on Trafalgar Square had been his pick. He had graduated from flying school only the day before, white wings pinned to his left breast. Modest about his own achievements, he had played this down, but she would bet that he made a good pilot, clever with his hands, cool under fire, the sort to coax the best performance from a temperamental machine. She was so proud of him she wanted to shout it out loud, but that might startle the matronly woman contemplating the *Equestrian Portrait of Charles I.* She settled for squeezing his elbow closer to her side.

Sebastian steered Helen through the busy rooms, commenting on his favourite works as he went. With every step, he shed the military officer and became the artist she had first met – it was beautiful to watch. She was listening, really she was.

No, she had to confess that she was so busy watching his expression of delight or distaste as he reacted to the works that she could only hazard a hum when he asked for her opinion.

'Is that a good hmm or a bad hmm?' he asked, pointing at a rural scene by Constable.

Helen forced herself to pay attention. She liked the clouds in the picture. 'It was a good hmm.'

'I agree. He would have loved to go up in my plane with me and look at the clouds from up there. Just think what a marvellous painting he could have done from that perspective.'

'From the date, I'd say he could have gone up in an air balloon – he looks like a man who knows his clouds.'

Sebastian peered at the painting more closely. 'I think you're right. I've never heard if he did so, but I'll have to look that up when I get a chance to return to studying.'

It was rare to hear Sebastian talk about 'after'. No one could see beyond the end of the war – in fact, it was hard to believe the war would ever end. It had been going on so long, the prospect of an end felt like a mirage constantly moving away from a wanderer lost in the desert.

'You'll return to the Slade then?'

'I think so. Would you mind?'

She touched her chest. 'Me? Mind? Of course not.'

'We'll be married then, naturally. You'll be the wife of an art student.'

'Living in a garret?'

'Not quite.' He smiled and put his arm around her

waist. 'Not that that wouldn't be very appealing with you there. Ah, here's a picture you might find interesting.'

They had paused in front of a depiction of Venus from the back, looking in a mirror held by an obliging Cupid.

'Why are you showing me this? I think she looks as though she should put some clothes on – she has to be cold.'

He chuckled. 'Yes, she could do with a fire in her room. It's the *Rokeby Venus*. One of the campaigners for women's suffrage had a go at it three years ago.'

'Had a go at it?'

'Attacked it. She was making a point about women being treated as objects not people, I think.'

'Good for her.'

He nudged her to keep her voice down. The guard was keeping a very close eye on anyone who showed particular interest in this work. 'So you agree that women should have the vote?'

'Of course.' She frowned up at him. 'Don't you?'

'Oh yes. In fact, it might be a good idea to let *only* women have the vote for a few decades – see if they can sort out the mess we men have made.'

And that was why he was absolutely perfect for her. 'I love you, Sebastian.'

'Well now.' He cleared his throat. 'You don't say that very often. Not without me prompting you.'

'But I think it all the time. And just now it bubbled up.'

'You know, Helen, I have a strong urge to kiss you too.' His smile was glorious.

'Is that even possible here?' She looked around at the respectable people wandering the halls.

'I think it could be arranged. An art student knows a thing or two about this place. I know a corner with some completely dull bowls of fruit where no one goes. Come with me.'

Trying not to give away their plans by running, she walked swiftly alongside him.

'Will this do?' He pulled her into a little room with some florid canvases.

The lurid colours momentarily took Helen aback. 'Is that a dead rabbit?'

'Yes. Artists are funny fellows. I think that one is having a joke about still life – you don't get more still than something dead, now do you? Shall we go somewhere else?'

She shook herself, remembering what he had in mind before ugly pictures had derailed them. 'No, here will do very well.'

He bent his head, then paused. 'Your turn.'

She frowned. 'What do you mean?'

'You kiss me.'

'Oh.' She blushed at the notion of being the one to start the kiss.

'Please.' He was enjoying every second of her discomfort, the cad.

Never one to shy away from a challenge, Helen licked her lips. 'As you asked so nicely.' Going up on tiptoes, she curled her hand around the back of his head and pulled him down to meet her mouth. She kissed him softly, putting all her yearning for him, wishes for his safety, into the gesture. She dropped back to her heels. 'How did I do?'

He smiled. 'Not bad. But you might need to repeat it just so I can be sure.'

She went up again and this time did not stop him as he took over the progress of the kiss. It was far easier with his arm supporting her, anchoring her against his chest. Magic – that was what it felt like. Their shared touch split off the fear and loneliness that she carried – a smooth, sweet chestnut of love bursting from the prickly husk that had contained it.

'Excuse me, sir, madam, you cannot do that kind of thing here!'

Sebastian kept her face hidden in his chest. 'What thing, sir?' He stared down the guard.

'Kissing! *In a public place.*'

'Kissing? How dare you, sir! My companion had become overwhelmed with grief for the rabbit in this picture – I was comforting her.'

Helen's shoulders began to shake with giggles.

'See – she is sobbing. She's very sensitive.'

The guard paused, weighing up the worth of accepting Sebastian's version of events against further challenging with his own. 'Then I trust you will escort your companion to a room where she is not disturbed by the exhibition on the walls.'

'Capital idea. Come along, my love. We'll away, back to the clouds.'

They walked with heads held high past the guard. Once out of sight, Sebastian pulled her hand and they ran through the gallery and out until they reached the lions in Trafalgar Square.

'You are so bad, Sebastian Trewby!' She swatted his chest, still gasping with laughter.

'Am I?' He grinned down at her. 'I wasn't the one initiating kissing in a public place.'

She bit her lip. 'True – but you told me to.'

'Ah me: it seems I'm leading you astray.'

'I'm rather enjoying the process,' she admitted.

He smoothed his finger along her cheek. 'I've got something for you. I've had it a while but wanted to wait for the right moment to give it to you.'

She turned her head to nuzzle his fingers. 'You don't need to keep giving me things.'

'Whyever not? It is one of life's greatest pleasures.'

She rolled her eyes. This was one of their frequent disagreements, he insisting on surprising her with little gifts, her protesting, as she couldn't afford to reciprocate.

'Here it is.' He pulled a beautiful silver locket from his jacket and fastened it around her neck. He pressed her palm to it, trapping it against her breast.

'Oh, Sebastian!' She lifted it up and flicked it open. He had put his photograph and a lock of hair inside.

'I wanted you to have something so I can always be

near you.' He looked a little anxious that she wouldn't like so lavish a present.

'It's beautiful. Perfect.'

'Like you.'

She gave a chuckle. 'I wish I were.'

He moved closer. 'No: I know you are.'

Secretly thrilled by his romantic words, she continued to laugh and shake her head. 'I'm glad you think so. It is so lovely when a boy has these illusions about his girl.'

'Then we will have to agree to disagree on the subject. I was rather hoping you'd say *I* was perfect.'

She looked up into his dancing eyes. 'I'm afraid not – I will not perjure myself, Mr Trewby.'

'Oh, is that so, Miss Sandford? And what is wrong with me?'

'You are almost faultless, except you have this foolish belief in the perfection of your fiancée.'

He laughed and shook his head. 'What am I going to do with you?'

'Come back safe to me: that's all I ask.'

'I'll do my very best.' He touched the locket where it lay against her heart.

Poplar, 15 June 1917, 8 a.m.

'Is Joan going to die, Miss Helen?' asked Maddie as they worked together on the Get Well card, heads close over the kitchen table.

The two little boys playing with soldiers on the rug by

the fire stopped what they were doing, big brown eyes turned to hang on Helen's every word. They were too young to be worrying about death, but the attack right on their doorstep had stripped that blissful ignorance from them.

Helen rubbed her throat. 'I hope not, Maddie. She's in the very best hands. Your mum is with her day and night, and the doctors are very skilful.'

'Why can't I see her? I'm her big sister. She'll be missing me.' Maddie cut out a flower from an old magazine.

'She spends most of her time sleeping, love. She'll know you are thinking of her if we finish this pretty card. Let's stick that one there – see, a lovely posy of roses for her.'

The baby, asleep in a big wicker laundry basket, whimpered, then settled. Helen wondered what time Grandma Betts would be in to help. She had not been able to go to work since the attack, and her employers were coming to the end of their patience, granting leave for a child who wasn't even a close relative. The 'distant cousin' story Elsie had put about had only bought Helen a few days' compassionate leave.

'Morning, my loves!' Grandma Betts shuffled in without knocking. Stooped-shouldered like a crow pecking at scraps, her black skirt had gone rusty brown in patches with wear, but she was always as neat as a pin. Not a real grandmother to the children, it was just the name everyone called her. Widow of a painter and decorator, she supplemented her meagre pension with child-minding for the locals.

'Grandma!' Maddie got up and waved the card immediately under the old lady's nose at great risk to the barely dry glue. 'Do you like my picture?'

Grandma took the spectacles that hung on a ribbon round her neck and peered. 'Beautiful, my little button. Just like you.' She patted the girl's cheek.

Caught unawares, Helen felt a lump in her throat. She turned away to put on the kettle, to hide her distress. Would anyone ever call little Joan a beauty again? One side of her sweet face was likely to be permanently marked by burn scars, if she survived the next few weeks. Still, they would be fortunate to have the problem of how to help her adjust, so long as the little girl had her life. She would always be beautiful to every member of the family, whatever she looked like to outsiders.

The two little boys now crowded Grandma's skirts, thrusting their favourite soldiers in her direction.

'Look, he's like Daddy!' said Joe, the twin with the spiked crop of brown hair that gave him a striking resemblance to a hedgehog.

'Mine's Daddy too!' Freddie held out his preferred little man. His hair lay flat against his scalp like an otter's – Helen found noting these details the easiest way of telling them apart, as their capability for mischief was equal.

Helen put a cup of tea in front of Grandma Betts. 'Will you manage from here?'

Grandma sat down at the table with a huff and took

out her knitting. 'Of course, love. I've been looking after little ones since well before you were born.'

Helen knelt down to kiss the boys. 'Be good, won't you?'

They nodded solemnly. 'We promise.'

It was always better if they had a scheme to occupy them rather than rely on such good intentions. 'What are you going to do?'

Joe held out a sardine tin. 'We make a tank.'

Freddie cradled some cotton reels in his hand. 'With these.'

'Good plan.' Helen got to her feet, kissed Maddie and reached for her coat.

'You saw tanks when you were at the hospital with Daddy, Miss Helen, didn't you? Did they look like that?' Maddie gestured to the tin now rolling across the hearth-rug on improvised wheels.

Helen faltered as she pinned her hat to her hair. 'I . . . yes, they did. Much bigger though.'

Grandma Betts looked puzzled. 'You were in France, dear?'

'She was a nurse. Daddy said she was a very good one. A proper Florence Nightingale, he called her.' Maddie imparted her compliment with great pride.

Helen did not like the way Grandma was putting two and two together. She may be elderly but there were no dusty corners in her mind. 'I have to go.'

Grey eyes peered at her over a pair of clicking needles.

'Why are you working in the factory and not in a hospital, dear, if you don't mind me asking?'

Helen did mind her asking. 'I had to come home. Family reasons.' It wasn't quite a lie. 'I'll see you later. Thank you for coming over. Elsie is very grateful.'

Reminded of the calamity that had befallen this little family, Grandma Betts was distracted from her thoughts on Helen's past. 'No trouble at all. That's what neighbours are for.'

Waiting for her bus, Helen hugged her arms to her sides, feeling the chill shadow of doom stretching out for her, even though it was a warm day. She did not regret using her skills at the school – how could she? – but it had made her an object of interest in the local area, and Grandma would not be the last to wonder about her. Would any of them put it together with the story about the German nurse that circulated last autumn? Her assumed name was hardly much of a change from her real one. Helen Sandra *Ford*, she had proclaimed herself; she had concocted a story that the Sandford on her old documents was a clerical error, should anyone ask, and so far no one had.

Watching the bus rumble down the street towards her, she regretted not taking up Sebastian's offer to change her surname when she'd had the chance.

Mrs Hopper nodded as Helen came in ten minutes late. 'How is the child, Miss Ford?'

'As well as can be expected, thank you for asking.' Helen sat down, already feeling weary after a busy morning of getting the children ready for Grandma Betts.

Nelly snipped off some threads holding the piece she was working at on the machine. 'I hear the girl was badly burned.'

'I'm afraid that's true.'

'Poor little mite. All the great and the good are flocking to the hospital – even the Queen, can you believe it? They'd be better doing something to stop it happening rather than holding our hands once the damage is done.'

Several of the women within earshot muttered their agreement.

'I also heard you were quite the heroine down at the bombsite, doing first aid like a professional.' Nelly looked at her hard.

How to answer? Helen picked up her sewing. 'Thank you. I just used the first-aid training I have. I couldn't stand around and do nothing.'

'No, I don't suppose you could.' Nelly signalled the conversation was at an end by running her machine hard. 'Guilt does that to a person.'

Helen's heart missed a beat. Nelly knew – or was half-way to knowing. A trickle of sweat ran down her spine like the touch of dead fingers. She hunched over her machine, half expecting the blow to fall, but Nelly said nothing. None of the other women acted any differently towards her, but there was a definite Arctic wind blowing from her nearest neighbour. Scared now, Helen kept her head down and worked as hard as she could, taking only the minimal breaks, making sure they did not coincide with Nelly's. She did not want to give the woman a chance to get her on her own and interrogate her some more. She did not want to lie outright; so far she had got by with half-truths and silence. A full-blown lie was likely to catch her out much more quickly. Sitting in the high-ceilinged workroom among the rows of women, Helen felt like she had a spotlight shining down on her, illuminating every flaw, every crack in her story. She wished she could crawl away and take shelter somewhere – Sebastian's arms being her preferred haven. The precarious loneliness of her position was too much to bear. She was only eighteen and yet on days like this she felt eighty, carrying the burden of an unjust condemnation. Lightning rod of national hatred. Scapegoat.

Mrs Hopper examined her basket of finished goods. 'Excellent work today, Miss Ford.'

'Thank you, Mrs Hopper.'

'We've had a collection in the time you were away – for the families of those affected by the incident at the school. Will you take it and see that it is fairly distributed to help with hospital and funeral expenses?'

Helen held out her hand, Nelly's eyes raking her back. 'Of course I will. I'll give it to the headmaster – he is ensuring the money that comes in is divided equally.'

'Perhaps we should give it to him directly,' said Nelly, leaving her seat.

Helen withdrew her palm. 'If you prefer.'

Mrs Hopper frowned. 'Mrs Hilton, I'm sure Miss Ford here is a perfectly safe messenger. I've written the amount down quite clearly and put it in this little parcel here. Do you have any reason to think she might lose it or have it stolen from her? She is a most reliable worker as far as I can see, not given to such lapses of attention.'

'Perhaps Miss Ford can explain herself why I might think the money is not safe with a thief.'

Helen swallowed, refusing to look ashamed of something she had not done.

'Nothing to say, Miss Helen Ford? You see, I remember those stories even if others have forgotten them. Thought you could get away with hiding among us, did you?'

The axe had finally fallen.

'I don't know what you think you know, Mrs Hilton, but you are wrong about me.' Helen picked up her handbag. 'Perhaps you should deliver the money yourself, Mrs Hopper, as my colleague objects. I have to go.'

'Not so fast, Miss Ford.' Mrs Hopper held up her hand. 'Not while that accusation stands. Mrs Hilton, are you saying that Miss Ford has been stealing from us? I have never noticed any irregularities in her output; nothing has gone missing to my knowledge.'

'I don't suppose it has. No, she stole from the hospital where she worked in France and was kicked out. Don't you remember the newspaper articles last year? It took me a while to work it out but I thought her name was familiar. Then when I heard about her nursing expertise, the penny dropped. The gossip is doing the rounds where I live. I'm not the only one to know.'

Helen began walking. There was no point, she had

discovered, of defending herself against accusations she could not deny. Being half German meant she was automatically guilty, with no hope of proving innocence.

'Miss Ford, wait! Haven't you anything to say?'

She paused at the door. 'Would it make any difference? I've tried my best to help, but that is never good enough.'

Nelly pointed at her. 'She's German – you realize that, don't you, Mrs Hopper.'

'And she's been among us all this time?' exclaimed Bernadette, coming to stand beside her friend. 'Is she a spy? Do you think she's planted herself in the East End to signal to the planes where to drop their bombs?'

Nelly folded her arms. 'I wouldn't go so far as to say that, but it looks very suspicious.'

Helen took her record card out of the time puncher by the door and ripped it up. Leaving the two halves to fall to the floor, she walked out.

9

The long summer evening seemed an insult. Helen wished for dark to hide her distress, but the sun refused to cooperate. Happy shafts of light broke between the terrace housing, gilding the dusty roads. Children played in the streets, a fierce marble competition on one corner, skipping on another. Two days ago these same children had been cowering in basements and underground stations; now they were enjoying the open air and showed no signs of fear. Only the mothers, standing on doorsteps, arms folded, had the crease of worry etched between their eyes. Assessing the skies. On guard. Their little ones were more sensible: you had to snatch moments of calm and pleasure, as they never stayed long.

And certainly never for her. Each refuge she reached was to be blown down, scandal chasing her like the wolf pursuing the little pigs from house to house in the fairy tale. She had thought Elsie's home had been built of bricks, but once again it was sticks and straw for her. She knew she had to go home but feared to arrive back in Poplar dragging her trouble behind her.

What should she do?

Passing a little church, on impulse she entered. It was empty. At peace. She sat in a pew near the front and gazed up at the stained-glass window put in a few decades ago by well-fed Victorians, an elaborately robed angel sticking a spear into an obligingly passive dragon like a cook testing the Sunday joint. She preferred the haunted suffering on the face of the Christ on the altar crucifix – that spoke more about struggle and warfare than the Angel Michael playing at battling beasts as the twins did soldiers on the hearthrug. The dark wood of the carving made Christ a man of any time, any race, at home in trenches as well as Judaean deserts. It was an answer of sorts, wasn't it? He did not stop suffering but shared it. Hard to keep hold of these old certainties in the furnace of world war, but that one part of her childhood faith did at least still make sense.

A priest entered from the vestry and nodded affably to her. Taking a box from his pew, he knelt at the altar rail and began praying, taking out one by one a collection of photographs and cap badges. With great care, he spent a moment on each one, then put it aside. When he had finished, he must have said a prayer for at least twenty-five young men. He got up and put the box back in its place.

Helen rose to go.

'Would you like me to say a few words for anyone, my dear?' the priest asked. 'You see, I pray at this time each day for my boys out there.'

Helen settled the strap of her bag on her arm. 'Your boys, father?'

'My parishioners.'

'And does it help?'

He lifted an eyebrow. 'Well, that is the question for the ages. Does it help them? I pray so. I say a few words for those who have died as well as those still living because I believe they are still with us here.' He tapped his heart. 'But I tell you one thing: I know that it helps their families and me. We can do so little but this we can do.'

'I have to admit that I'm struggling to believe anything. It all seems so unfair.' She felt a little angry with the priest for having his answers. If God weren't here to rail at, then the priest would do. 'I can't bear it – all this suffering!'

'I agree, my dear. The loss of life is an obscenity, a sin. But we were never promised fairness. Persecution, hatred and rejection – we were told to expect all those. It is a realistic saviour we have, not a fairy godmother. I hope you haven't made the mistake many do of confusing the two?' He spread out his hands in a questioning gesture.

'So what's the point in believing if all we get are bad things?'

'Ah, I didn't say it was *just* bad things – we get love and joy too from time to time.' His eyes twinkled. 'But for the hard patches in life, we were promised the strength to endure. If we trust in Him.' He nodded to the crucifix. 'You need to just keep putting one foot in front of the other. It's not a perfect answer but it is the only one I've found reliable.' He patted her arm. 'Now, who shall this old man pray for, eh? It can't do any harm and it may well do a lot of good.'

He was right; there was no point ignoring every possibility in the mystery of living, every little ounce of help that could be begged, borrowed or stolen from Heaven. 'His name is Sebastian. A pilot. But can you also remember Joan — she's five and was hurt in the bomb at the school?'

'I'll add them to my box. Do you have something you can give me to remember them by?'

She dug in her handbag and pulled out a pencil. 'This is for Sebastian — he is an artist.' She tugged the button off her cuff. 'And this is for Joan.'

He held the two objects in his hand with care. 'And you? Shall I say a few words for you too? Something tells me you need it.'

After the scene at the factory, it was almost a relief to find that there was no more need for hiding. 'My name is Helen Sandford. Yes, strength to endure is what I need.'

'I've heard that name before, have I not?'

'Yes, I'm quite infamous.' She wondered if he would take back his offer to pray for her.

'I think you do not speak idly of fairness and unfairness?'

'I am guilty of being half German but not of the rest.'

'Ah, my poor child, you say that as if expecting me to be the first to cast a stone at you! But you see, I am too old for this fuss about nations; I know only people, men and women. I pray that you will find the strength you seek.'

Helen wanted to kiss the old priest for his acceptance. 'If I can, may I come back and see you again?'

'I'd be delighted if you did. I'm always here at this time and now you know where to find me.'

Touched by this encounter, Helen felt ready to return home. Looked at another way, every time she sank beneath the waves, there was someone there to pull her above the surface: Elsie and Reg, the old priest, and most of all Sebastian. She just had to remember that.

Grandma Betts was sleeping by the stove when Helen arrived home. The boys had got into the sewing box and like inquisitive kittens had wrapped themselves up in darning wool. Maddie was trying to untangle them and looked close to tears as they made her attempts worse. She always tried so hard to be responsible and good – it was quite a burden for her. The baby was sitting watching the excitement with avid interest, beating a pot with a wooden spoon. Helen swept into the kitchen, saw what was going on, and picked up Maddie for a big hug.

'Have they been naughty?'

'Yes.' Maddie buried her head in the crook of Helen's neck.

'Shall we leave them tied up forever or shall we set them free?'

The boys stopped tugging on the knots on hearing that threat, shocked such a punishment could be suggested. Maddie bit her lip, sorely tempted. 'I think Mummy needs the wool.'

'All right: freedom it is. Sit still, you terrors, and I'll sort you out.'

The twins sat, only wiggling with irrepressible giggles when Grandma let out a particularly loud snore.

Helen had almost finished releasing the two boys when a voice called out by the front door:

'Anyone home?'

'Daddy!' squeaked Maddie, dashing to greet him.

'Oh, thank God!' murmured Helen. She would no longer be facing the gathering storm alone. 'There you go.' She unlooped the last strand of wool and the boys were off like greyhounds slipped from the leash. She shook Grandma awake. 'Grandma Betts, Mr Cook is back.'

The old lady took a second to come to her senses. 'Their father? Praise be. I'll make space for him then. He won't want me cluttering up his kitchen.'

Helen heard her exchange greetings with Reg on her way out. Deciding he would be hungry after his journey, she set about finding something for supper, moving around the kitchen with the baby balanced on one hip. She was a little nervous seeing him, knowing that he would want her to tell him his daughter would be fine and she really didn't have the words.

'Yes, I'm here for a few days.' Reg entered the room in mid-explanation to Maddie. He had a boy hanging off each leg, catching a ride on his boots, which didn't seem to bother him. 'Hello, Helen. Thank you for looking after this lot.' He kissed the baby and then Helen's cheek.

'No thanks required. I wouldn't be anywhere else. Have you been to the hospital yet?'

'Yes, love, I've just come from there. There's not much I can do so Elsie thought you might need a hand by now.'

'How is Joan?'

'Oh,' he looked down at his children, 'fair to middling.'

'As far as I could tell, she's receiving the best care there is.'

He cleared his throat. 'Good to know. Oh, I bring greeting from your young man.'

'You saw Sebastian?' In surprise, Helen lifted her hand to her mouth, lips just touching the ring.

'I did. He had had a little accident and ended up in the hospital —'

'What!'

'Nothing serious, just a few bumps and scrapes. He happened to be with me when I got your telegram.'

'But he's all right?'

'Yes, he's right as rain. And how about you? How are you managing?'

His question brought back the problem she had left behind at work. 'I'm afraid I can't report the same for me. They know — at the factory.'

'About you?'

She nodded. 'It's getting out. Even Grandma Betts is getting suspicious. I'm not sure what anyone can do about it, but I'm not welcome back at the factory.'

'I see. Is there anything I can do?'

She shook her head. 'Don't worry, please. You've enough on your plate. I think I've found a kind of peace about it. I can't stop what is going to happen, can I?'

'You don't know how guilty that makes me feel, love.'

She smiled wistfully. 'I can guess. Now drink your tea and I'll see what there is to eat.'

The police officer arrived at dawn. Reg was already up, in the kitchen feeding the baby, and so answered the door. In the small house, their conversation was audible in Helen's bedroom.

'Is this the residence of a Miss Helen Sandford?'

'I'll have you know it is the residence of Reginald Cook and family.' Reg sounded quite put out. The baby began to wail, her cries gaining in power as she sensed a new crisis had arrived.

'But does Helen Sandford also live here, Mr Cook?'

When he didn't reply immediately, Helen knew he was contemplating lying.

'She registered this as her home address when she took her job at the garment factory. Was she lying about that too?'

'Now hang on a minute, Miss Sandford is not a liar!'

Helen slid out of bed and dressed rapidly.

'So she does live here.'

'And what business is that of yours?'

'Do you know who she is?'

'Of course I know who she is!'

'Did you know she was thrown out of a military hospital for theft after it was revealed she was German?'

'When will your lot realize that she's innocent? She didn't take nothing – and she's not German! If you have to persecute her for having a German parent, what are you going to do about the Royal Family, eh? They're bleedin' cousins to the Kaiser!'

Helen didn't bother with stockings. Reg was going to get himself arrested if he carried on like this.

'It's all right, officer: I'm here. How can I help you?' She remained half-way up the stairs. 'It's fine, Reg,' she added in an undertone.

'Miss Helen Sandford?' The policeman was looking at her as if she were about as welcome in the household as rising damp.

'Yes, that's my name.'

'I'd like you to accompany me to the station. I have a few questions for you.'

'What kind of questions?'

'As to why you are hiding your nationality, for starters.'

Reg bristled. 'Bloody stupid bureaucrats – can't you get anything right? I told you – she's English. Sandford. Does that sound German to you?'

'She has a German mother and communicates with her relatives in that language. A complaint has been lodged that she poses a threat to the local people by living among them.'

'What kind of threat?' Helen asked.

The policeman rubbed his nose, perhaps – in one sane

corner of his mind untouched by the anti-German hysteria – aware he was talking nonsense. 'Well, bombs did fall in the area. Fifteen children are dead.'

'That's a bleedin' insult, that is! This young lady did nothing but help. You take that back!' Reg had his fist curled. It was just as well he was carrying the baby or he would have taken a swing at the man.

'It's not what I think, Mr Cook: it's what's being said. And to clear the matter up, she needs to come with me.'

Helen tried to stay calm but found her legs refused to support her. She sat on the step and wrapped her arms around herself. 'Are you arresting me?'

'Not yet, miss, but you'd better come prepared for a longer stay, just in case. I'll give you a minute to pack up your things, but best be quick: I came early so the locals don't decide to see you off in their own fashion. There's been some unpleasant business with your sort.'

'Her sort! You couldn't find a truer English girl if you spent the rest of your life searching! Look, mate, she didn't take a thing from that hospital! That was me, all right? Arrest me for it but leave the girl out of it!'

The policeman ignored Reg's outburst. 'Miss, I really think it best you come along quietly now while you can.'

Keep putting one foot in front of the other – that was what the priest had said. 'I'll just get my coat then.' It was hard to believe any of this was real, though it had a terrible logic to it. Retreating to her bedroom, she stood looking blankly at the window. She briefly contemplated climbing out that way, but knew there was no escape for her.

Maddie stirred in the bed. 'Is it time to get up yet?'

'No, love. Go back to sleep.'

'Are you going somewhere?'

'Yes, I think so.'

'When will you be back?'

'As soon as I can.' She bent down and kissed her fore-head. 'You're not to worry about me.'

British Airbase, La Houssoye,
France, 15 June 1917, 6 p.m.

Sebastian stretched out on the old sofa, listening to the chatter of his fellow pilots as they relaxed off duty. It had been a good day: no one lost and two Germans downed over British lines, a little plus in the Allied column against Richthofen's flying circus.

'I think I saw him this morning, you know,' said Bunty Taylor, a rather imaginative pilot of Sebastian's age who claimed more hits than was his due.

'What? You went up against the Red Baron and lived to tell the tale?' Bob Nunn, one of the older men, scoffed. 'Come on, Bunty, that isn't very likely! You are barely out of greenhorn stage. If he had you in his sights, you'd not be here to tell us.'

'It looked like him – at least, I think. It was a triplane. I let loose a few rounds from the old gun and he went running.'

Sebastian smiled at the ceiling. That last detail confirmed that Bunty was inventing again. Richthofen never ran – he was the Sir Lancelot of the joust in the air and for that reason was the kill most British pilots lusted after. The man's legend was becoming more embroidered, the longer he came out top in the air combats.

'I'm looking for volunteers, chaps.' The captain strode into the tin shed that served as the officers' mess. 'Command is calling the 46th back to England to defend London. We need experienced pilots to join them, preferably those due some leave.'

Every man in the room stood – no one would fail to put himself forward for a plum assignment like that.

'Oh, I say, sir!'

'Pick me!'

'At your service, captain.'

'Ah, I see I'm going to struggle to find suitable recruits.' The captain smiled sourly. 'Looking through the leave roster . . .' he glanced down at his notes, 'I'd say that makes Tennant, Cordel and Trewby the lucky volunteers. You are to report to Sutton's Farm in Hornchurch, Essex, as soon as possible.'

Charlie Cordel, who had been with Sebastian since training days, punched the air. 'Yes!'

'This isn't a holiday, Cordel, but an assignment to fight the Germans like any other.'

Charlie did a poor job of looking sober. 'Of course, sir.'

'The people of London are counting on you.'

'Yes, sir.'

Charlie waited until the captain left the mess before carrying on his celebration. He did a handstand over the

138

back of the sofa, landing with a flourish. 'What a stroke of luck, Trewby! Tennant, are you ready to charm the ladies of Essex?'

Over in his armchair by the window, the shy hedge sparrow of a Scottish pilot, who transformed to a hawk when behind the controls of his plane, stammered something that could have been an agreement.

Sebastian had already calculated how close Hornchurch was to Poplar. Not far. He rubbed his hands in anticipation. 'Yes, a lucky break for us. Not sure what they expect us to do though. How are we going to stop the planes getting through? It strikes me we are being asked to catch minnows with a harpoon.'

Charlie was making himself a nuisance, dancing around the other men who had not been so fortunate. He called across their heads. 'That's beside the point, old man: we are going home.'

It might not be the first consideration for Charlie, but Sebastian thought it was rather important to the likes of Reg and his family that the military come up with some sensible defences.

10

The cell in Poplar police station smelt of . . . well, Helen didn't want to put a name to the odour, but it made her want to curl inside her skin and shut it out like a hedgehog rolling up. She perched on the corner of the bunk and turned up the collar of her coat so she could sniff the material – a little smoky but clean. She had sewn it herself last winter and it brought back happy memories of sharing the fireside with Elsie, chatting about their menfolk in France and their hopes for the future. She had never dreamed then that this is where she and the coat would end up.

A door banged somewhere else in the building. She had been here for hours. The policeman had made the effort to come for her early, but that had not resulted in an immediate interview; instead she had been left to stew all day, staring at the walls. After six hours she had decided it was deliberate. Respect for authority had been drummed into her as a child, but if someone didn't come soon she would have to take action – demand they tell her what was going on at the very least. It was hard, though, to find the courage to do that in this masculine world of prisons and policemen.

A key turned in the lock and a man, but not a uniformed officer, stood in the doorway. Was he a lawyer for her?

'Miss Helen Abendroth-Sandford?'

She stood up. 'I've never used the name Abendroth. My name is just Helen Sandford. Are you a solicitor?'

'No. Why? Do you think you need one?'

Her brief hope that he might be on her side puffed out. 'I don't know. I don't understand why I'm here.'

He shook his head at her. 'So that is how you are playing it. Follow me.'

No 'please', no manners allowing her to go first through doorways – the man made his opinion of her plain. Outside the cell, a constable waited to accompany them down the corridor: two big men to escort one small girl. It was as if they expected her to turn rabid and bite them.

'The sergeant said you were welcome to use his office, sir,' the policeman said, opening the door to a little room not far from the front desk.

'Thank you, constable.'

Ah, so they could both be polite, at least to each other. Helen wondered who the man was – he was wearing a suit, had slicked-back brown hair and a moustache, looked fairly well-to-do by Poplar standards but not top drawer, not like Sebastian and his family. She clung to the locket around her neck, hoping his picture and lock of hair would warm the chill in her bones.

'Take a seat, Miss Abendroth-Sandford.' The man

gestured to an upright chair placed in front of the desk. He took his own seat behind it, then sat observing her in silence for a few moments. Helen rubbed the seam of her skirt, trying not to reveal how nervous she felt.

'How old are you, Miss Abendroth-Sandford?'

'Miss *Sandford*,' she said in a low voice.

'Pardon?'

'I said, it is just Miss Sandford.'

He gave a cool smile. 'Your age?'

'Eighteen. Almost nineteen.'

'When were you last in Germany?'

Startled, she looked up and met his calculating eyes. They seemed small and mean, holding an expression she last saw on a dog that was about to attack. 'I've never been there.'

'When did you last communicate with someone from that country?'

'I have never written to anyone in Germany – except adding Christmas greetings and that kind of message when my mother wrote to her relatives.'

'What do you know about the organization called "The Unseen Hand"?'

'I've never heard of it.' She laced her fingers together, realizing that by letting them flutter in her lap she was betraying her anxiety. It was important for her pride that she didn't crumble. 'Excuse me, but who are you, sir?'

'My name is Brown and I'm from the Home Office.'

'So you're not a policeman?'

'My department is in charge of the police service of this country.'

'I see.' She didn't really, but he showed no inclination to be more forthcoming. Did he have any right to question her? She was too intimidated to ask.

He took another line of attack. 'How do you signal your compatriots?'

'My what?'

'Come, come, Miss Abendroth-Sandford, I'm not a fool: you have to be living in this area for a reason. You have no previous connection with Poplar, but yet here you are, sitting right on top of the docks, in the economic heart of the kingdom.'

'I'm staying with friends.'

'Ah yes, the Cook family. Interesting man, Reginald Cook: has quite a reputation in his regiment for bending the rules. Does he know about your activities? Surely not, as he would not be sheltering an enemy – that is a step too far even for one of his moral ambiguity.'

Helen brushed a hand across her face, at once both scared and confused. 'I don't know what you think I have done but perhaps you'd better just come out with it, sir.'

'We have reason to believe our enemy has a network planted in London – agents directing the raids and undermining morale at home. You are suspected of being one of the many heads of that hydra.'

This was all so strange – so absurd. 'On what grounds am I accused of this? I can't see what I've done other than go to work and help Mrs Cook mind the children.'

Mr Brown opened a file that lay on the desk in front of him – close-written pages of 'evidence' someone had been compiling on her. 'The circumstances speak against you – your conduct in France, your presence here where you have no business being, your concealment of your identity.'

These accusations floating around her were like clouds, impossible to dispel, intangible nothings. Helen had no experience with the law, but she did remember that they couldn't continue to hold her without charging her with something.

'I am willing to answer any question you may have, but are you going to charge me with a crime? I've been here all day, helping with enquiries –' she resisted a grimace at those ironic words – 'and so far no one has spelled out what I've done.'

Brown looked down at the papers on the desk in front of him. 'Slippery customer, aren't you?'

'Me?' Helen gave a shocked laugh. This whole interview was like crossing a river on rocky stepping-stones, each one threatening to trip her up and dump her in.

'I don't suppose you will tell me how much Lieutenant Trewby has told you and what you've passed on to your masters?'

Not Sebastian too! She shouldn't be surprised they had ferreted out that detail if they had been spying on her, but she had kept hoping that her private life would not be touched by their sullying accusations. She could only shake her head, praying she would wake up from this nightmare.

'I thought as much. Don't worry: we will make sure he is disabused of his illusions about you. We can't let a good man be used by the enemy.'

This was too much: this Brown person was taking the fragile stuff that was her life and stamping on it. 'Please, don't.' She lifted her hands as if to ward off a blow – but it wasn't a physical attack, was it?

'"Please, don't" what?' Brown looked curious for the first time.

'Please, don't involve him.' She let her hands drop, ring winking up at her from her lap. She knew in her heart that Brown wasn't worth her appeal, but she was hurting and could not help herself.

'Interesting. So he does matter to you.' He made a note on her file. 'We won't be charging you with an offence today, but know this: we have our eyes on you. Put one toe over the line and you'll be inside and the key thrown away. I advise you to think carefully. You are very young – it could be argued that you have been led astray – the folly of youth, filial loyalties in conflict. If you come clean and give up your associates, you may be able to strike a deal with us that sees you released after a few years.' He paused, waiting for her to confess her non-existent crimes. 'No? Hardened, are you? I must say, you are the most striking case I have ever seen where the outer package belies the inner person.'

She could see no sane reason why he was so convinced of her guilt. 'Why are you saying these things to me?'

'Do you really have to ask that?'

'Yes! I don't understand any of this. What evidence do you have? Could it not be that I am as I seem and not as you have decided?' It was hopeless – she could tell she had not moved him one jot.

'You have two days to consider my offer. Leave word for me here if you wish to make a deal.'

Was she angry or was this hurt clawing away in her chest? 'I'm English. I was a nurse. I did not steal. I have no "associates" – that's the only information I can offer you as I don't belong to any "network". I'm not a conspirator. I live under the same threat of becoming a victim of the bombers as everyone else. Why are you singling me out?' But she knew, oh she knew: it was because this war had sent everyone more than a little mad.

'You may go. Think on my offer – it won't remain on the table for long.'

Helen couldn't summon the will to move. The man calling himself Mr Brown got up and left first. The policeman entered, standing by the open door, perhaps to ensure she didn't vandalize the office. When she showed no signs of moving, he came over and took her firmly by the elbow. 'Time to go, miss – unless you want to spend a night in the cell?'

'Where's my handbag? You took it from me,' she said, still reeling from the interrogation. Emotionally ripped in half – her soul felt soiled by this hateful experience.

'The duty officer at the front desk will return it to you.'

'Very well.' *Just one step.* Taking a steadying breath, she got up.

'Filthy Hun,' muttered the officer as he escorted her down the corridor. 'Handbag for the baby-killer, Sarge.'

The desk officer practically threw her belongings at her. 'They letting her go?'

'For the moment.'

'Criminal, that is.'

Imagine they are talking about someone else, Helen told herself.

'I don't think she'll be running around out there for long, do you? The locals won't allow it.'

'Better think of getting yourself back to the Fatherland, Fräulein. While you still can.'

Saying nothing – what words were there in the face of such prejudice? – Helen walked stiffly out of the police station.

En route to Dover, 16 June 1917, 5 p.m.

Looking out over the choppy grey waters of the Channel, Sebastian wondered, not for the first time, at the smallness of the stretch dividing England from the horror of the land campaign. You could fly across the sea in twenty minutes, give or take. That would have been a fine way to return home, rather than crammed in with seasick Tommies.

'What will you do first, Trewby?' Charlie asked,

throwing his cigarette butt over the side. 'I vote we hold a squadron dance, rope in some local ladies, get a quartet of musicians on board – what do you think?'

'They might expect us to pass the time by flying a few sorties, you know.'

Charlie waved that away. 'Naturally, but we're only young once and I've not been to a decent dance in an age. I don't count those dull things with zee mademoiselles of France standing on one side and us on the other, wishing we knew what our partner was saying.'

'You should've paid more attention in your French class.'

'I would have done if I had actually thought I'd find the language useful one day. I'm determined to make up for lost time.'

It was hard for pilots like Charlie to understand the seriousness of the air threat to London – the damage there was pinpricks compared to the deep incision down the Western Front. For him, a home posting was a holiday from war. Sebastian realized how different it all seemed to him, with a loved one under the path of the bombers.

'You should invite your fiancée up.' In Charlie's mind the dance was already a certainty.

'I will. She's going to be very surprised to find I'm practically on her doorstep.' Leaving in a hurry, Sebastian had only had a moment to send Helen word that he was moving back to England. It was even possible he would arrive before his letter.

'I know, I know: we'll have fizz – if there's any to be

had – and a dinner, and a proper dance floor laid down! And we'll get a marquee set up for the mess. And to impress the ladies, we'll entertain them with stunts before the meal – you can loop the loop – that'll astound your fiancée no end.'

It was like some giant child had grabbed hold of Charlie-the-clockwork-airman, wound him up and left him to scoot round the deck until he ran down – he would not stop until he had settled every last detail of the mythical dance. Sebastian imagined stuffing him into a teapot like the dormouse in *Alice in Wonderland* – half listening to the extended monologue, he even drew the sketch. He added himself as the White Rabbit and their quiet companion, Tennant, as the Mad Hatter. Not a good piece of casting, that. The Scot would be better as the caterpillar. He quickly drew him again in his new role.

'I never knew you were a dab hand at drawing!' exclaimed Charlie, taking the picture and showing it to anyone who evinced the least inclination to be sociable, and a few who didn't. 'Let's have a look at the rest.'

Before Sebastian could protest, his sketchbook was whipped out of his hands.

'These are dashed good!' Charlie sat down on a kitbag beside him. He paused over a picture Sebastian had done from the perspective of high up above the battlefield, planes passing below him. 'Where did you learn to draw like this?'

'I was at the Slade Art School in London before I joined up.'

'Dark horse you are, Trewby! You never said. You should put in to be one of those official war artist chappies.'

Sebastian just smiled and shook his head. He didn't want to turn his art to something the government could command from him; it was his one remaining area of freedom.

'Oh and who is this little beauty?' Charlie had found one of his pictures of Helen.

'My fiancée.'

'You are a lucky dog. Wish I had a sweet thing like this at home waiting for me.'

The shy Scot, Fred Tennant, cleared his throat. 'The lasses love a laddie with wings.'

'What's this? Why, Scottie, don't tell me you have a wee bonnie lassie in the glens.' Charlie's attempt at the Scottish accent was an insult to all north of the border.

'Aye, I do. I'm wed and got a bairn.'

Charlie slapped his forehead. 'How did I not know this? And that makes me the laggard with the ladies – one wed, one engaged and me all lonesome.' He grinned. 'Now I know my true mission on this home posting – find my lady before all the good ones are taken.' He turned to Sebastian. 'Does your fiancée have a sister or some pretty friend we can invite to our dance?'

Sebastian paused before answering. Complicated – Helen's sister was an unmarried mother in New York with a little boy to look after, while Helen's supply of friends was running dangerously low. 'I fear, Cordel, you'll have to go hunting yourself. But do not be too anxious: with all the men away in France, even a sad specimen like you should have no difficulty.'

Charlie, who was in truth a fair-looking fellow – as far as Sebastian could judge these things – chuckled and stretched out on his kitbag. 'I hope you are right, Trewby.'

Helen waited for night before making her way home, all too aware that the policemen's muttering about the threat of reprisals from locals was not idle. Her own eyes were witness to this truth. After leaving the station, she sheltered in an alleyway off the High Street, watching as several shops with German-sounding names were looted, the locals running wild, hacking at the shutters, throwing the goods out into the street to be made off with by gangs of children. The crowd wasn't too picky – turning their attention to the neighbouring premises if they held things they fancied – shoes, furniture, bread – everything was fair game. A free-for-all – except the unfortunate shopkeepers. The owners protested, but the policemen present seemed unmoved. One officer pocketed an orange from a Jewish greengrocer's and turned his back on the mayhem.

Then one idiot decided to set light to a butcher's shop.

'We'll 'ave a roast tonight!' he crowed, shoving a lit petrol-soaked rag into the debris littering the shop. It caught with a whoosh that was cheered by onlookers. The householders either side, however, were less enthusiastic.

'You fool!' shrieked a woman, driving the crowd off

her doorstep with a broom. 'You'll burn my family in our beds, would you?' She applied the brush to the side of the idiot's head with a solid thwack.

Seeing they were about to have a major incident on their hands, the policemen who had so far been little more than spectators decided belatedly to take action. Approaching the site, whistles blowing, truncheons swinging, they scattered the looters and organized a chain of buckets to dampen the blaze. No one spoke to the butcher and his family, gathered in a sad huddle on the pavement on the far side of the road. The wife wept on the man's shoulder.

'Twenty years we've had this shop!' Helen heard her lament. 'Twenty years.'

The East End had gone mad. Like a lion with a thorn in its paw, it had taken to trying to gnaw off its own limb – a senseless destruction that hurt only itself. Helen leaned back on the grimy bricks and let the tears run down her cheeks unchecked, weeping for the families, for Joan and the other victims of the bombs, for herself.

When the fire was a heap of smoking ashes and the German butcher and his family were left picking over the remains, Helen slunk home, head down. She said nothing to Reg when she came in, just nodded, hung her coat on the peg by the door, and went through to the kitchen.

'You all right, love?' He stood in the doorway awkwardly. 'I came over earlier but they said you'd been released. No charge.' He dug his hands in his pockets.

'How are the children?'

'Fine. In bed.'

'Joan?'

'She had a good day.'

Helen washed her hands of the day's filth and then cut a slice of bread.

'You've not eaten?'

'No. Tea?'

'I'll make it. You sit down.'

She sat at the table and nibbled at the bread. *One step at a time.* 'I'm going to have to leave.'

'You don't have to do that, love.' Reg put a cup of tea in front of her.

'No, I do. Really, I do.' Oh but it hurt. 'I watched the crowd set fire to a house containing a German family tonight. I can't risk your children.'

Reg puffed out a breath. 'No, I don't suppose you can. Do you have somewhere to go?'

'I appear to be running out of places to run.' She gave a short laugh. 'Ironic.'

'Your mum and dad?'

She shook her head.

'Then we'll ask the lieutenant. He's not short of a bob or two. He'll be able to help.'

'I'm not sure he'll want to help me.'

'Now see here: none of that nonsense! The lieutenant is devoted to you!'

'I don't doubt that. It's just that the only place I can think of to run to now is my sister in New York.'

'And he won't want you to go so far?'

She nodded and gulped the tea.

'Don't blame him. Sea's a dangerous place, for passenger ships too.'

'I know. The ship that took my sister was sunk on the return trip.'

'You'd prefer to risk that than stay here?'

'I'm not sure I'm being left much choice.' Reg had a right to know just what trouble he and his family were touched by, as his name had been mentioned. 'There was this strange man from the Home Office at the police station. He had it in his head that I'm some secret agent for the Germans. They've been watching me and apparently I act suspiciously. He knew about you too.' Wearily, Helen let her head fall to rest on one hand, elbow propped on the table. 'I can't do anything right, so perhaps I should just give up trying. Start again somewhere else.'

Reg had no time to reply as a fist thundered on the front door.

'Bring out the German bitch!'

'Jay-sus!' Reg leapt to his feet as the door crashed open and six dockyard workers invaded the kitchen. 'Get out of my house, Harry Dalston!'

The answer from Harry was a punch to the jaw that laid Reg out cold on the floor. Helen screamed. She tried to run for the backyard but was grabbed around the waist and hauled out the front. Flailing to get a grip, she struggled in iron-muscled arms but could not wriggle free. Dragged down the street, her captor dropped her to the pavement. She staggered to her feet, and found herself in the middle of a hostile crowd consisting of people she had thought of as neighbours. It was the worst kind of scenario, because the very ones she would have appealed to for help before today were surrounding her, faces ugly with hate and bitterness.

'I've done nothing,' she said hoarsely. Her hair was falling from its bun, straggling down one side of her face, the sleeve of her blouse ripped from the rough handling.

'Child-killer!' shrieked one woman. She picked up a stone and threw it at Helen. It missed, bouncing off the brick wall beside her.

Oh God, this couldn't be happening. Helen threw her arms over her head, trying to protect herself from the missiles that were beginning to come her way.

'My son's dead because of you!'

A sharp sting caught her back when a pebble found its mark. Then another – a rain of tiny shots pinging off her back as someone threw a handful of gravel at her. Helen knew she had to get off the street or they'd kill her. Rubbish, mud, anything they could lay hands on, now ricocheted off her. Small cuts and bruises mixed with heavier blows.

'We don't want no Huns living here!'

'Get out!'

'Go home!'

The door to the nearest house was six feet away – but that seemed a mile, and she doubted any refuge would be offered inside. Terror numbed her brain. All she could think was that by crouching down, head curled in, she would minimize the target and they'd lose interest in her. She knew not to expect any help from the police.

A half-brick struck her thigh. Someone was whimpering. She realized it was her.

'What the hell do you think you're doing?' Out of a crack in her lids, she could see Reg wading through the crowd, beating them aside with a poker, blood running down the side of his face. 'Picking on women now! Have you all run mad?'

'But, Reg: she's a German spy!' protested one dockyard worker, blocking his path through to her.

'Would I 'ave a spy in my 'ouse? With me own kids there? Would I? You know me better than that, Jim. Get the hell off the street. Go 'ome, the whole pack of yer.'

With a disgruntled murmur, the crowd began to disperse.

'Jay-sus, are you all right, Helen?'

'Reg.' She pushed her hair off her face.

He was on his knees beside her, folding her to his chest. 'Christ Almighty, what have they done to you?'

She began to shake. Her fingers plucked at his jacket. He scooped her up and lifted her. Cradling her in his arms, he carried her back into the house. The front door was still wide open. Putting her down in the parlour, he went back to it and shot the bolt. He then took her coat from the peg and hung it round her shoulders.

Helen shrank back, aware that she was covered in muck. 'I'm filthy – you mustn't get dirty.'

Her words had the opposite effect to the one she

intended. 'You, Helen, are the sweetest, purest girl Elsie and I 'ave 'ad the privilege to know. Remember that or I will be very cross with you.' He headed for the kitchen to heat some water for a bath.

Helen knew she should go and help, but somehow she couldn't find the energy. She clutched the coat round her shoulders, shivering. The noises on the street had returned to normal, almost as if the murderous outpouring of hate had never happened. It made her distrust everything she thought she knew about people, this capability to shift on a sixpence from friendly chat to fists and missiles.

She would have to run again.

Sebastian had never been to Reg's house before, so had to ask several times for directions. On the last occasion, knocking at a likely house, the reaction he got was bizarre: the man who answered pointed to a black front door over the road, then spat.

'You come for 'er, 'ave you? About time. Good riddance.' The man slammed his own door shut.

Sebastian crossed the street and knocked. No reply. He tried again, a bright little tap-tap-tap. 'Cook? Cook? Are you in there?'

The door opened a crack, and then Cook threw it wide. 'Christ, lieutenant, what are you doing here?'

'I'm on leave.' He produced the bunch of flowers from behind his back with a flourish. 'These aren't for you.'

'Come in, quick.'

Something was wrong. Sebastian entered the tiny front room, flowers dipping in his hand. 'Where's Helen? She is still here, isn't she?'

'Yeah, bless 'er, but no thanks to my sodding neighbours. They bloody well tried to stone 'er, they did!'

'What!'

'Shhh!' Reg hopped on the spot, gesturing upstairs. 'The kids don't know about it and I'd rather they didn't.'

'Where is she?'

'In the back –' Reg grabbed his sleeve – 'but you can't go in. She's 'aving a bath, to get clean like.'

With very deliberate care, Sebastian put the flowers down on the table before he crushed them. He did not know what to do with the hot river of fury that flowed in his veins. To have his Helen attacked – he wanted to put his fist through something, preferably one of her attackers' faces.

'Who were they, Cook?' he asked tightly, having wild thoughts of marching into the nearest police station and demanding the whole pack of them be arrested.

'Neighbours. I would've called them good people until this evening. Maniacs.'

'Give me their names and I'll report them.'

Reg sat down and gave a weary laugh. 'Yeah, fat lot of good that'll do, sir. Your little lady spent the whole day being harassed at the police station – they probably encouraged them out there to have a go at her when they couldn't find a scrap of evidence to charge her with.'

It knocked Sebastian's belief in an ordered society to find the police involved. Who could he and Helen rely on if not them? 'What on earth do they think she's done? It's not that old stuff from France, is it?'

'No, sir, though that don't help. It's because they've

gone stark raving mad – can't do anything about the Huns in the sky, so are inventing an enemy on the ground.'

'Then she's leaving. With me. Tonight.'

'That's best.'

They sat looking at the wilting flowers on the table between them; a white petal drifted to the cloth, curled like a feather. In the kitchen, the splashing had stopped. Sebastian had a fair idea that Helen would be suffering in there and that only made his anger more potent, a great fiery heart that beat against his ribcage. It was no good him losing his temper – that would be of no help to anyone. He reached for the calm and focus that he had learned on the battlefield. There was more than one sorrow here.

'How is your little girl, Cook?'

Reg grimaced. 'We hope she'll pull through. Infection is one of the biggest threats at the moment, the doctors say.'

Sebastian pulled a banknote from his wallet. 'Please, I want you to have this to pay for the medical bills. If you need any more, let me know.'

Reg, who would never have accepted for himself, had no misplaced pride when it came to the well-being of his little ones. 'Thank you, sir.'

'Hire a nurse with it. It seems your neighbours won't let you keep the best one in England under your roof.' He couldn't stop his bitterness seeping into his tone.

Reg swore colourfully, but cut off when Helen appeared at the door, her damp hair loose over her shoulder, wearing a clean set of clothes. Towelling the water off the long strands, she didn't see they had a visitor.

'Thank you, Reg. I feel much better now. Can you give me a hand emptying the tub?'

Reg waved that away. 'Leave it, love. I'll do it later. You'd better get packed up – your young man has plans to take you somewhere tonight.'

She dropped the towel. 'Sebastian? You're here – but how?'

'Yes, I'm here, darling.' He picked up the towel and ran it over her hair tenderly. 'I got leave unexpectedly. Just a few hours, but thank God I did.'

Helen swallowed. 'Reg told you?'

He nodded. 'Tell me what I can do, please. I need to help you.' She rested her forehead on his shirtfront for a moment, still shaking in the aftermath of the assault. 'I'd prefer to go after your attackers, but Reg says the police won't take your side.'

'No.' Her trembling subsided. He was immensely moved that she chose him as her port in this storm, but what if he could not live up to her expectations?

'You'll have to go somewhere else then.'

'Yes, it is the only thing I can do now.'

'Pack a bag. I'll make sure you're safe tonight.' He vowed that he would do that much.

'All right. It won't take me long.'

Sebastian felt her trusting smile directed at him like an arrow to the heart. She brushed her fingers over his as she passed on the way to the stairs. He had no idea where he was going to take her. He was due to report to his squadron the following day and was staying at his club. No ladies allowed there.

Then he saw the answer, like finding the airfield after being lost in fog. Of course: the Ritz. She deserved a treat after the horror of the night. He would use his family name to make sure she was shown to the best room the hotel had available. She should like it there, as they had once had a very memorable tea dance in the Palm Court in the early days of their courtship, his first attempt at impressing her.

Helen returned with a small case. 'Say goodbye to the children for me, Reg?'

'Of course, love.' Reg kissed her forehead. 'I'm sorry – for everything.'

She smiled up at him. 'You and Elsie have been wonderful. If I can, I'll come back for a visit. Give Joan a kiss from me.'

He patted her cheek. 'I'll do that. Let us know where you are, promise?'

'Yes, I will.'

Sebastian held out his hand for the case. 'I'll be carrying that.'

'Can you manage it with your cane?' Helen asked, holding on to it with both hands on the handle.

He was damned if he was going to let his injury stop him being a gentleman. 'Helen,' he said severely.

She passed it over.

'Now, you take my elbow and we'll manage very well

until I can find us a cab. Where do you think I'm most likely to get one round here, Cook?'

'We're not exactly a cab kind of area, sir, but try the High Street.' Reg unlocked the door and poked his head out. He shot out like a dog spying a cat. 'That's right: run! Get your ugly face indoors, Dalston! Punch me out in my own home, would you? You and I have a score to settle!'

'Cook, you've children at home,' Sebastian reminded Reg, pulling him by the back of his shirt as he kicked at his neighbour's door.

'I'll get even, I will.'

Knowing the quick mind and fists of his old comrade, Sebastian was sure he would. 'But not tonight. Thank you for everything you've done and tried to do for Helen.'

It took all the weight of the family name and a larger-than-usual tip to see Helen safely to a room at the Ritz at such a late hour. Sebastian returned to his club, half expecting everyone to have retired to their beds, but Charlie Cordel was still up, enjoying the pleasures of a quiet brandy in a library after living in a shed in France for the last few months. He beckoned Sebastian over and poured him a glass from the bottle the staff had left for him when they'd gone off duty.

'I hope you found your lady well?' he asked cheerfully.

Quite out of the blue, Sebastian felt his spirits sink – a sensation not unlike plummeting from the sky with no engines. 'I'm in a hell of a hole, Cordel.'

Charlie's merry face sobered. He nudged the glass towards Sebastian. 'Don't tell me she gave you the old heave-ho?'

'God, no.' Sebastian took a sip, wondering how far he could trust his friend. Charlie had always seemed a decent chap, but then no doubt so had Reg's neighbours. 'She's in desperate need of a new place to stay. Her own family are a wash-out, and where she's been . . . let's just say, it's no longer very welcoming.'

Charlie stroked the glass with his fingers. 'There's something in this that you're not telling me, isn't there?'

Sebastian sighed. 'There is.'

Charlie sat forward. 'I may seem a bit of a flibbertigibbet to you, but I hope you consider me a friend.'

'I do, Cordel. I'd have you at my back in any battle, no question.'

Charlie raised an eyebrow.

'Oh, all right then.' Sebastian surrendered. He was not ashamed to admit when he needed help. 'Helen has a German mother. Completely through no fault of her own, the authorities have decided she is a suspicious character.'

Charlie snorted in disdain, which Sebastian took as encouragement to continue.

'Their attitude has infected the people where she's been living; it's suffered from the raids, you see, and they are running mad with anti-German feeling. When I got there, I found that a crowd – the very same people she has been living among for months – had just attacked her. She helped save their children, for heaven's sake, when the Poplar school was hit, little ones killed, and now they turn on her!'

'Crikey! Is she hurt?'

'Cuts, bruises; but I can't leave her there. I'd marry her tomorrow if that would help, but my own family have already been hostile to her and she wouldn't want to go and live with them, and there's no provision for married officers in our game, what with being moved from airfield to airfield. And besides, I don't want our wedding day to be forced on us in such a horrible fashion, tainted with this business. I really don't know what to do. Set her up in a flat somewhere, I suppose, but I worry that word will leak out again and on her own she'll be a target, no one close to defend her.'

Charlie grimaced and swirled his brandy.

'She's such a sweet, wonderful person, Cordel. I can't bear it that people are doing this to her.' Sebastian felt a little better for unburdening himself, not that he expected Charlie to come up with a miracle. 'Anyway, that's my problem – and I've got to find a solution before we head up to the airbase tomorrow.'

'Do you know what, Trewby: I think I might just have an answer for you.'

'Go on.' Sebastian was ready to listen to any idea, having run out of his own.

'You need someone who will look after your lady, not care two hoots about her German origin or the opinion of others – correct?'

'Yes, that about sums it up.'

'I think I have the perfect person for you. My aunt.'

Sebastian had to laugh. 'Don't tell me the solution is someone called Charlie's Aunt? How perfect!'

Charlie grinned at the reminder of the popular farce, staple of the London stage, about a student impersonating his friend's relative to great comic effect. 'Funnily enough, Aunt Dee-Dee does bear a stunning resemblance to that character. We think she's a she, so to speak, but she does wear trousers and smoke cigars, so the jury is out on quite what she thinks of herself.'

'Are you pulling my leg? If you are, I'll tell you I'm too tired and this is too serious to joke about.' Sebastian wiped his hand across his face, weariness catching up with him.

'Never been more serious, old chap. Aunt Dee-Dee is a sculptress – one of the Bohemian set. The family black sheep – though I've always considered her more of the interesting multi-coloured sort of ewe, making the rest of us look a very dull flock.'

'You don't mean to say your aunt is *Delia* Cordel?'

'Yes, that's her. Do you know her?'

'Only by reputation. I've sketched some of her works as part of my training in anatomy at the Slade. She is brilliant at rendering the human torso. Her bronze of a boy Actaeon is famous.'

'Really? That's very pleasing. I posed for that, you know.'

'No!' Sebastian wondered how he felt about having sketched his friend at one remove for hours. The chances were he knew his bone structure better than Charlie did.

'I swear that's true. She is very skilled at bribing friends and relatives to take off their kit for her – in an artistic manner, I hasten to add. She can't help herself – we are her raw material, you see. But don't worry: your fiancée will be safe with her. She might find herself roped in for the odd pose or two, but will emerge unscathed.'

'And she wouldn't mind being asked to offer Helen a room?'

'Lord, no. She has a soft spot for underdogs, stray kittens, fledglings fallen from nests – that sort of thing.'

'Then she won't be able to resist Helen.'

'I'll call her in the morning and we'll take your young lady round and see what they make of each other. It'll still give you a few hours to sort something out if it turns out they don't suit after all.'

'No, no, it sounds a really good idea. Thanks, Cordel.'

Charlie finished his brandy in a gulp. When he noticed Sebastian's interest, he added: 'Just preparing myself to face Aunt Dee-Dee. I've remembered what she's really like in the flesh.'

The tall town house on Gower Street did not look promising: black bricks, black front door, white paintwork – the building equivalent of a man in a dinner-jacket. To Helen's eyes it looked far too respectable for her.

'Are you sure, Lieutenant Cordel?' she asked Sebastian's friend. He had struck her when they had first met thirty minutes ago as a charming man, sandy hair combed back, brown eyes sparkling with mischief. He reminded her of a golden Labrador who had never lost its puppyish ways. It was easy to trust his good intentions, but she wasn't entirely convinced he would judge others very well, assuming kindness where it might not exist.

'Very sure, Miss Sandford. Aunt Dee-Dee knows we're coming.' He rapped on the door, and in barely a couple of heartbeats it was opened, to reveal a severe-looking woman with grey hair pulled back in a bun. She frowned at Charlie. If this was his aunt, she was not very pleased to see him. Helen reached for Sebastian's hand, noting that he too looked dismayed.

'Muffin! How are you, old girl?' Charlie smacked a kiss on both of the cheeks of the door warden. 'Is my aunt ready to receive us?'

'Miss Cordel is in her studio, Master Charles,' the lady said, with no sign that she welcomed his enthusiastic greeting.

'Did she say we were to go up?'

'She did, sir.'

Charlie bounded past the housekeeper. 'Excellent. Come on, chaps.'

Helen found she liked being treated as one of Charlie's 'chaps'. His lively manner gave her the courage to pass the woman he called Muffin despite her less than hospitable manner. 'He is rather fun, your Charlie, isn't he?' she commented over her shoulder to Sebastian.

'Very.' Sebastian gave Muffin a wide berth. 'I'm just beginning to realize that he's got depths too. I'd mistaken the surface fizz for the whole.'

'Easy to do as it is so distracting.'

They shared a smile of understanding as they followed Charlie up the stairs.

He knocked on one of a set of double doors on the first floor – leading to what in most houses would be the principal apartment. 'Have to wait to be invited in – Aunt Dee-Dee is very strict about that.'

'Come!' called a gruff voice.

Charlie threw the doors open and swept into the room. 'How are you, Auntie?'

'Charlie! What a nice surprise for you to call me this morning!' Aunt Dee-Dee was standing by the window, a mass of modelling clay on a bench before her. Her hands were grey with the stuff. Dressed in a splattered smock and loose trousers, she stood six feet tall – quite an Amazon warrior with her fierce, square jaw and steel helmet of short hair. 'You can help me out – I need a ribcage but all the young fellows I normally use are abroad, leaving me just Mr Viner and he's got a paunch. Take off your shirt for me, dear.'

Helen was pleased that Sebastian had warned her about Aunt Dee-Dee's occupation, but she had not believed him when he mentioned she was ruthless about recruiting. The sculptress's approach was like a bucket of cold water in the face.

Charlie blushed. 'Auntie, there's a lady present.'

Aunt Dee-Dee glanced over at Helen where she stood with Sebastian by the door. 'Heavens, you brought me another one. Young man, you too – take off your jacket.'

Helen didn't know if she should be embarrassed or collapse into giggles – neither seemed to be right for Delia's studio. She settled for what she hoped was an expression of intelligent interest.

'Do you always greet your guests like this?' asked Sebastian, who had evidently chosen to be amused.

'Only the handsome ones. Charlie told me you were an artist so I know you understand the imperative of my craft. I know you don't have time to waste, so chop-chop.'

'Helen, would you like to wait outside while we satisfy that imperative?' Sebastian asked, undoing his tie and thus proving he would do almost anything to earn her a safe haven.

'And miss this? Absolutely not.' Helen was surprised by her own boldness but since yesterday she was feeling reckless, ready to take chances. Playing safe had so far served her badly.

The sculptress beamed at her as if she were a very talented pupil who'd just turned in her first finished piece. 'Splendid. She'll do very well. Had to check she wouldn't make a fuss about my work. Welcome to Gower Street, my dear.' Aunt Dee-Dee gestured for her to come nearer. 'Can't offer to shake hands –' she waved the clay-stained fingers in evidence – 'but consider it done.'

'Pleased to make your acquaintance, Miss Cordel.'

'Call me Aunt Dee-Dee – I prefer it to Miss Cordel. Only Muffin gets away with that because it makes her unhappy to call me Delia. Offends her sense of propriety.' Aunt Dee-Dee's eyes shone, showing that the family resemblance to Charlie ran to mischief-making. 'I imagine that I am one great offence to what's right and proper to her, but she does carry on trying.'

Charlie stopped undoing his shirt buttons. 'So it was just a test? You don't need Trewby and me to pose?'

'Charlie, you know me better than that. Yes, it was a test, and yes, I need you to pose. Do you realize how hard it is to find models these days? There's a war on, you know. Miss Sandford, do ring for some tea.'

Helen pulled the servants' bell that was set on the wall by the fireside, then took a seat in the old armchair. Once Charlie and Sebastian were shirtless, Aunt Dee-Dee forgot everything but her clay, allowing Helen to make a careful study of the place that was to be her new home. The lovely apartment was as stripped to the floor as the boys were to the waist – bare boards, no painting on the wall, a cold stark light coming in from the windows. North facing, she guessed, remembering Sebastian telling her that this was the light favoured by artists, as it did not overwhelm. Sculptures in various stages of creation were set around the walls. Most were in stone but a few were in bronze. It was almost impossible to get hold of that material since the war started, so those were probably older pieces. Aunt Dee-Dee had switched to marble and clay so she could continue her work. Sketches of projects were tacked to the walls or scattered in piles on the floor. There was an air of creative chaos to the studio; something that Helen remembered from Sebastian's own room when she had first met him. Yes, she decided, she would like it here.

'What do you think, Miss Sandford?' Aunt Dee-Dee was gesturing to the two figures she had rapidly moulded. 'They're two centaurs – human bodies on horse legs.'

Helen allowed herself now to look over to Sebastian. She had never seen him in this state before and she realized, when her cheeks burned with a betraying embarrassment, that she wasn't quite as sophisticated as she hoped. He had darker rings around his wrists and neck where he had been exposed to the sun, the rest of his skin paler, muscles defined in a way quite unlike a female body. She wished she could run her fingers over the contours as the sculptress did her model. 'He's very lovely – I mean, the centaur's very lovely.'

'I quite agree – they both are.' The door opened and Muffin appeared with a tray. 'Youth is so attractive. Excellent timing, Muff.'

Helen took the cup that was offered to her. 'Thank you, Miss Muffin.'

Aunt Dee-Dee threw her head back and roared. 'Lord! She's not Miss Muffin, child. She is either Mrs Yeats or Muffin – one or t'other.'

'Oh, sorry.'

'You weren't to know. I don't suppose this nephew of mine bothered to introduce you properly. Charlie, you've lost a bit of weight. Do something about it.'

Charlie patted his trim stomach. 'I'll do my best, Auntie.'

'Shame you can't filch this German girl off your friend. There's a nation that knows about baking, I can tell you. Never saw a thin German before the war. Stuff and nonsense, all this fuss over who's to be top dog in Europe. We're all losing to the Americans, can't they see that?' Aunt Dee-Dee dispatched her tea as swiftly as she did the subject of Helen's nationality predicament. 'Are you a good cook, Miss Sandford? Lord, I can't call you Sandford if you're going to live here. Sounds far too ordinary – and we are not a mundane household, as I'm sure you have gathered.'

'You can call me Sandy if you prefer.' The girls at the theatre had called her that; it felt appropriate to have her old nickname revived here. 'Or Helen.'

'I'll do that. So, do you cook and whatnot?'

'Yes, I can cook, bake, boil, slice and fry.' Helen gathered one was supposed to answer with matching attitude, so gave it her best shot.

'Good. You could show Muffin here a few recipes then. Her cakes are a complete disaster, aren't they, Muff?'

'It's the ingredients, Miss Cordel.'

'They were a disaster before the war too, Muff, and you know it. You just have an excuse now.' She turned back to smooth another ridge on the model she was making.

Helen worried that the much-put-upon Muffin would get upset, but she took the criticism in her stride. 'If you hadn't scandalized the last cook by insisting she cater for the models you had up here for the bacchanalian piece, then you wouldn't be relying on my skills.'

'I can't see what she thought was so wrong – we all have bodies. My art is to show them off, reveal the life surging just below the skin, make dead materials seem to breathe. It's the closest one can get to being God.'

'God or not, she reported you to the police.' Muffin began picking up a few used cups that were scattered around the studio.

'Ignorant woman. There was nothing going on in this room that would have embarrassed anyone. A vicar could have sat where that girl is sitting and not felt one twinge of shame.'

'And you told the chief inspector exactly the same thing before persuading him to offer his head and shoulders for a bust of Plato.'

'Bribing an officer of the law, aunt? Tut-tut.' Charlie grinned at her affectionately.

'Not bribing: converting. And besides, he had exactly the right look.' She gestured to a clay bust standing in one corner, a man's hat perched aslant the brows. 'Just waiting to have the chance to cast the bally thing. Damn war.' She grabbed a rag to wipe her hands. 'There: that'll do for today, boys. You can cover up.'

Sebastian grabbed his shirt and went over to Helen while still doing up the buttons. 'Enjoyed that, did you? You were smiling like the cat who had got at the cream.'

Had she? Helen shrugged, pretending nonchalance. 'I was a nurse. Not much I haven't seen before.'

'Little liar.' He kissed the tip of her nose. 'You couldn't take your eyes off us.'

'I only had eyes for you,' she whispered.

He smiled tenderly and rubbed his thumb across her cheekbone. 'How can you still make me feel this way?'

'What way?'

'Hopelessly, helplessly in love with you.'

'Because that's what I feel about you.'

He put his finger under her chin, tilted her face to exactly the right angle and kissed her.

Charlie cleared his throat. 'I say, Trewby, old chum, we've a train to catch.'

Helen pulled away reluctantly. 'You've got to go.'

'You'll be all right now?'

'I think I will. This is going to be interesting, challenging.'

'But fun?'

'Oh yes, definitely fun.'

'Good.'

'Try to keep yourself safe, won't you?' She absolutely hated that every goodbye could well be the last one. Life should not have to be lived on this knife-edge the whole time.

'I'll do my very best, I promise you. I'll let you know when I next have leave. I'll settle the matter of the rent before I go.'

'Sebastian!' She protested but knew she would have to agree. Chances of being employed again were very low, with the government hounding her.

'No, I'm not going to be moved on this. You and I are a team for life and we will share everything, including money. Anyway, looks as though you'll be earning your keep teaching Muffin how to cook.'

12

Sutton's Farm, Essex, 7 July 1917, 4 p.m.

Sebastian brought his Pup down for a smooth landing, bumping over the runway until he could taxi to the hangars. He cut the engine, killing the vibration that had juddered through his bones since take-off. The waiting mechanics rushed out to help him climb down from the cockpit and begin servicing the plane so it would be ready for immediate deployment. Balancing himself with a hand on a mechanic's shoulder, he jumped to the ground, stripping off his goggles, helmet and gloves.

'How was it, sir?' the mechanic asked.

'Frustrating.' He rammed his fingers through his hair, stuck to his scalp after having been under the helmet for hours. 'I could see the damage, but the Germans were dancing rings round us. Didn't catch sight of a single one.'

Charlie's plane glided in to land, lifting that little piece of worry Sebastian carried when he knew his friend was aloft.

'The pilot who came in before you said the anti-aircraft guns almost got him.' The mechanic opened the engine housing, listening to the clicks of the cooling mechanism. Nothing sounded out of kilter.

'She's running well – low on fuel but otherwise in good shape.' Sebastian watched Charlie's plane taxi in – no sign of damage. 'As for the gunners, you'd think they'd be able to distinguish one of ours from a Hun, but no: if it flies, they shoot. The Gothas got a big target in the East End; I saw the smoke plume.'

The mechanic wiped an oily hand across his nose. 'There must be a better way than this. Each time, we're shutting the stable door after the horse has bolted. The Germans will be back at their base by now, laughing at us.'

'I think I'll go in and find something to kick.'

'You go right ahead, sir – as long as it's not a mechanic, we're right with you on that.'

Sebastian was sleeping under canvas in a tent he shared with Charlie and Fred Tennant. It was pitched in the orchard, shaded by trees in full leaf, little pebble-hard apples forming where recently had been blossom. He tried not to think of them as little bombs waiting to fall but the image was there, especially after the June drop had thinned out the crop, scattering the ground with immature fruit. Oddly, life in the orchard often felt like a holiday: fine weather, pretty surroundings, convivial companions, not too much work, a lot of time spent playing cards and waiting for the Germans to come their way. The knowledge that he was having it so easy grated, like whistling a happy tune at a funeral. He threw his flying-gear on his bed, guiltily aware that his servant, an invalided signals sergeant, would be along soon to clear up after him, but he was too angry to be tidy. If only he could score a kill – knock one of the bombers out of the sky – but he had not been joking when he'd said to Charlie their task was like using a harpoon to catch minnows. The German aircraft just skimmed away, going back to their base. The only real enemies the Huns faced were adverse weather and mechanical failure. The British pilots had made very few hits, as this was sneak warfare rather than the dogfights over the trenches. Those combats seemed clean by contrast with this messy business involving high explosives and civilians under the flight path.

Charlie came in, yawning. 'Any luck, Trewby?'

'No. You?'

'Not a scrap. Heard they got a garment factory in the East End. The chap who told me said that the women got out unscathed.'

Memory stirred. 'Do you know which factory was hit?'

'No, but the mechanic said it made shirts and blouses.'

'It has to be the same place. I think Helen used to work there until they kicked her out.'

'Lucky for her they did then. Oh, by the way, there's some government suit wants to speak to you. He's in the commander's office wearing holes in the carpet.'

'Is this my official summons?'

Charlie shrugged. 'Well, the CO did say to inform you but, if you like, I can say I didn't see you.'

Sebastian changed shirts and put on his uniform jacket. 'No need. I suppose I'd better go see what he wants.'

'Don't let him lure you back to France. You'll miss the dance if you do that.'

Sebastian smiled sourly. 'And that is my first consideration, naturally. Not winning this war or anything like that.'

'Ah, that is where you and I part company, my friend. You take the burden on your own shoulders; I'm quite ready to allow someone else to worry about that nonsense because, as far as I can see, there is precious little I can do to change the course of history.'

'Actually, Cordel, I'm with you there. I realized that when I had my little walk on the Somme. One man versus History: it's like a ladybird taking on a steamroller.'

Charlie flopped on his bed and picked up a newspaper. 'I forget that you've seen combat in the trenches. That rubs out any last illusions a person might hold. You might even have fewer than me, as I still believe I might get lucky at the dance and find my princess.'

Sebastian's foul mood lightened a little as he thought of Helen, whom he had hopes of luring up for the ball. 'I think I've clung on to a few dreams about romance too.'

'Exactly. Knight in shining armour – that's you. Me, I'm hoping to be someone's Prince Charming.'

'I hope she appreciates the effort you're going to for her, whoever she is.' Charlie had been the driving force behind the entertainment, spending all his free time refining the details. 'I'll see you at supper.'

The commander's office was housed in a brick building on the far side of the airfield. It had once been a farm agent's place of work, now requisitioned for the RFC, but continued to smell vaguely of pigs. Sebastian took his time crossing the airstrip to reach it, allowing a space to ponder why he was summoned. His father might have pulled some strings and come up with an offer for work away from the front line. That would fit his family's concern, but he did not believe his father would do it without warning him what was afoot. The other possibility was his connection to Helen had sent up flags in some department somewhere. She had told him that his name had been mentioned in her interview at the police station, so he had to be prepared for trouble.

He tapped on the door.

'Come in.' Sebastian's CO, Major Kennington, sat behind his desk; a sharp-looking man in civilian clothes occupied the chair opposite him. 'Took your time, Trewby, didn't you?'

Sebastian felt no need to apologize for not running to a non-emergency meeting. 'I've just got in, sir.'

'Status?'

'I was up for three hours, sir. Signs of German activity but no visuals on aircraft. No damage to my plane. I returned when it was clear they had all left the area.'

'I don't know about you, lieutenant, but I'm getting heartily tired of this game.'

'Yes, sir.'

'Waste of good men, machines and fuel. You'd be more use on the Western Front. Still, that's not for now. This is Mr Brown.'

Sebastian took a closer look at the official: the same one who had made Helen so upset.

'He is from the Home Office,' continued the major, 'and would like to ask you a few questions. Do you wish me to remain?'

Mr Brown cleared his throat. 'No, that won't be necessary, major.'

'Mr Brown, with respect, I wasn't asking you. I was asking Trewby if, in my capacity as his commanding officer, he wishes me to be present. I have met your type before, Brown, and I've always found your questions to be very – how shall I put it? – sticky.'

'Yes, sir, I would appreciate it if you would assist me with said stickiness.' Sebastian hadn't realized the gruff major was such a good man, having only dealt with him on straightforward matters of flying.

Mr Brown did not look too pleased to have a senior officer interfere with his plans for the interview. 'Major, I would ask you to step outside. I have confidential matters of the highest national security to discuss with the lieutenant.'

Major Kennington smiled – but it was a shark's smile: all teeth and danger. 'Careful, Brown, you are on my turf here. I assure you that I have the necessary clearance to sit in on this interview. I am running a key part of our national security here, after all.'

A plane flew overhead, the rumble underscoring his claim.

'Very well. If you would take a seat, lieutenant.' Brown

was holding himself like a cat given sight of his bath, offence bristling from every pore. That cheered Sebastian up as nothing else could. He took the only remaining chair, a hard wooden upright that looked as if it had been brought in from the local school. He decided he would say nothing, no offer of cooperation, until he had heard Brown's entire pitch.

'I don't imagine you know why I am here, do you, lieutenant?'

He had a shrewd idea but confined himself to a neutral 'No, sir.'

'I have examined your record and find you are an exemplary officer. Decorated after the Somme.'

Like a Christmas tree. Medals and commendations to hang on his chest when many a better soldier was dead in the mud.

'You have served in France since the beginning of March and now here, called back to defend the people.'

The major shifted in his seat. 'Is there any point in all this, Brown? I'm sure Trewby knows his record better than you do, and I reviewed it before adding him to my squadron.'

'My point is that no shadow hangs over the lieutenant in the eyes of the military or government authorities, which is why it is more important than ever to ensure he is not used by the enemy against the very country he serves so well.'

'As Trewby has just come back from chasing that enemy from our skies, we can rest assured that they have no reason to think they can "use" him. Even the suggestion is an insult!'

With the major doing a better job of defending him than he could have done himself, Sebastian studied his hands where they rested on his knee, folded one on the other at ease. He knew exactly where this was going and he promised himself that he would not lose his temper. Freeze the man out with sarcasm was the best approach.

Mr Brown did not want the major as an opponent in this match. 'Forgive me if it sounds insulting; I have no intention of doing so. No, I am referring to a matter in the lieutenant's private life. Did you know, major, that he is engaged to a person who is of interest to the authorities – a half-German nurse who concealed her identity and was dismissed from her post near the front line for stealing vital supplies?' Mr Brown turned to Sebastian, faux regret in his tone. 'I'm sorry if you would have preferred privacy for me to break this news to you, but you did insist on the major being present.'

The major had not been expecting this turn of events. A chink appeared in his defence of his man. 'Is this true, lieutenant?'

'Yes, I am engaged, sir. Yes, my wife-to-be has a German mother and an English father, but has always lived in this country so considers herself English.' He hoped his tone of voice conveyed just how tired he was of this old bundle of accusations. 'Yes, she was dismissed but no, she didn't steal. She was dismissed wrongfully and given no chance to defend herself as the charge rapidly moved from stealing to her heritage. Since then, men like Brown here have been dogging her footsteps and convincing themselves and those that surround her without any proof that she is up to no good. She has just turned nineteen, sir: hardly had time to make herself the femme fatale that Brown seems to think her.'

'So you know about her and the network of German spies, do you?' Brown began taking notes, excitement evident in his scrawling handwriting. 'She told you what we thought she was doing?'

Sebastian wanted to rip the pad from his hands and follow through with a left hook to his jutting jaw. 'You're wasting your time, Brown, slinging more mud at her — it won't stick because there is nothing there for it to cling to.'

'I'm sure she has convinced you of that, but we have the evidence in the blood spilt and the rubble of the East End. People are dying thanks to the targets pointed out to the planes by the enemy among us.'

Civilians, Sebastian thought with disgust. 'I don't think you understand the first thing about flying, Mr Brown. What you are looking at is evidence that the Germans are outstripping us in the race to make a decent long-range plane and have navigators who can read maps. It's really not that hard to cross the Channel, look for a mass of housing that matches London — the Thames is a bit of a giveaway there — and drop your bombs. Why you feel the need to add in a layer of spies on the ground is beyond me.'

Brown scowled at the implication that he was ignorant. 'You are naive, lieutenant, if you think the enemy has not put his agents among us.'

'I don't doubt there are some, but not Helen. You know only one thing *about* her – her parentage – but I know *her*. She would no more betray this country than I would.'

The Home Office man turned to the major, to appeal to his experience. 'Now you can see what we are up against, sir: an innocent man being taken in by a clever, scheming young woman. It has been noted at a senior level in government, considering whose grandson he is – grandfather in the House of Lords – and I can tell you they are not pleased. I would ask you to throw your weight in with us, to ask him to break off all contact with the woman. If he does not do so, he will jeopardize his career, reputation, and possibly the safety of this country.'

Sebastian did not want to hear what the major would say on the matter. He stood up. 'No.'

'No, what?' asked Brown, taken aback.

'No, I will not throw over my wife-to-be on hearsay. No, she is not a risk to my safety or that of this country – to suggest this is a deep insult both to me and to her. Paint her as you may, I know what she is: kind, loyal and true. Sir –' he met the major's gaze – 'may I go? I have nothing more to say to the Home Office.'

The major had been disturbed by the allegations, Sebastian could tell. 'Lieutenant, my advice is you should seriously reconsider your position. It could hurt you.'

'I'd hurt far more if I dug out my heart and handed it to this man here. Sir.'

'I see.' The major drummed his fingertips on the desk, no doubt thinking lovers were a hopeless breed when it came to reason. 'Yes, you may go, Trewby. I need to discuss this with Mr Brown and my superiors. There is nothing more to be gained by prolonging this conversation. Consider carefully what has been said here. In fact, that is an order. However blameless your lady may be, or not, perhaps it would be best for all of us if you put your relationship with her behind you.'

'I will obey your order, sir, but I already know what my considered opinion of this matter is.'

'Does she know where you are?' asked Brown before Sebastian had reached the door.

'Yes, of course.'

'Major, you should look to your security. If she's passed on the information about the location of this airbase, you may find you have become of interest to the saboteurs at large among us.'

'She has no links to sabotage. Dammit all, sir, this is nonsense!'

'You are dismissed, Trewby. We will discuss this again tomorrow when you've had a chance to think it over with a cool head.'

It took all of Sebastian's training not to slam the door when he quit the office. He now had a tiny insight into how Helen had felt when the authorities had come after her: every innocent action became something suspicious.

Breathing was probably a crime in Brown's book. With no door on the tent to kick open, Sebastian had to content himself with tossing back the flap. He found Charlie still stretched out but his bed area tidied, thanks to his efficient servant.

'Ah, not good, I take it? What's the news? Back to France already?' Charlie tossed his paper aside.

'I wish it were that. It's Helen – the man at the Home Office came to tell me to break it off with her in the interests of national security.'

'By George, what a rotter!'

'Thanks, Charlie: I'm glad you see sense. The major was persuaded by the argument that there's no smoke without fire.'

Charlie chewed his thumbnail thoughtfully. 'He has to be careful and he doesn't know her. Still, you can introduce him to her when she comes up next week.'

'I'm not sure I can do that. They'll arrest her for breaching security or something idiotic like that.'

'Lord above, we are led by fools. But you can't go to the ball without your princess.' Charlie sat up, face alight with inspiration. 'I know: I'll invite Aunt Dee-Dee – no one will turn her away. And no one will think twice if she has a pretty young lady in tow.'

Sebastian felt a smile form despite his black mood. 'Splendid idea. Persuade the major he really must ask your aunt to dance – that would partially settle my score with him.'

'We'll smuggle Helen in, make the introductions without him being any the wiser.'

'I'm not sure about Prince Charming, Charlie; I think you are acting more like Niccolò Machiavelli.'

'Gosh: that's the first time anyone has called me devious. I rather like it.'

With a chuckle, Sebastian grabbed a towel and went to wash for supper. For all Charlie's optimism that they could ignore the problem, he couldn't help but feel the shadows stretching over the sunny path of his relationship with Helen.

13

Helen had become quite used to meeting unexpected things in odd places in Aunt Dee-Dee's house. Finding a brace of puppies in the bath was something new to add to the heap of kittens in the kitchen and the one-winged blackbird that lived in the attic. They were golden Labradors, tiny paws sliding on the ceramic, a towel rucked up at one end where someone had tried to make them comfortable. Helen couldn't resist. She picked one up, nestling the moist nose in the crook of her neck, wriggling body held on one hand.

'Aren't you gorgeous?'

The puppy agreed, little tail wagging.

'I wonder what she wants with you. I can't imagine you sitting for your portrait.'

'No, indeed.' Aunt Dee-Dee came in with a bowl of mince. 'I rescued them from a sack bound for London Bridge. I keep an eye on the ironmonger in Tottenham Court Road. He lets his bitch run wild and never looks after the pups that result. Should be tied up in a sack himself.'

'What will you do with them?'

'Find someone to look after them for the moment, then

homes in the country. I have a history of doing this. I think nearly all my friends have benefited from my strays.'

Helen smiled into the dog's furry neck. 'You mean you twist their arm and they take them in?'

'Exactly – and it does them the power of good, so they should be grateful even if they aren't.'

'I'll look after them for you. I'd like to do that.' She had been feeling at a loose end and this would fill the hours nicely.

'Excellent. I was hoping you'd say that. Now, will you come and pose for me again?'

Helen was standing in for her Greek namesake. It involved standing in the chilly studio draped in a toga, but it was a small price to pay for the warmth of Dee-Dee's welcome to her house. 'I'll be right with you.'

Modelling for the sculptress was never boring. Dee-Dee kept her amused with sharp observations on her friends and neighbours, surprising anecdotes and vocal complaints against the politicians making a meal of the war. They rarely spent an hour alone. Her acquaintances – all Bohemian types who seemed to survive by cadging off their more affluent connections – drifted in, made a few acerbic comments about each other and drank copious amounts of tea. Muffin appeared to hate them all with equal passion. If looks could kill, the studio would be littered with bodies like the closing scene in *Hamlet*.

One frequent visitor, a photographer, Alfred Preston, was as delicate as Dee-Dee was robust; he liked to take pictures of the artist at work. Helen considered him one of the few of the hangers-on to have true talent. He had set up his camera that morning and was busy framing Helen in the background of the shot, ignoring the puppies pulling on the bottom of his trousers. Elderly, with thick white hair swept back from a beak of a nose, he reminded Helen of a swan rooting in the water as he dived under the black hood of his camera lens.

'Lord, Alfred, you are looking positively unkempt these days,' the sculptress scolded when he emerged, hair flopping over his eyes.

'That is not my fault, Dee-Dee. This idiotic government has incarcerated the only man I trust to give me a decent haircut.'

She used a knife to smooth the upper arm of her model. 'That sounds interesting. What did he do? A conscientious objector?'

'No, no, nothing as rational as that. Leopold is from Munich. They've bundled him up with the others interned in Alexandra Palace.'

'You should go to him then, if he can't come to you.' Aunt Dee-Dee would never let a little something like a prison camp get between her and what she wanted.

He began packing up his equipment. 'You know what? I might just do that.'

The sculptress glanced over at Helen. 'And I think we might come with you.'

Alfred rolled his eyes. 'Dee-Dee, they're in prison. We can't just waltz in there.'

'Oh, pish! No one will notice us.'

'For a practical woman, Dee-Dee, you are terrifyingly short-sighted when it comes to how you strike other people. You blend no more than a giraffe among sheep.'

Helen had to agree with him.

'So, are we going?' Aunt Dee-Dee wiped her hands. 'I've done as much as I can this morning.'

Alfred sat back on his heels. 'What? Right now?'

'But of course — you can't go around looking like a snow-covered haystack. The birds will start nesting on you.'

He ran his fingers through his hair. 'That bad, is it?'

'I am your friend, Alfred, and a true friend does not pull her punches.'

'Then I suppose we could – an experiment to see if we can get in.'

'Of course we'll get in: the walls are only to keep the foreigners inside, not to keep us out, as I will explain forcefully and at length if necessary. You are coming too, Helen. Get dressed.'

'But . . . is this wise?' Helen slipped a dressing-gown on over her robe.

'Naturally. We might need you to interpret for us.'

'Speak German, do you, my dear?' asked Alfred, closing his box of lenses.

'She is German – from her mother's side.'

'Lovely people, the Germans, I've always thought. Very interested in photography. Before the war, some of my best clients came from Berlin.' And with that, Helen knew she had found another ally.

★

The taxi dropped them at the gates to the old pleasure gardens in north London. Alexandra Palace sat at the top of the hill, a pale wheat-coloured brick and glass structure, like a grand railway station without the steam engines. This used to be given over to concerts and exhibitions; now the occupants were there with no ticket and no way home. War's waiting-room. Alfred explained to Helen that the anxious authorities had swept up any man who had a connection to the enemy nation, ironically often young men from Germany sent to relatives to avoid military service. They may have been safer than on the Western Front but they had ended up fenced off, treated like lepers, to be kept separate from the population at large.

'Leopold told me they sleep in large halls on plank beds – thousands of them. No privacy, barely any washing facilities, food ghastly.' He shuddered. 'No servants.' Alfred had come from what Aunt Dee-Dee called 'money', so life without a valet was unthinkable.

After Aunt Dee-Dee had talked her way in, it turned out not to be the hellhole Helen had been expecting from Alfred's description. Thanks to the fine weather, most of the inmates were outdoors, lying under trees or doing some form of exercise. If you pretended very hard, it could look like a day's outing. A fierce football match was under way on one of the pitches enclosed by the fence; the watching guards seemed more interested in the scoreline than intimidating their charges, leaning out of their sentry box to observe.

Aunt Dee-Dee and she strolled along the terrace, garnering their own share of interest. The men had the look of people forced to wait for a delayed train: a mixture of resignation and frustration. It was a fairly accurate analogy, for their lives had been put on hold while the engine of the war chugged slowly along its tracks.

'You do know,' said Helen to Aunt Dee-Dee as Alfred went off to seek his barber, who had apparently set up shop inside the building, 'that by bringing me here you will have only added fuel to the fire where the Home Office is concerned.' She leaned against the stone balustrade of the terrace, enjoying the sweeping view across London.

'I am not a complete fool, Helen.'

'Never said you were.' She grinned. 'I wouldn't dare.'

The sculptress chuckled. 'I wanted to show you who the idiots in the Home Office thought you were. Not bad company to keep.' Dee-Dee's eyes lit up as one young German began his morning exercises.

'You think they might do this to me?' Helen had always known it was a possibility. The law had been changed to allow for internment.

'So far they don't have these places for women. That's probably why they have left you alone. But I thought you should be prepared for the worst.'

'Do I say "thank you"?'

'No. You file it away and remember. A girl has to be prepared for anything, far more than a man who has life served to him on a silver platter. I will do all in my power to stop them, but you are not to be scared if they do get it into their heads to seize you. This is what they have in mind.'

It did help to have a picture of that possible future; she had been imagining some dungeon in the Tower of London.

'And now, if you don't mind, I'd like you to do me a favour.'

'A favour?' Helen was ready to do anything for her kind landlady, but she couldn't imagine what she meant.

'Just stand here for a moment and look – I don't know – lost. Yes, lost. Feminine and helpless – not something I have in my repertoire.'

'You want me to stand here and look feather-brained. Why?'

Aunt Dee-Dee patted her cheek. 'Bait, my dear, you are bait. I'll just walk round the corner.'

Obligingly, Helen stood. As her eyes took in the scene, she began to have an inkling of what the sculptress might be planning. Aunt Dee-Dee had one obsession and coming here was like bringing a child with a sweet tooth to a confectioner's. She knew men well, for it didn't take long for her lure to attract a nibble of interest.

'Fräulein, you need help? You are lost?' The handsome young athlete had broken off his exercises to come to Helen's rescue.

'No, sir. I'm waiting for a friend.' Helen was torn between amusement and embarrassment at being made use of in this way.

'Are you visiting?'

'Yes, we're with a gentleman who is visiting his barber.'

'Ah yes, he must be seeing Mr Leopold. He is a very good cutter of hair.' He held out his hand. 'My name is Walter Wenninger.'

'Helen Sandford.' His hand swallowed hers up. She noticed he checked the third finger of her other hand. He couldn't miss the engagement ring. She was pleased she had started wearing it openly now she had accepted that Sebastian would never back out of their engagement. Aunt Dee-Dee had banked on the young men here being eager for some diverting conversation with a girl of their age and she had been spot-on.

'We don't get many lady visitors. It is good to see someone from outside,' Walter continued, eager to make their conversation last.

'How are they treating you?'

'All right, I suppose. We are . . .' His gaze went to the green fields beyond the fence.

'Bored?'

'Yes.'

'Young man,' boomed Aunt Dee-Dee, marching round the corner with a determined expression, 'I've always thought the cure for boredom was to find employment.'

Walter looked taken aback to find himself on the receiving end of one of Aunt Dee-Dee's pep talks. 'Indeed, Madam.'

'Mr Wenninger, this is my friend, Miss Delia Cordel.'

'Do you want a job, Wenninger?'

'What? Um, of course. But I am here, no?'

'Exactly. All the lovely young Englishmen are abroad or too busy for me. Only the other day I was racking my brains to work out where I can find a pool of talent. And here you are: I need you.'

'Now steady on!' he protested.

'She's a sculptress – she needs you for a model,' Helen quickly explained.

'If you can organize a small group of young men willing to pose for me once or twice a week, then I would make it worth your while.'

'She'll pay you in kittens if you don't watch out,' Helen muttered in an undertone. 'Puppies, if you are lucky.' The German smiled in confusion. 'I'm serious.'

'I most certainly will not pay him in kittens! No, I will pay normal artist rates, exactly what you would get if you sat for the Slade or the Royal Academy. How does that sound?'

Poor Walter did not know what to make of the event that was Delia Cordel. 'Well, I suppose . . .'

'Come, come, boy: it's not as if you've anything else to do! Tuesdays and Thursdays. You won't get another offer like it.'

That much was certain.

Walter took the leap. 'Then I agree. How many of us do you want?'

'Oh, four or five. Different physical types, but no old bow-legged ones – plenty of those outside the fence.'

Walter grinned, looking the carefree young man he must once have been before the war cut short his freedom.

This unorthodox job offer amused him. 'Then, Miss Cordel, you have a deal.'

In the taxi home with the newly shorn Albert, Helen shook her head in admiration.

'Confess, Aunt Dee-Dee: did you have that plan in mind before we went?'

'Naturally.' The sculptress flicked through a notebook, checking off dates in her diary.

'So the visit wasn't for my benefit?'

'Oh, that too. I can hold more than one thought in my little brain at any one time, you know.' She wagged the pencil at Helen.

'I realize that.'

'But I have you to thank for it. I wouldn't have thought of the internees if you were not staying with me, and the shortage of potential subjects was reaching critical point.'

'I'm surprised you didn't ask Mr Wenninger to take off his shirt.'

'I thought of it but decided he might run scared.'

'Scared of you? What? Never!'

Aunt Dee-Dee laughed, a great gust of joy. 'It has been known, my dear. Some people find me a little intimidating.'

Sutton's Farm, Essex, 23 June, 6 p.m.

The last time Sebastian had attended a ball had been the disastrous one in the autumn when his family had ousted Helen from the house and prevented her coming to ask for his help. It had taken months to set that wrong to rights and he was determined that this midsummer dance would see no repeat. She should be able to get in without raising any alarms, as there were a number of local girls invited who were not personally known by the major. And if his impression of Delia Cordel was correct, she usually managed to steal the limelight once she entered a room. No one would notice Helen until she had disarmed all opposition.

Charlie was sitting at the camp-table in their tent, running through the final preparations. 'At nineteen hundred hours we'll have the aerial display. Dancing starts at twenty hundred hours. Carriages at twenty-three hundred hours.' He ran his fingers through his hair. 'Have I forgotten anything?'

'The Germans, maybe. What happens if we get a call to muster?'

'They've not done a night flight yet – we've made it too easy for them by day, so I doubt that will change.'

Sebastian checked his dress uniform was in good repair. 'Pretty scary, flying by night. Have you done it?'

'Once or twice when I was late back to base. They lit oil drums to help me down, but relying on my wits to guess the speed of approach without visual clues was a touch hair-raising.'

'Does it not strike you as odd that we are hoping they don't change their tactics so our evening's entertainment isn't spoiled?'

'Trewby, old chap, have you not noticed the whole war thing skews our priorities? I'm just hoping to make it through to the end – but if these are the last few weeks of my life, damned if I'm not going to enjoy them.'

Aunt Dee-Dee had ordered a special evening trouser suit made for her – more of a divided skirt than male apparel.

'Don't want to embarrass the nevvie in front of his commanding officer,' she had explained brusquely when Helen had remarked on the fetching garment. It was a rich wine-red colour, trimmed with black velvet. Topped with a feathered headdress, it would be a brave man who asked the Amazon to dance, particularly as she had not surrendered her cigars to propriety. She would look like a chieftain in her corner of the ballroom, puffing out smoke signals.

'You're very fond of Charlie, aren't you?'

'Can't help myself.' She tweaked her jacket straight across her ample bust. 'He's an amusing chap – quite the best of my brother's brood. Comes across as a lightweight but there's ballast there under it all. Now, Muff, do something for Miss Sandford's hair. I'm sure I have some jewels I can lend you – left over from my debutante days.'

It was hard to imagine Aunt Dee-Dee making her entrance on the London social scene as a young girl. Helen could only conjure up an image of a younger version of the same forthright woman striding manfully across the ballrooms.

'Did you enjoy your debut?' Helen asked as Muffin fixed some jewelled pins in her hair.

'Hated every moment. Waste of time and fabric. I was too shy to protest at the time.'

'You? Shy?' Helen smiled at the thought.

'I'm afraid I was. I know I have a face that looks more like a hatchet than a houri, but I did let my father fool me into thinking I'd find my husband and a conventional future on my dance card. Ridiculous. It took me a few humiliating years to realize that was not what I wanted. My parents eventually gave way when I took to trousers and sculpture.'

So her dress was more a declaration, a defence against rejection. Helen could understand that. It was a clever plan and it helped that she was fearsomely talented, of course.

'None of it would have been possible without my own money. Yes, that looks very nice, Muff: classical. It suits you, Helen.'

Muffin held a mirror so Helen could admire the back of her head where the diamond-topped pins had been threaded. With her pale yellow dress, chosen to match her ring, she looked quite pretty by her own standards. 'Thank you, Mrs Yeats, you've worked a miracle.'

'That's all right, miss. Long time since I've had the chance. I'm pleased I haven't forgotten a trick or two.' Muffin actually smiled at her in the mirror. Recently, since Helen had taken on the care of the puppies and proved useful in the kitchen, the housekeeper seemed to have moved her from the liability column to that of a household asset.

'The car is waiting for us, my dear.' Aunt Dee-Dee swung an opera cloak over her shoulders, red satin lining flashing.

Helen felt a tingle of excitement. She was aware this was a risk, brazenly ignoring the warnings from the Mr Browns of this world that she should distance herself from Sebastian, but that did not outweigh the simple pleasure of going out for an evening, dressed up to the nines, with her fiancé. They had missed so much normal courting in their topsy-turvy lives over the last two years so she was determined to enjoy herself now she had been given this chance. It was entirely too decadent travelling by car; she decided not to ask where the petrol came from – Aunt Dee-Dee was full of such mysteries. As the miles between Gower Street and Sebastian's airbase passed, she felt her spirits bubble, a champagne bottle waiting to be popped open.

They arrived on the stroke of seven. A crowd was already gathered in the entrance of the marquee but all eyes were fixed on the sky rather than the new arrivals. Helen searched the guests, looking for the familiar tall figure of Sebastian, but he did not appear to be there.

'Do you think they were called away on patrol?' she asked Aunt Dee-Dee anxiously.

But the sculptress had spotted her nephew. 'Charlie! What a splendid party you've organized.' She smacked hearty kisses on his cheeks.

'Aunt, you look marvellous!' Charlie grinned but seemed a little distracted, half his attention also on the sky. 'Miss Sandford,' he said in a lower tone so no one could overhear, 'charming, absolutely charming!' He kissed her hand.

'It's lovely to see you again. Where's Sebastian, Lieutenant Cordel?'

Charlie's eyes shone with amusement. 'He'll be along in . . .' The rest of what he said was lost as a plane flew low overhead, dipping its wings at the audience.

'When?' asked Helen, when the noise abated.

'That –' Charlie gestured aloft – 'was him. He's doing a few stunts to get us in the mood.'

'Stunts!'

'Perfectly safe, I do assure you. He's quite the best pilot among us, though don't tell him I said that.'

Helen watched with horrified fascination as the plane began to climb. 'What's he doing?'

'A loop-the-loop, I think.'

She dug her nails into her palm. With the long rays of the sun behind them, she stood with her shadow stretched out across the lawn, keeping her gaze on the little plane as if she could will it to come out of the stunt safely.

'It's easier not knowing, isn't it?' murmured Aunt Dee-Dee. 'I imagine my nephew in the sky but the details I keep purposely vague. It's terrifying to witness.'

That was it exactly. She could live in the knowledge that he was risking his life every day, but to be forced to see the gravity-defying reality removed the comforting distance she had maintained in her imagination. The plane climbed and climbed and then went over backwards.

'Oh my word! Is it supposed to do that?' she squeaked, clutching Charlie's arm.

'Yes, my dear. He is performing a textbook manoeuvre, very useful in combat situations.'

The plane slid out of the loop like a toboggan down a slope – then immediately entered another climb.

'What's he doing now? Has something gone wrong?'

'No, no, I think he's planning a spin. It saved his life the other month against two of the enemy. Don't be concerned: no one does them better.'

The plane appeared to falter, then tip its nose down, rotating like a sycamore seed. Helen muttered a prayer, much to Charlie's amusement.

'Ease up on the arm, old girl,' he chuckled, patting her rigid fingers, 'I'll want that to hold my partners in the dance.'

Helen looked down and noticed with horror that she had been squeezing his forearm to the point where he would have bruises. 'Oh, I'm so sorry, lieutenant.'

The plane eased out of its spin, circled the airbase once more, then landed with an elegant fast glide, followed by a taxi to a stop by the hangars. The onlookers applauded.

'Bravo!' called Aunt Dee-Dee in her foghorn voice.

The pilot stood in his cockpit and waved an acknowledgement.

'Now let me get you both drinks while we wait for Trewby to join us. I have some very superior pre-war fizz. I advise you to bag one now as the wine goes rapidly downhill after this has finished.' Charlie guided them inside the marquee and plucked two flutes off the drinks table, handed them to his guests, and then took a third for himself. 'To safe landings!'

Helen echoed that toast with utmost sincerity.

14

They had barely finished their toast when a stout man with a handlebar moustache appeared at Charlie's side. He had the well-fed look of a man who rode the desk rather than the skies. 'Ah, Cordel, are you going to introduce me to your guests?'

'Major Kennington, this is my aunt, Delia Cordel, and her companion.'

'Delia Cordel? My word, I had no idea my lieutenant hailed from such distinguished stock!' The major kissed Aunt Dee-Dee's hand. 'I believe I went to an exhibition of yours three or four years ago.'

'Major, delighted to make your acquaintance. Actually, we have met before: a garden party in '88.'

'You do have a good memory, ma'am. Thirty odd years ago – I was still very wet behind the ears.' His eyes drifted back to her features, trying to place the memory. 'I say, are you the same Miss Cordel I met then, daughter of Sir Peter Cordel?'

'Hard to credit it, isn't it? I was somewhat different in those days.'

The major struggled to find something flattering to say about the contrast between the shy, plain debutante and her flamboyant successor. 'You are always charming company, no matter how many years have passed.'

'Very nicely put, major, but I was a silly goose then and you were kind, so that makes you all right in my estimation. I have enjoyed getting my own back on the people who tormented me in those days – they don't know what to make of my transformation.'

'I'm sure they don't.' The major now turned to Helen. 'And this is a young relative perhaps?'

'No, my companion and a friend of Charlie's. Helen, Major Kennington.'

'Pleased to meet you, sir.' Helen felt his whiskers brush across the back of her glove in the same gallant gesture he had used on Aunt Dee-Dee. Charlie moved a little uneasily beside her but when the major gave her an impersonal smile, he relaxed. The major had filed her as an unthreatening, ordinary sort, nothing compared to the intriguing sculptress.

'The pleasure is mine. We can't have too many pretty English girls at our ball, that's what I say. Cordel, I hope you'll start off the dancing. It seems half of the local population are here to enjoy themselves; we had better not disappoint.'

'Absolutely, sir.' Charlie winked at Helen. 'May I have this dance?'

Helen accepted his hand. 'Of course. What was that about?'

'What?' Charlie tried to look innocent, but failed.

'Why did you get nervous when the major met me?'

He steered her on to the dance floor and nodded to the little orchestra he had put together from local musicians. He winced as one hit a flat note, seizing on the opportunity to avoid answering. 'It's not going to be quite London standards but it's the best I could get.'

Helen smiled up at him in reassurance. 'They'll be quite acceptable – everyone here is wanting to enjoy themselves, so I don't think you'll get any complaints.'

'I've asked them to start with some sedate waltzes.' He twirled her round the floor in time to the Viennese tune.

'And then?'

'I've requested a few more interesting dances for later, when the old folk start to think about bedtimes and slippers.'

'Dare I ask what kind?'

'What would you say to some ragtime and a tango?'

Helen looked at him in wonder. Both styles of dancing had been criticized by the conservative press as leading the youth of Britain astray, a dangerous American import. 'They'll allow that here?'

'That is what we are going to find out.' Charlie smiled and spun her in three revolutions. 'We can't keep doing the dances of our grandparents, can we? We are the new generation – what's left of us.'

'True. But let's put the war away for one night.'

'Absolutely. I apologize. Just feeling a tad fragile these days. Lost too many friends.'

'I know. But it's a heavenly night and you've done a wonderful job with the arrangements.'

Her compliments helped restore his good mood. 'I think there might be a future for me as a stage manager.'

'Any theatre would be lucky to have you.'

He laughed and spun her round again. Helen found the exercise exhilarating: there was nothing like a good canter round the dance floor to blow away the cobwebs. Charlie was a skilled dancer, light on his feet and confident in the way he guided his partner. Still, he owed her an answer.

'Charlie, why are you worried about the major?'

Their waltz ended and Charlie escorted her to the edge of the ballroom marquee where tables and chairs had been set up.

'It's not important.'

'I think it is.'

Charlie did not have it in him to withstand her appealing look. 'It's just that the Home Office have been sniffing around and spooking the brass. Trewby's been told to throw you over. He gave them short shrift, of course.'

Helen had been expecting something like this. 'I see.' She glanced over to where the senior officers were gathered at the drinks table. 'So they don't know who I am?'

'No. And perhaps it would be best for everyone's enjoyment if we kept it that way, eh?'

It hurt to be made to feel ashamed once again of who she was, but she could see Charlie's point. 'Yes, I agree.'

'Thank you. Will you be all right until Sebastian gets here?' Sebastian had already warned Helen that his friend was on the hunt for his true love. He would not want to waste a moment longer than he had to, dancing with someone else's fiancée.

'Of course, I'll wait for him. You go and find her.'

'Very well.' Charlie tugged at his collar, looking at once both determined and daunted.

'Try that one there.' Helen nudged him towards a girl she had noticed slide a few sideways looks at the handsome young lieutenant.

'Righto. Wish me luck.' Charlie walked up to the young lady, a pretty little blonde with a sprinkling of freckles over her nose. He bowed. He needed no luck in his conquest: she very happily accompanied him on to the floor in time for the next dance.

As usual during the war, there were more females than male partners in the room. No one came over to ask Helen to dance as they were already spoken for, so she stood this one out, admiring the flare of the skirts and the swirls of colour as the couples went past. She drifted to stand behind the flower arrangements, out of the immediate notice of the major and his cronies.

Then two hands pouncing on her from behind blinkered her eyes.

'Guess who?' Lips brushed the exposed skin of her nape and pressed a kiss to the top of her spine, sending shivers through her. Finally he was here!

'Is that my handsome, brave hero?' Helen teased, pleased that they were shielded from all eyes by a display of potted plants.

'Could be.' He dotted another kiss on the spot where her shoulder met her neck.

'The bold pilot who sweeps all before him?'

'You're getting close.'

'Oh, Major Kennington, I'd know you anywhere.'

She got a little nip for her joke. Hands dropped from her eyes and Sebastian turned her round. 'Minx.' He kissed the tip of her nose.

'That's to pay you back for scaring me witless with your stunts.'

'Fair enough.' He rubbed his thumb over the back of her hand in reassurance. 'But really there was no danger.'

'Sebastian Trewby, how can you say that when I saw you hanging in the sky upside-down?'

'You only have to start worrying when I'm not hanging up there but heading for the ground.'

'Yes, like when you sent your plane into a spin?'

'I had it under control. I'll have to take you up one day and show you.'

She shuddered. 'Not in this lifetime.'

He laughed and tucked her arm through his. 'Don't tell me: you are one of those who think that if we were meant to fly, God would have given us wings?'

'I wasn't – but I think I've just been converted to that view since you threatened me with a demonstration.'

'I'll let you into a little secret.' He bent his head to her ear, breath tickling her lobe.

'Yes?'

'It.' Kiss. 'Is.' Kiss. 'Fun.' Kiss.

'I'll take some persuading of that.'

'I'll make a bargain with you: if we get through this war safe and sound, I'll take you up.'

'That's my reward for peace?' Helen groaned. 'You are the only person who could make me regret the prospect of this all ending.'

'Do we have a deal?'

'You'll keep yourself safe to see it through?'

'If I can.'

'Then I agree. I'll use every incentive you have to come home to me.'

'You are incentive enough. Now we've got that settled, shall we dance?'

Helen glanced down at his leg. He was all spiffed up in his regimentals and looked gorgeous. He had left his cane behind and was walking with only the lightest of limps. 'Will you manage?' She wanted to ask if he dared in this company, but she already knew that Sebastian would not have insisted she came here if he wasn't fully prepared to risk exposing their connection.

He arched a brow. 'Is that a challenge?'

'More an honest question, but take it as you will.'

'Yes, I will manage. I can't say I'll be very elegant, and I might have to sit out the more strenuous ones, but I am not sitting back while other chaps twirl my fiancée around the dance floor.'

'Good.' She leaned against him to whisper. '*I'll* let *you* into a secret: I don't want to dance with anyone else.'

He set his palm firmly at her back, the other holding

her hand at shoulder height, and led her into the waltz. The tempo was slow and smooth, allowing them both time to adjust to each other's touch. She could feel the warmth of his palm through the silk at her waist.

'Do you remember the first time we did this together?' Sebastian asked.

'At the Ritz when you took me there for tea? Yes, I do. I was so worried I would trip over my own feet and disgrace myself.'

'So was I.'

'I got cream on my nose when I bit into a cake.'

'I have very fond recollections of that: I wanted to lick it off but decided that would get us thrown out.'

'I didn't know.'

'No, you were quite oblivious to my attraction to you.'

'Not entirely. I thought you were warming to me.'

'Warming, darling? I was already succumbing to the fever. I would call myself a goner.'

She leant back in his hold. The first time they had danced, she had been so nervous she had tensed up and barely remembered that he was supposed to be leading. On this occasion, she happily let him guide, fully confident he would steer them clear around the room. She closed her eyes, savouring the occasional pressure of his hand nudging her in a new direction, the movement of his legs against her skirts, brief touches as they spun.

'Enjoying yourself?' he asked, tone rich with amusement at her blissful expression.

'I love you.'

He paused, then carried on with the dance before another couple could collide with them. 'I know, darling. And I love you – from the tip of my toes to the top of my head.' He whirled her expertly out of the marquee to stroll under the apple trees. 'I think this might be quite the most perfect evening of my life.'

She looked up at him, sure her heart was in her eyes. 'Mine too.' The roof of the hangar loomed over the marquee, reminding her of the world beyond the reach of the music. She began running, pulling him away from all that. 'Sebastian, let's stop time and never go back.'

He caught up and led her through a gate and into an orchard dotted with little tents. 'Excellent idea. At least, let's try to hold this moment for as long as we can. I don't know how many more we'll be granted.' He pulled her into the shadow of a tree and bent down to her lips.

When they returned to the ball, they discovered that Charlie's suggestion of more modern dances had gone down well with the participants. The pilots all had the reputation of being quite the most dashing of the military, so they were game, and the young ladies wanted to look sophisticated. A lively foxtrot was under way, Charlie now with a tall brunette in his arms.

'I think he is sampling the market,' whispered Helen.

'He won't take long in deciding. He is a sentimental chap; he wants a picture in his wallet and lovelorn letters to savour. He envies me my good fortune.'

She squirmed at the thought of how her writing would

appear to a neutral audience. Many of the letters she had
sent him had wandered into the kind of talk only lovers
could stand. 'You are just as bad.'

'I know – and proud of it. If I'm not on hand to whisper sweet nothings in your ear, then the postal service
will have to do it for me.'

The foxtrot ended and the band shuffled their music.
There was a moment of indecision, some shaking of heads
and mutterings, then the leader beckoned Charlie over.

'I wonder what's the matter?' Helen asked.

'Let's go see if there's anything we can do.' Sebastian
steered her through the crowd to the little stage. 'Problem, Cordel?'

Charlie was looking flushed with excitement and high
spirits. 'Revolt in the ranks. These chaps here claim no
one will dance the Argentine Tango – too risqué. I'm
telling them that we like risqué here, seeing how risky
life has become.' He grinned at his own pun. 'I'll dance
it. You ready to give it a whirl, Miss Sandford?'

'I'm afraid I've never learned it.' The dance had been
too notorious for the village dances in Suffolk where she
grew up.

'Charlie, why's the music stopped?' Aunt Dee-Dee
strode over.

'They are balking at a tango, Auntie.'

'Fiddlesticks!' She snapped her fingers under the
nose of the first violin. 'I'll show you all how it is done.
Kenny!'

The major, who was deep in conversation with

the local MP, looked round on hearing his name rapped out.

'You tango, don't you? You were always one for the new dances.'

'A bit after my time, Delia.'

'Stuff and nonsense – you've kept up to date. I saw your foxtrot. You –' she dug her finger in the chest of the hapless violinist – 'start playing.'

With Aunt Dee-Dee ordering him, he could not refuse: no man could hold out against her for long. With aggression perfectly suited to the dance, Dee-Dee collared the major and dragged him on to the floor.

'Oh well done, Auntie! Bravo!' Charlie whistled as the older couple did a creditable job of the staccato style of the tango. He turned round and took the hand of the blushing blonde who had been his first partner. 'Miss Wells, let me show you some of the steps.'

Sebastian was still enjoying the sight of the power tussle going on between his commander and the sculptress. 'A dance made for her, I think.'

Helen tapped her toe, feeling the pulse of the music. It had an earthy quality that the waltzes lacked, mirroring the push and shove of a relationship trying to find its feet. She and Sebastian butted heads on issues enough to recognize that this too was part of romance. Too much sweetness and a relationship would founder; a little creative tension added spice.

'You want to try it, don't you?' Sebastian ran his finger over the curve of her jaw.

'Can you do it?'

'Oh yes. The Trewby training included many hours with a dance tutor – Mother made sure of that.'

'Then show me.'

'If you insist.' He brought her into hold.

'Oh, it's much closer than a waltz!' Helen was surprised to find her upper body in contact with his.

'Exactly – why do you think Charlie wanted it on the programme?' He winked. 'Now, this is a dance I can actually do even with my leg, as it is essentially a walk around the floor. I'll provide the frame for you while you cross and flick your foot between mine.'

'How does that work?'

'Watch Miss Cordel.'

Aunt Dee-Dee was currently stepping and crossing the poor major into a heap of cowering masculinity. 'I think she's winning.'

'Yes, her caballero is close to surrender and she'll discard him like a rag – that's the passion of the dance: take, use, reject.'

'Ooo, cruel! I like it.'

Sebastian laughed. 'But I'm not going to let you throw me away, darling, so rein in those bloodthirsty tendencies. Let's try it. A few basic steps to start with – but the tango also allows for improvisation, so don't be scared of having a go.'

They joined the small number of couples who had ventured on to the dance floor. The beat was clear and it was easy to drop into the steady walk that Sebastian instigated.

'Now, swivel and flick.'

Helen threw her head back and laughed. It was wonderful – a spiky dance that burned up some of the passion the kissing in the orchard had engendered. It made her feel a powerful, sensual woman moving with the perfect partner, one strong enough to withstand her little bites at his position holding her. Sebastian was right: he wasn't going to let her go. This was a scuffle between equals, not one dominating the other.

The music ended far too soon. Helen felt she was only just getting the hang of the steps. 'Play another! I want to do that again.'

Sebastian led her to a seat at the side. 'I think that's it for now. The good news is that there are many more nights of tangoing before us.' He kissed her cheek. 'After we are married.'

'Oh you!' Her face had to be fiery red from that particular comment.

'Trewby.' The major arrived at their table, Aunt Dee-Dee on his arm. He had the battered look of a man who had just come in from a gale-force wind. 'I hope you are not embarrassing Miss Cordel's companion?' He clearly thought that his lieutenant was getting too fresh with a stranger.

'No, indeed, sir. Lieutenant Trewby is being the perfect gentleman,' Helen replied.

'Pleased to hear it. Very pleased to see my men squiring some good *English* girls about the floor; we don't do enough of this, thanks to the blasted Boche.'

'Indeed, sir,' said Sebastian stiffly. They both had heard the major's emphasis on her nationality. It would have been nice to throw the truth back in his face but it was safer for them if they kept quiet.

Aúnt Dee-Dee came to the rescue. 'Come on, Kenny, let's leave the youngsters to enjoy themselves.'

The major turned to his partner. 'I think there's just time for one more dance. What about it, Miss Cordel: rematch after that tango? I feel more myself with a Viennese waltz, I must admit.'

The major led his partner back to the floor.

'Is that a romance in the offing?' asked Helen.

Sebastian shook his head. 'I don't think Miss Cordel is in the pool for a husband. I would say we are witnessing the rebirth of a friendship.'

'Somehow I find that even more heartening. There are some good things that come out of this horrible war.'

'My little philosopher.' Sebastian took her in hold. 'And if this is the last dance, I say we make sure we enjoy every second of it.' They revolved into the swirl of couples, movements instinctive and harmonious, losing themselves in each other's eyes. Time did not quite stop, but for a few moments it became golden.

The next morning over a late breakfast in Gower Street, Helen received a postcard from Essex. Sebastian and Charlie had been ordered to return to their squadron in France. The Home Office had recommended Trewby's immediate redeployment away from his suspect connections.

PART THREE

Telegram

15

Helen nudged open the door to the studio, backing inside with the tray of tea. The bone china cups rattled, pale blue flowers shivering on the fragile white porcelain. 'Here, Aunt Dee-Dee, you must have some breakfast. You haven't eaten or drunk anything since last night.'

The sculptress sat like one of her own statues, facing her latest creation that she had just unpacked from the crate the foundry had sent her. She must have hefted it out without assistance, no mean feat, and placed it on a low marble-topped table like an altarpiece, where it shone with a dull-gold glow. Helen knew Aunt Dee-Dee had sacrificed other pieces to provide enough bronze to cast this one.

'I made some toast. Best eaten while hot.' Helen put the plate on a little table beside her. She couldn't bring herself to look at the statue – she knew what it was, had seen it through the various stages of sketch to model to casting, but it held too many memories. She tried for a bright tone, though instinct was telling her this was a misstep. 'Muffin says the papers are full of rumours that

221

the German high command is going to sign the armistice.' No reaction. 'It's the end of the war. The troops will be coming home.'

'Not all of them.' Aunt Dee-Dee's voice lacked its normal power. She was speaking from a mental distance, miles away from current events. She had black days like this, though they were fewer than in spring.

Helen cleared the lump in her throat. 'No, not all.' She poured the tea, catching the leaves in the strainer for second usage.

'Aren't you going to tell me what you think of him, Helen?'

Digging deep for her courage, Helen took a low stool at the sculptress's side. She made herself look up. A young man in bronze, a third of life-size, half transformed to a stag, being brought down by dogs. His body was twisted in anguish, turning back to look at his doom biting on his heels, arms outstretched in hopeless appeal to Artemis, the heartless huntress. You could tell his cries were going to be ignored from the look of despair on his face.

'It's a brilliant piece, but I think you know that. Even better than your first Actaeon.'

'It's the best I've ever done. The legend of the young hunter who dared to look on a naked goddess and was transformed, chased and torn apart for his accidental sin. The dogs of the hunt. Dogs of war.'

The statue was the result of months of suffering in the studio, frantic work, sleepless nights and tears. 'He would be impressed.'

Aunt Dee-Dee sat back in her chair, closed her eyes, and angled her chin to the ceiling. 'No, he would laugh and tell me to cheer up, stop dwelling on pain and agony.'

'I think you're wrong.' Helen felt very daring challenging the sculptress, but lately the distance between them of experience and age had been collapsed by shared loss. 'He might say such things but underneath, the solemn part, would know exactly what you wanted to achieve, and you've done it.'

Dee-Dee did not have time to reply as Muffin came in with the morning's post. 'Oh, Miss Cordel, you've finished it!' She placed the letters next to the uneaten toast.

'Muff, join us.' Aunt Dee-Dee held out her hand and gestured to her housekeeper to take the spare seat beside her, a little audience of three for the new exhibit.

Breaking with habit, Muffin sat down, her bottom lip quivering. 'Your Actaeon.'

'My elegy for our lost boys.'

'Exactly.' Muffin patted her employer's knee. 'You've done well by them. They would appreciate it.'

'I doubt that – not with so many lying in Flanders mud. What's a statue to them? Why am I playing about with myths and legends when there is so much real death out there?' Aunt Dee-Dee wiped the moisture from her eye; tears of a strong woman were more moving than the easy ones of others.

There were many ways of answering that, but Helen

went for the one she felt truest. 'It's a memory, a promise. We are not going to forget. That would be the ultimate insult.' Her generation felt like a scrap of old lace, so many rips and holes where friends had once been; it needed something as substantial as bronze to solidify the fading memories.

'There is that, I suppose. It's the best I can do.'

The three companions sat in silence, admiring Actaeon, and letting the tea get cold.

British Airbase, Houthulst, West Flanders, 8 p.m.

The accommodation in the English orchard of summer a year ago now seemed a very distant memory – like a Garden of Eden from which Sebastian had been ejected. In his mind he tried to keep the image of himself whirling around the dance floor with Helen, but in reality he was trudging down the ruined high street of Houthulst on his way to the canvas hangar, about to go on a night patrol. He stumbled over a rut, cursing the mud, bricks and debris that littered his path. After years of relentless shelling, this corner of Flanders was nothing more than a wasteland of holes, filled with dank, evil-smelling water. To fly over it was to look down into Hell. With the lid of November clouds shut during the day, there was not even the glint of blue to lighten the bruised land beneath.

The mechanics had his plane ready for him.

'Is it true, sir, do you think?' one asked, tucking a spanner into the back pocket of his oily overalls.

'That the Germans are about to throw in the towel?' Sebastian put a boot on the tread spot on the wing. 'I think so. They're on the back foot and they know it. They've been pushed back to where they started in '14.' After a terrifying spring offensive, when it looked like the enemy would carry all before them, the tide of war had shifted in the summer, and now there was little prospect of them being able to answer the Allies, not with the power of the United States added to the Allied forces. Like a boxer fighting back after being on the ropes, the forces under Marshal Foch had delivered their knockout blow and it was only a matter of the Germans acknowledging it.

'Does that mean we'll be home in time for Christmas?' The mechanic winked. That phrase had become something of a joke ever since it was bandied about in 1914 so erroneously.

'You think the RAF is going to be that organized, do you?' Sebastian swung his leg over the rim and climbed into his cockpit. The RFC may have got a new name and status but the personnel were essentially the same old hands – every man jack that worked for them knew that. Sebastian strapped himself in. He had become used to the difficulties of flying by night, but he had to check the light on his instruments was working or he would be in deep trouble.

'I live in hope.' The mechanic moved away.

'Nah, you don't, Bill: you live in cloud-cuckoo-land,' teased the other mechanic. 'Stand clear. Contact!' He spun the propeller and the engine clattered into life.

Sebastian took her up, using the oil-drum lights along the runway as his guide. When he had first tried a night mission he had been terrified; now he loved gliding in the moonlight. It was the closest he had ever come to entering a trance: chasing shades of grey deepening to black in the clouds, the pinpricks of lights below, plumes of smoke looking like mother-of-pearl oyster shells bubbling up from the inky depths. Stripping away the colours narrowed his focus. It felt like the mood he entered when deep in a painting or sketch, a place where the hand could move without conscious thought.

A flare to the right – an ammunition dump had just gone up some miles away. Was this a hit from Allied shelling or were the Germans destroying their supplies as they retreated? Not a question he could answer from up here. No sign of enemy patrols. The pilots hadn't seen a Fokker for a few days; it was almost as if the Germans had already given up.

He followed his agreed route, scanning the skies. Empty. What had been the point of it all? What had anyone won? Looking down at the devastated landscape below, it was hard to make even the slightest bit of sense of the sacrifice. Charlie had always said it was nothing but an annoying pause; something to get through, if possible, so life could begin again.

Or end.

The moon rose, a half-slice of silver in the sky. Sebastian indulged his melancholy mood by turning his plane to fly towards it, not really thinking of his patrol any longer, as it seemed clear that no Germans had ventured up here tonight. He had the sky to himself. The moon had a ghostly beauty, recalling the Peter Pan stories of his nursery days, the star that led to Neverland. He could fly straight on till morning if he so wished, to the country of those that would never grow up. So many of his contemporaries had not known what lay ahead, that they, like Peter, would never see adulthood. It would be some comfort if he could believe they had ended up in some heaven, some land of make-believe, of mermaids, wild animals and Red Indians – Charlie would have loved that. He would have dived straight into the pool with the fishtailed girls and fallen in love with one – or all – of them.

Sebastian wished he could believe.

British Airbase, Bailleul, France, 13 August 1917, 5 p.m.

'Do you think I should write to her?' Charlie asked Sebastian earnestly.

Stretched out on his narrow camp-bed, Sebastian nobly restrained a sigh. 'You wrote to her yesterday.'

'I know, but still: should I?'

Poor Miss Wells – object of Charlie's devotion. 'You don't want to smother her, Cordel. She might get spooked.

One letter every other day is about right: we agreed that, remember?'

Charlie sat down on a camp-stool. 'I'm going to ask her to marry me.' He let his hands dangle between his knees. 'I think she'll say yes. She'll say "yes", won't she, Trewby?'

Sebastian closed his eyes. 'Yes, she'll probably say "yes", if you don't manage to scare her off with your pursuit. You've spent how long with the girl? A few hours?'

'But I've written at least fifteen letters to her and she's sent me ten.'

'Congratulations for single-handedly keeping the postal service going.'

'Diana Wells. Mrs Charlie Cordel. Hmm. I wish I had a more distinguished surname. She's a peach, isn't she, Trewby?'

'Yes, a peach.'

'Do you think I'll get to kiss her next leave or would that be too soon?'

Sebastian wondered what evil god had decided to make him the expert on romance for Charlie. It wasn't that he minded the occasional conversation on the subject, but Charlie's appetite for the topic was inexhaustible. 'I think you should see how things pan out first. Charm the girl; make sure she's the one for you. The kissing will happen when it's right to happen.'

'I've not kissed a girl before, you see. I don't count aunts and that sort.'

'One doesn't.' Sebastian smiled up at the canvas ceiling.

Charlie had many pleasurable new experiences coming his way.

'The other men have suggested I go into town with them to . . . you know.'

'Visit the ladies of the night?'

'Yes. But I don't want it to be like that. I want to be in love.'

'I got that message somehow.'

'I want to be like you: committed to the girl through thick and thin.'

'I'm certainly that.'

'She's a plum, your Helen.'

'Peaches and plums – we have a fruit salad of a romance mixing.' Sebastian sat up. 'Seriously, Charlie, she is a lovely girl, your Miss Wells, but don't rush your fences.'

'I know, I know. It's my fatal flaw to get ahead of myself.'

'I know: why don't you start your letter today and add to it tomorrow? Then you can send it so she gets two days of news.'

'Good idea.' Charlie grabbed his writing-box. 'I've just got time to tell her about this morning's breakfast and the joke Benn played before we have to report for the briefing.'

As Charlie bent his head over his letter, Sebastian got out his sketchpad and started drawing. '*Lover at work*'. He caught the golden tumble of hair, the glitter of the brown eyes, tongue occasionally poking out between teeth as he searched for the right word. He and Miss Wells would make a handsome couple and doubtless produce a pretty batch of flaxen-haired children, if given their chance.

Charlie looked up. 'Oh I say, Trewby, that's first-rate. Can I send it to Diana?'

Sebastian held out the sketch. 'It's all yours.' He stretched out again and folded his hands loosely on his chest. A chilly, rain-bearing wind had called off flying for the remainder of the day over their part of the Western Front. The bad weather also had the pleasing result of deterring the Germans from launching more raids across the Channel. The British airmen were celebrating the news that the raid of the day before had resulted in the loss of a large number of Gotha planes; the new defence measures put in place were finally bearing fruit, unlike Sebastian and Charlie's own aimless patrols earlier in the summer. He hoped that meant that Helen would be a little safer, at least until the Germans tried new tactics – a slippery foe, as the British airmen knew to their cost.

'When did you realize that your Helen was the one?' Charlie asked, folding his half-finished letter and putting it between the leaves of a book of sonnets.

'It crept up on me.' Sebastian rolled on to his side and propped his head on his hand. 'I think it might have been the moment she agreed to pose. Studying her for her portrait made me see her – really see her. I've always thought that my art is about what lies under the surface; I didn't expect that it would also teach me what to love in someone, but it did. You need to look at your Miss Wells straight, Charlie. Ask yourself if you will make her happy and if she will suit you.'

Charlie smoothed the hair off his forehead. 'Oh, she makes me very happy. I hope she doesn't mind that I'm such a lightweight chap. I don't have your artistic depths, or my brothers' ambition for that matter.'

Sebastian considered that his friend's ability to enjoy himself in the dark times – what Charlie considered a sign of being frivolous – was one of his strongest qualities. 'There is nothing lacking in you, Charlie.'

'If a perceptive chap like you thinks so, then that's all right.' Charlie beamed. 'It's settled: I'll propose next time I go on leave.'

Sebastian bit back the words on the tip of his tongue. There was no point preaching caution to Charlie, as it would not stick.

Bloomsbury, London, 3 September 1917, 3 p.m.

After a brisk walk through a local garden square, Helen turned into Gower Street, carried along by the Labrador puppy she had chosen to keep from the rescued litter. She had naturally gone for the clumsiest and least handsome of the pups, spotting a fellow underdog when she saw one. Dimly excited by everything in his simple life, Rolly pulled enthusiastically on the lead, then stopped and sniffed with no warning. Helen knew she should be better at discipline, but somehow she couldn't inject the tone of command that Aunt Dee-Dee naturally had with other creatures.

'Come along, Rolly.'

The dog looked up once, chocolate-brown eyes quizzical, then returned to his investigation of the lamp-post.

She tugged the lead. 'Home time.'

Only when he was ready did Rolly potter along the street to the area steps that led to the kitchen.

Muffin looked up from the vegetables on the kitchen table as Helen came in. 'Had a nice walk, dear?'

'Lovely, thank you.' Helen hung the lead on the back of the door. Rolly joined the old boxer on the rug by the stove, nudging his way in to make space for himself. A litter of kittens spilled out of a crate by the coal-scuttle like popping corn from a saucepan. Dee-Dee's ménage of rejects was always being replenished. Helen scooped up one escapee and put it back in the blanket nest. 'Can I do anything?'

'No, no, dear: you're expected upstairs. You've visitors.' Muffin nodded at the door to the rest of the house.

'Me? What kind?' Helen's recent experience of visitors had been unpleasant ones in authority looking for her. They had stopped coming after Aunt Dee-Dee chased them off a couple of times.

'Family.'

Helen shook her head. 'That can't be right. My father's disowned me and my mother is too afraid to come to London.'

'I mean your in-laws to be.'

Her fingers froze on the pearl buttons at her cuffs as she prepared to roll up her sleeves. 'Really?'

'Yes, upstairs. I took up a tea-tray a quarter of an hour ago.'

Helen gulped. 'Did they look friendly?'

Muffin patted her arm. 'Only one way to find out, dear. Courage!'

Checking her reflection in the mirror by the back door, Helen hurried upstairs. Aunt Dee-Dee's voice could be heard from the library, a cosy room at the back of the house on the same floor as her studio. If Muffin had taken the visitors in there, it meant she and Aunt Dee-Dee approved of them. Taking a fortifying breath, Helen turned the handle and entered.

'Ah, here she is!' said Aunt Dee-Dee in her booming voice. 'Enjoyed your walk, Helen?'

'Yes, thank you.' Helen's eyes went to the visitors: a tall gentleman with light brown hair and an elegant lady with a pearl necklace and silk blouse. She recognized Sebastian's parents at once from the sketches he had done of them. Clasping her hands tightly, she braced herself for rejection. The only reason she could think for them to visit was for them to appeal to her to remove herself from their son's life.

'Miss Sandford?' Sebastian's father had risen to his feet on her entrance. His smile reminded her of his son. 'I'm Theo Trewby and this is my wife, Lady Mabel.'

Helen wondered if she was expected to curtsy or shake

hands. A bolstering look from Aunt Dee-Dee decided her: she came forward and offered her palm.

'Sir, I'm pleased to meet you both. Sebastian has told me so much about you.'

'And we have heard quite as much about you, I'm sure.' He folded her hand in his big palm. It felt warm and welcoming, not the chilly rejection she had been expecting.

'Lady Mabel.' This time Helen did bob a little curtsy. The woman's expression suggested this was in order.

'Miss Sandford. I'm pleased to meet you after all this time. I still don't understand why Sebastian didn't bring you to see us earlier.' His mother's voice was upper crust, crystal tones ringing in the room, a little querulous, like a magpie to Aunt Dee-Dee's bittern call.

'You know why, my dear: your press and government have hounded the poor girl.' Theo's American tones thickened as he disassociated himself from the witch-hunt. 'Seb didn't want to expose her to our family after the last attempt. Your sister and the Glanville girl were very unkind.'

Helen felt the sickening tumble-turn of humiliation in her stomach again as she remembered the hostile reception she had received in Somerset the year before.

'They didn't understand,' said Lady Mabel.

'I say that's no excuse for being cruel to a stranger in need. Our son suffered for months afterwards, not knowing where she had run away to. No more of that nonsense, I hope?'

Helen knew that question was directed at her. 'No, I'm staying put.' She took a seat. 'Does Sebastian know you are here?'

Theo sat down. 'No, he doesn't. We agreed before he left England not to discuss you in his letters to us. The less the censor knows, the better.'

'I don't know how they dare open our letters,' sniffed Lady Mabel. 'It is not as if the Earl of Bessick's family would plot treason.'

'Only truly democratic thing in this nation – the censorship of the mail,' grumbled Theo.

'I see.' Helen had recently been smuggling her own letters to Sebastian disguised as fond messages from Dee-Dee to her nephew. It made for a challenging time for both of them as they tried to think of suitable phrases that would pass the beady eyes of the officials. Sebastian was under close watch thanks to his relationship with her, but so far they had not questioned the affectionate letters to Charlie. 'If you tell him you met Rolly, he'll guess the rest.'

'Rolly?' asked Lady Mabel. The snap in her voice amused Helen; surely she couldn't be suspicious that her son might have a rival?

'My Labrador.'

Lady Mabel relaxed her spine a tiny bit. 'Ah. Sebastian has one too at home. Most useless dog in all creation.'

'See, my dear, Seb and Miss Sandford are obviously well matched,' said Theo.

'Because they share the same taste in dogs?'

'I seem to remember we first met at the Derby in '89 when we admired the same filly. Well, maybe we were not appreciating quite the same filly, as my interest rapidly transferred to one who had two legs and not four.' He winked at his wife.

'Theo, you mustn't make fun of me in front of these people!' Lady Mabel tried to scold him but she looked flattered, the glimpse of a warmer woman peeking out from her high-class reserve. She turned to Dee-Dee. 'Those were the days when my father could afford race-horses, Miss Cordel.'

'He never could afford them, darling: he just thought he could.' Theo patted her hand.

The easy teasing between Sebastian's parents fascinated Helen. Her own father bludgeoned her mother in every discussion, never doing anything as light-hearted as making a joke. She realized how little she knew of a successful marriage.

'In any case, Miss Sandford,' continued Theo, 'we thought it well past time to visit you and assure you that you have the full support of Sebastian's family behind you now. No need to feel you have no friends in England.'

'I've been very lucky with my friends,' Helen said softly, smiling at Aunt Dee-Dee. She also had the priest at the little church near Poplar on her side. She had dared to go back once or twice to talk with him and found him very wise. She hadn't managed to see the Cook family, but the priest had visited for her and kept her abreast of Joan's recovery. The little girl was home and there was talk of her going back to school soon. She was far from the only one bearing scars of that terrible day.

Theo put his cup and saucer on the tray, brushing a few crumbs from his thigh. 'And one day soon, if our boy gets his way, we'll be family. Isn't that right, Mabel?'

'Indeed. I've told Sebastian that I insist that you get married properly, from our home. The earl, my father, would be furious if we did it any other way.'

'And the Earl of Bessick furious is not something any of us like to see,' said Theo, a twinkle in his eye. He checked his watch. 'We must go if we are to catch our train, and we've taken up more than enough of your time. I hope you feel welcome to visit us in Somerset, Miss Sandford, with or without Sebastian.'

Helen wasn't sure she was brave enough to face that alone, but appreciated the offer. 'Thank you.'

After the Trewbys had left in their taxi, Helen stood at the window for a long time, watching the traffic jostle for position on the street below. Black cabs, lorries and delivery vans shuttled across Bloomsbury. Shop workers, museum officials, servants and local householders wove past each other, separate threads in the tapestry, barely aware of each other yet still making up the whole. It struck her as unaccountable how her life had become hitched to that of an aristocratic family down in a county she had visited once, and that only briefly. Their acceptance of her was hard to trust; their rejection had been much easier to understand. During the war, all things were thrown up in the air – careers interrupted, families scattered, women's roles changed; when they settled down in that mythical time of 'after', would things go back to the old ways or would the new shape stay? Would she still be regarded as the right bride for the privileged son or be thought of as a wartime embarrassment best forgotten?

The long rays of the late afternoon sun struck the windows in a dazzle. Suddenly, she couldn't bear to be penned in among the houses.

'I'm going out for a walk,' she announced to Aunt Dee-Dee.

The sculptress only nodded, already engrossed in moulding a piece for her latest project now she no longer had to be nice to visitors. Helen was out of the house before Rolly got wind of her intention.

Taking a chance on the first bus to come along, Helen jumped on one heading towards Westminster and got out at Parliament Square, remembering that she could reach the river from here. The Houses of Parliament looked splendid in the early evening light, a ridiculous fairytale palace considering the prosaic men in black three-piece suits who worked inside. It should be the home of Oberon and Titania, not Lloyd George and Churchill. Smiling at the thought of the MPs being turned, Bottom-like, into ass-headed creatures and fairies, she walked south across the bridge, side-stepping the late workers heading home and the people out for a night on the town. Finally she could breathe, the expanse of the river flowing under the arches defeating the city's attempt to trap and cage its inhabitants. She went half-way across and looked down at the tide rushing through the channels, muddy waters flecked with leaves and unidentifiable scraps, prose to the poetry of the architecture behind her. The view of the river connected in memory to her emotional confrontation with Reg at Christmas by the Tower just two miles downstream. She hoped the Cook family were also enjoying a peaceful late summer evening and that Joan could finally sleep without pain.

Some instinct made her turn. Scanning the crowds, she could see nothing out of order. There was a commonplace man in a grey raincoat reading a newspaper as he leaned against the parapet, but otherwise everyone else was in motion. She turned back to the Thames and watched the seagulls fight for scraps on the shore.

'Move along, miss.'

The policeman's voice in her ear made her start. She clutched her throat, heart thumping.

'Excuse me?'

'You've been asked to move along.' The policeman rocked on his heels, boots squeaking as if he were squashing mice beneath his soles, dark uniform with dully shining buttons down his chest.

Helen glanced about her. By no means was she the only Londoner who had taken a moment or two to admire the river, but she was singled out to be asked to move.

'Is there a problem, officer?' she asked politely.

'Not if you move along.'

'Move to where?'

'You have been pointed out as a suspicious character and I'm just obeying orders, miss, so I suggest you don't make a fuss and do as I ask, or we can go to the Yard and discuss this in less congenial surroundings.'

Indignation stopped her being scared at this threat. 'You would arrest me for standing on the bridge? Why?'

The policeman raised his eyes to the clock tower of Big Ben, guardian of the government's seat. 'Obvious, isn't it, miss?'

The man in the grey raincoat folded his newspaper and approached. For one second Helen assumed he had noticed her being bothered and come to her defence as a gentleman might take it upon himself to do – that was, until she saw his expression.

'Is the young woman giving you trouble, officer?' he asked.

'Nothing I can't handle, sir.' The officer took her by the elbow and steered her towards the steps off the bridge down to the Embankment. 'Just keep walking, miss.'

Astounded by his action, Helen could think of nothing else but to do as the constable said. The man in the over-coat followed, staying ten yards behind her but definitely shadowing. He was probably the very one who had asked for her to be 'moved along'.

One of Mr Brown's men. Had to be. But why were the Home Office wasting their time having her followed? If they had had her under surveillance since June, that would have been one very boring assignment, as she never did anything but walk her dog and help Aunt Dee-Dee with her visitors.

Darkness was falling, and with it her mood soured. She stopped. The man copied her. She started walking again and he fell into step. He was no longer even hiding the fact that he was tailing her. How long had this been going on without her noticing?

She swung round.

'Haven't you got somewhere better to be?' she snapped.

He ignored her.

She stomped on, debating all the ways she could make his life miserable: shopping for female intimate apparel, spending hours in the powder room of the nearest hotel, walking in circles around Nelson's column until they both got dizzy. These petty revenges were almost as satisfying in contemplation as they would have been in reality. Then she realized that, to be following her now when she rarely went out after dark, the man had to be part of a watch kept on her lodgings; they would have noted her afternoon's visitors and probably knew Sebastian's parents were there before she did. Inadvertently, between the Trewbys and herself, they had rekindled the blaze of suspicion that would punish Sebastian for standing by her. She imagined letters were being typed and conclusions drawn even as she walked.

Before she could work out what to do about that, the bells of a local church began to ring; the piercing whistles sounded in a nearby street. Another raid had been spotted.

'It can't be,' Helen whispered to herself. It was dark now and the Germans never flew at night. They hadn't been seen in the skies over London for two long peaceful months and people had begun to relax. The last thing anyone was expecting was a night bombing raid.

Fists clenched, she whirled round to her shadow. 'I expect you are going to blame me for this, aren't you?' She stabbed her finger to the sky.

The man just looked at her.

'Go away and take cover, you idiot!' Helen began running. She didn't know this part of town very well but remembered there were some bridges further up the Embankment that could shelter large numbers of people underneath. They would be better than nothing if she couldn't get into the overcrowded Underground station.

Her shadow ran after her.

The drone of approaching Gothas told Londoners under the flight path that this was no false alarm. A flash, closely tracked by a boom: the first missiles were already falling. She counted the gap, estimating how far away the bomb had been. Not that that mattered much, with the planes moving at random overhead. At least, with the Thames on one side, she had some protection. With a stitch in her side, she arrived at the vaulted bridges she remembered. Already there was a crowd to swallow up her tracker; if he kept with her, she no longer knew nor cared. They had been rendered equal by the danger. Both became just two more of the scared, pale-faced onlookers scanning the skies to see if their number was up.

More and more people joined the refugees: women in evening gowns, men in spats and uniform, tramps, bus drivers, waiters and waitresses, street sellers, women carrying babies, men clutching children. And then the most extraordinary arrivals approached. A string of elephants paced solemnly down the Embankment, herded by men in glittery costumes. Lockhart's Performing Elephants seeking shelter from their evening's performance.

'Dammit, man, you can't bring them under here!' shouted a gentleman, monocle dropping from his eye socket. 'There are women and children.'

The lead herder shrugged. 'Easier to move people somewhere else than these, mate.'

A few bystanders relocated away from the elephants but most stayed, parting to the edge of the tunnel under the bridge, leaving the centre of the wide road to the elephants. The creatures moved with heavy grace into a circle, heads pressed together as if in serious conclave, little sequinned cloths on their backs fluttering like totally inadequate wings unable to lift them from the earth.

Helen sat down on an abandoned packing case, hands folded in her lap, her mind quite taken from the threat in the skies. The vision of the peaceful elephants was a gift, a reminder of the absurdity of life, its weirdness and splendour. What was the small threat of falling victim to a bomb compared to the chance of watching, without the price of a ticket of admission, the gentle twining of trunks and slow stepping of huge feet? A blessing.

'Marvellous creatures, aren't they?' said the woman next to her.

'Wonderful – until they stampede,' said her companion, a cheery prophet of doom.

But that night the bombs fell elsewhere, dispatching tram drivers and soldiers, mothers and children, leaving the elephants untouched to entertain their impromptu audience of admirers under the arches.

16

British Airbase, Bailleul, France,
22 March 1918, 10.30 a.m

Sebastian stood in the makeshift cemetery in front of the
rows upon rows of plain white crosses and the two new
heaps of soil. Around him, his colleagues joined in the
responses of the familiar funeral service as the chaplain
rattled through the words; he had no need to look at the
page of his book, as he conducted this ceremony with
horrible frequency. Wind fluttered the pages and whipped
his white surplice in a mockery of the flag of surrender.
Black soil, leafless trees, crows circling. White and black.

A sudden swoop of unreality seized Sebastian like an
eagle snatching a fish from a loch and then dropping it
from its claws, leaving him in free fall. Was he really here,
standing with his boots in mud, his head uncovered, as
the sun danced in and out of clouds? The last few years
felt like a dream – a nightmare – too many friends now
nothing more than a pathetic cross of bone-white sticks.

The bugler played the last post, notes hanging aching
in the air. With a sombre, slightly shamed demeanour,
the priest sketched a blessing and dismissed the men. The
pilots filed back to their camp, the living moving on and

already thinking of the missions that lay ahead. The Germans had begun a new offensive that week which was rapidly gaining ground, and there was every chance that those at the funeral would be the next ones in the ground as they attempted to deter it. *Who would be the last pilot standing? Who would bury him?* Sebastian wondered sourly.

He couldn't find it in himself to move. Patrick Benn, one of his friends in this squadron, approached and patted him on the shoulder.

'Come on, Trewby. You won't do him any good standing here. What say you to a good old singsong tonight in his honour? That'd be more his thing than standing maudlin in a cemetery.'

Sebastian dipped his chin in assent and forced his feet to move. All that separated Benn and him from their friends in the graveyard was chance. None of them were superior pilots; no skill ensured survival. Fate played dice with lives and you could do nothing but take your chances with everyone else. With that thought, his last scrap of faith in some benign god puffed away like a feather. He felt naked in a world of random, meaningless events.

He wasn't sure how he made himself climb inside his cockpit that morning. He was running on the engine fuel of duty. He kept reliving the moments the day before when he had done the same thing, giving Charlie the jaunty OK sign as they lined up for take-off. They had been celebrating late into the night before. After months of humming and hawing over Charlie's proposal, Miss

Wells had agreed to marry him on his next leave in the summer. You would never find a more contented man than Charlie that morning. *If I die today*, he had joked, *I'll die happy*, daring Fate to take him at his word. Sebastian taxied behind him as they took off on patrol, neither of them thinking about the risks they took every day; the routine was too familiar to take alarm.

Half an hour into their flight, they ran into trouble: the Germans were bombing the railway line again. They drove those off, but then crossed paths with some Fokkers out to hunt Allied fighter pilots. The dogfight that ensued was crazily confused. Sebastian didn't see what happened to Charlie, too busy saving his own skin from a persistent German who sat on his tail like a hawk chasing his dinner. He cursed himself for that, even though he knew there was little he could have done to help. It wasn't until he got back to base that he heard about the crash. Jumping in a tender, he went with the team to recover Charlie's plane, hoping against hope that his friend had survived. The first crew of mechanics had already arrived on the scene and done what they could for his friend. They'd recovered his body and placed it on a tarpaulin at the edge of the field in the shelter of some newly budding blackthorn.

The mechanics knew Sebastian was a particular friend of the casualty, more than just the ordinary comrade in arms, their lives entwined beyond the narrow world of war. Pilots insulated themselves from such sorrow by keeping friendships limited – deaths were too frequent for any other strategy – but most had experienced the devastating loss of someone who had crept inside those defences. The senior mechanic took him to the spot and lifted the cover from Charlie's face. Blond hair flapped in the breeze, but that was the only animation on the body. His expressive face was blank – not peaceful, just empty of Charlie.

'Shot through the heart, sir. Hardly a scratch on him otherwise, as the plane crashed into the canopy of that oak there and broke up. We found him still in his seat.'

Something snapped inside Sebastian. He sank to his knees, head bowed in utter defeat.

The man cleared his throat. 'I'll leave you with your friend, sir. We're all very sorry to lose him. Lieutenant Cordel was a great favourite with us mechanics.'

Sebastian wanted to howl; instead he dredged up some suitable words so as not to distress the man at his side. 'Thank you.' It came out as a rasping whisper.

The mechanic walked away, casting a worried look over his shoulder at the grieving lieutenant.

Shot through the heart by a bullet from a German machine-gun. Charlie would have laughed at the absurdity of his fate. No wonder the enemy had found his target with eerie accuracy: Charlie had had the largest heart of any man Sebastian knew.

Lieutenant Charles Cordel had been buried with a Canadian pilot, also lost on that morning flight, and the mess would hold a wake for them that night, celebrating the men with the songs they had liked, the funny stories the airmen knew about them. That was if they all returned from today's combat duties.

Pull yourself together. Sebastian taxied to the end of the runway, every nerve in his body aware of Charlie in the cemetery behind him. *The show must go on*. He took off with a strange dead sense of fatalism, so unlike the happiness of the day before. He went through the motions of the patrol, easing back the joystick to lift the nose, banking to the left to clear the airfield, wiping his goggles with the end of his scarf when condensation formed. The vibrations of the engine travelling through his seat failed to shake him out of his torpor. Even shooting down a straggling German triplane did not penetrate his numbness. He watched the plane spiral to the ground, taking no satisfaction in the little spurt of flame that confirmed his 'kill'. Eye for an eye? Hardly. That anonymous pilot who had just died was no revenge, just a job that had to be done.

The sixth sense that a pilot develops warned him that he had just turned from hunter to prey. He couldn't see him, but he could feel the enemy sitting in his blind spot behind. Stalling the engine suddenly and pulling up, he lost momentum so quickly his pursuer had to overshoot. The German swung away to the east, circling in the hopes of coming back round to get another shot at him. And so began the ballet of the skies, two planes vying for the best position, machine-guns rattling in sharp bursts in the few seconds when advantage was gained. Sebastian steered his plane through instinct, locked in his fatalistic mood that kept everything at a distance. The usual rush of adrenalin that accompanied such battles failed to trigger.

This was the way to get killed, he thought vaguely, going through the motions of the deadly *pas de deux*. If you didn't care enough to survive, you were unlikely to do so.

Then, out of the corner of his eye, he caught sight of a curl of cloud weaving up like an elephant's trunk reaching for fruit on a high branch. It brought to mind the vivid letter from Helen in which she had described her strange encounter with the creatures on the Embankment, an incident she called a beautiful gift on a night of horrors.

Helen.

The thought of her zipped through him like an electric charge. What on earth was he doing here, dicing with death and the German pilot like some half-wit, when he had her to consider? He'd slipped down into a mood where nothing mattered; now he kicked himself into action. *Stop playing the fool and start fighting for her sake*. He couldn't believe how close he had been to letting her down, losing his focus. Helen counted on him and he wasn't going to fail her. He pulled back on his joystick to take his plane over in a loop that should bring him down once more as hunter rather than prey. Taking the Pup on a path that echoed the curve of the trunk, he hung upside-down, then slid down the other side. A rattle of his gun and the Fokker banked sideways, engines coughing a horrible black smoke. The pilot turned tail, heading back to base. It was possible he wouldn't reach it, as he'd had to cut power to stop the fire spreading. Sebastian found himself wishing his foe good luck; fire in the air was every pilot's worst nightmare. Personally, he'd prefer to crash rather than burn.

His hands were shaking on his controls now he had cleared the skies of his enemy. Sebastian was shocked how close he had been to not caring if he lived or died, especially when he knew what effect his death would have on those he loved. Never again would he hold his life so cheap. Helen cherished it, so he damn well would too. Vow made, he checked his compass and headed back to base.

London, 23 March 1918, 10 a.m.

Helen stood outside the door of the studio, flinching as another crash reverberated within the room. Muffin hovered beside her, knocking on the wood panel.

'Open up, Miss Cordel, please open up!' she pleaded.

The only response was the tinkle of glass.

The news had arrived with the morning post. A brief note from Charlie's parents. Aunt Dee-Dee had thrown the open letter on to the table and stormed out to lock herself in her studio.

'What's she doing in there?' Muffin said hoarsely. 'Will she hurt herself, do you think?'

From the sounds of it, Aunt Dee-Dee was destroying her studio rather than herself, though maybe it was the same thing: all that work being smashed and overturned, the most vital parts of her imagination being ground into dust.

The front doorbell rang. Brushing Muffin's arm in a gesture to say she would answer it, Helen hurried down the stairs, hoping to see friends of Aunt Dee-Dee who could help console her. She threw the door open to find a government official accompanied by two policemen on the step.

Oh Lord.

If only she could go back and relive those last few seconds, she would have avoided this, disappeared into the depths of the house where officialdom couldn't touch her.

'Yes?'

'Miss Abendroth-Sandford?'

'No.'

The man looked at his piece of paper. 'Are you denying you are Helen Abendroth-Sandford?'

'Yes.'

'Her twin sister, are you?' he sneered.

'No.' She began to close the door. 'You have the name wrong.'

'Miss Sandford then.' He cleared his throat in an irritated manner. 'I have an order here for your removal from this address, so I advise you very strongly not to shut us out.'

'It isn't my house, so I cannot ask you inside even if I wished to cooperate. And this really is not a good time. We have just received news of a death in the family.'

'Then I'm sure you will not wish to add further to the distress. You have ten minutes to pack a suitcase and leave peacefully with your escort to the train before we enforce the order.'

'I beg your pardon?'

'This is an official notice for your internment as an enemy alien.'

'Show me.' Thrusting her hand through the narrow gap, she snatched the paper from him and quickly scanned the contents. Mr Brown and the Home Office had finally acted after months of stalking her. 'I . . . give me a moment.'

'Ten minutes, Miss Sandford.'

She slammed the door on them and dashed up the stairs to pound on the studio door.

'Aunt Dee-Dee, open up! Open up! Please! I need you!'

After a brief pause, the door swung open. The sculptress stood in the ruins of her studio.

'It's my fault. I baited Fate by making him into young Actaeon,' Aunt Dee-Dee said faintly.

Helen had no time for such delusions – she didn't even have time for grief, terrible as that sounded. 'Nonsense: Charlie loved that statue. Fate doesn't care two hoots for such things. Please, I'm sorry to interrupt you – I miss him too – but something else has happened.' She thrust the paper at Aunt Dee-Dee.

The sculptress waved it away. 'I can't read it. Nothing makes sense today.'

Now was not the moment for a spiritual collapse; Helen needed Aunt Dee-Dee to be her indomitable self. 'They're arresting me – sending me to prison.'

Muffin gasped. 'But they can't! You're English – you were born here!'

'They jolly well can. They don't care for facts, only suspicions. I've been given ten minutes to pack.'

Aunt Dee-Dee ran her hands over her face. Her knuckles were laced with tiny bleeding cuts. 'I . . . I don't know what to do.'

That made two of them.

'I thought you would.' Helen felt as if her last safe footing was crumbling. She had been sure that, even in mourning, Aunt Dee-Dee would save her. 'I . . . I counted on you.'

It was Muffin who surprised them both by stepping into the breach. 'Pack a case, dear.'

'What?' Helen reeled.

'Just for the moment. We don't want them to make it a criminal offence if you resist this court order. Miss Cordel will ring her friends in the government – and the Trewbys. Isn't that right, Miss Cordel?'

Aunt Dee-Dee nodded, her face still registering shock. 'Yes, that's the only thing to do. They won't harm you. Go quietly and we'll have you back here in two shakes of a lamb's tail.'

Muffin pushed Helen gently between the shoulder-blades. 'Hurry, my dear. I was a suffragette before the war; I know how cruel the police can be with ladies who resist them.'

Helen took the stairs two at a time to reach her bedroom, somehow managing to make rational choices among her belongings while she continued to fizz with panic. She'd need money, warm clothes . . .

The doorbell rang again. This time Muffin went down to answer it. Helen could hear her high angry voice barking at the intruders. She returned to the hall, carrying her suitcase, frantically wondering if she had remembered all the essentials. She was on her monthly – the worst possible time to undertake a journey to an unknown destination, but she doubted the men would care or think of such things.

The official was issuing threats to Muffin as the two policemen stood silent either side, eyeing the slight woman with distaste. Helen got the distinct sense Muffin had already roundly insulted their profession.

'I'm here. I'm ready.'

'I do not like to be kept waiting,' complained the man. 'You are making this unnecessarily difficult.'

Rage flared up inside Helen. *She* was making it difficult!

Muffin passed her leather purse. 'It's all we have at home but we'll send more if you need it.'

'Thank you. I can't tell you how grateful I am for your kindness.'

Muffin poked the nearest policeman. 'Carry the lady's case, or are manners entirely dead in your service?'

Reluctantly, the officer picked up the case.

'We'll see you back here very soon!' called Muffin as Helen followed her escort out of the house. A car waited for them on the street.

'She has influential friends: be very careful how you treat her!' shouted Muffin as the car pulled away.

17

The train drew into Aylesbury station and released a great sigh of steam, making the wooden canopy look like it was momentarily floating on clouds. Helen had scant idea of where she was – north-west of London, she had been told, but this was a place she had not intended to visit and never spared a thought. Now it was to be her prison. She dried her cheeks. She had been mourning Charlie, raging against the stupid loss of a brilliant young life, fearing that Sebastian would be next, but neither policeman had cared. They had assumed she was weeping for herself.

One of the police officers escorting her dropped the window and leaned out to open the door from the outside. He appeared to be looking for someone on the platform. The second officer lifted her case off the rack, then took her firmly by the upper arm. The presence of the two law officers had been enough to ensure they had the compartment to themselves.

'Come along, miss – that's if you don't want to wear handcuffs.'

Face red with humiliation, Helen quickly jumped down to the platform. She knew her little party was attracting everyone's eyes. Mothers were steering their children away; old men were glaring at her; the porters turned their backs, knowing better than to expect a tip from a girl under police guard.

Two prison officers in dark uniforms were waiting by the ticket office. They looked very like the policemen, though their expressions were, if anything, even less friendly.

'Is that the German woman?' said the older man in a carrying voice.

'Yes, sir. If you'd just take the papers and sign here.' The policeman handed over the sheaf of documents that the Home Office had drawn up.

The warder shuffled through them.

'Got many others like her?' the policeman asked, curiosity piqued. Germans were as rare these days as hen's teeth, thanks to the war cutting off tourism and internment locking up the few who had ended up on the wrong side of the Channel.

'A few, under the provisions of the Defence of the Realm Act. The most hardened cases. We know what to do with her sort, never you mind.' The prison officer scribbled a signature on a receipt.

'This one here has friends in high places who'll take an interest,' warned the second policeman, handing over her suitcase. Muffin's threat had got through.

'She'll be treated fairly, just like all our other prisoners,' said the warder stiffly. 'It's not my fault if the inmates don't like the Huns among them.'

'Good luck to you then. We'd better hurry if we're to make the next train up the line.'

Without any further acknowledgement, the policemen left to cross to the opposite platform. It was as if she were a non-person, a parcel or a box that they had delivered.

The two prison officers moved to flank her, barring any escape – not that she was thinking of making a run for it. Where could she go? 'Miss Abendroth-Sandford, come with us.'

Not that again. 'My name is plain Sandford. I would appreciate it if you would remember.' Trying not to be terrified by the swift change of events, Helen found her voice wasn't as strong as she would have liked.

'You speak very good English – hardly a trace of accent,' commented the second prison guard, who up to this point had held his tongue. He had a cheerful moustache on his upper lip and a crop of wiry rusty-brown hair that reminded her of terrier fur.

'That's because I *am* English.'

'And no doubt as innocent as a daisy,' muttered the first guard sarcastically.

'Yes, exactly.'

'If I had a shilling for each time one of our women said that, then I'd be a rich man,' chuckled the other.

It was a minor relief to leave the audience on the platform and head for the prison van.

'In you go, miss,' said the nicer of the two men, helping her step into the back. He handed her the case.

'Where am I going? No one's told me what's going on.'

'Aylesbury Inebriate Reformatory. It's where we house all our bad girls.' He gave her a smirk and closed the door.

Helen quickly sat down before she was knocked off her feet by the movement of the vehicle. This was all like some ghastly dream that kept on getting worse: first the news about Charlie; then the waiting around at the police station for her fate to be decided; and finally this trip to a provincial town she had never heard of, to be thrown in a women's prison that sounded like it was more concerned with drunkards than German aliens. She kept expecting that the door would open and someone would rush in to rescue her, but so far every time a new person arrived to deal with her case, events had taken another, darker turn. She would have to get to grips with the fact that she had to rely on herself, not bank on the slim chance of the cavalry coming to her rescue.

The short journey from the station ended inside the prison gates. The van doors opened to reveal a handsome building of red brick with white detailing, reminiscent of a military barracks.

'Out you get, miss.' The one she had nicknamed in her head 'Nice Guard' extended a hand.

'I'm really not German,' she said, wondering if she could recruit a supporter.

'That's not for me to say. All the women are here at

the pleasure of His Majesty and I'm just doing my job.'
So niceness had its limits.

He took her over to the reception area where the other guard was already processing her papers.

'Youngest one to date,' he was telling the man at the desk. 'No more than nineteen. But that's the enemy for you, using even women and children to do their dirty work.'

'Shall I issue a uniform?' asked the clerk.

'She's allowed to keep her own clothes as she's technically an internee.' The guard rolled his eyes.

'Bleeding hearts in government,' muttered the clerk disapprovingly. Helen did not think he had once raised his gaze to look at her.

'Get one of the female staff to search her and her stuff.'

'I wasn't born yesterday, mate. Step this way, miss.' He used a heavy key to open the door into the women's prison wing. 'Go into the first room on the right and wait.'

Helen swallowed, finding her courage failing at this crucial moment. She had to remember she was innocent and had done nothing wrong. Just like the men at Alexandra Palace, there was no cause for her to be put behind bars other than war madness. She felt a brief moment of envy: she'd swap the open skies of the Palace for this prison any day.

'Do I need to find a translator?' asked the clerk, eyes darting to the officer.

'No, thank you. I understand perfectly.' Mustering her pride, she walked over the threshold.

Sebastian threw the telegram across the room. Helen – interned! The government was insane! His father's measured words still could not stop the explosion of rage and anguish he felt, enough to make him wish he could renounce his nationality and duty, stomp on his uniform cap and hurry back to England. His father was doing all he could for her, even the earl was stirring himself from his Somerset retreat to make life difficult for officials in Whitehall, but the Home Office would not see reason. The thinking was that if Helen had done wrong, she was where she deserved and, if she were innocent, anticipating and preventing treasonous activities was better than 'letting her run around London getting up to mischief'. His father said he suspected that the real explanation for the move was that the Home Office had grown tired of spying on her, as she gave them no leads, and had decided to cut expenses by locking her away. Normal rules of having to provide evidence for a conviction didn't work in time of war, when the government could do what it felt like.

Sebastian was desperate to be there for her.

Fired up by this resolution, he marched to the CO's office. Captain Duff-Taylor, commander of this frontline airfield, had always been pleasant in his dealings with the men; Sebastian hoped today wouldn't prove an exception. He tapped on the door.

'Come. Ah, Trewby, what can I do for you?'

Duff-Taylor had the sharp gaze of a man who had seen action, if his lack of an arm on the left side weren't hint enough. His face was etched with lines of suffering, though he was only in his late twenties.

'Sir, I'd like to request a special leave of absence.'

The captain leaned back in his antique chair. The temporary headquarters of Sebastian's squadron was in a small chateau like something out of a Perrault fairy tale, senior officers inside, with the junior pilots and mechanics billeted in tents around the landscaped garden. Sebastian woke each morning to see the round tower and moat of the oldest part of the building floating above the mist, a strangely poetic sight out of place with the rest of the day. The dusty heirloom furniture had been pressed into service for the officers, so Duff-Taylor might well have been sitting on a fortune. Not that such things mattered in war, when a chair became valued for its original purpose rather than its price in the auction room. If necessity demanded, it would also serve as firewood – such were the priorities of men fighting for their lives.

'If I recall, you aren't due any leave for a few months.'

'There's an emergency at home, sir.'

'Not bad news, I hope?'

'Bad news' meant death. 'Not that kind of news, sir. It's my fiancée.' Could he really say the next part of the sentence? How would the man take it? 'She's in difficulties.'

Duff-Taylor raised an eyebrow. 'Do you mean an early marriage is in order?'

'Excuse me?' Too late Sebastian realized his commanding officer had assumed he had got the girl pregnant and had to rush back to right that wrong.

'No disrespect to the lady, but we can't let pilots go running off home at this juncture in the war because of some bad timing. It won't have escaped your attention that we are fighting for our survival here and I can't release a damned good pilot for anything short of a life-or-death crisis.'

'It's nothing like that, sir. My fiancée has been interned – wrongly interned. Her only connection to Germany is her mother. She's never lived there or even been there.'

'They're not interning women, Trewby. You've got your wires crossed.'

'With respect, sir, I know what I am talking about. They've put her in Aylesbury Prison, sir.'

The captain sighed. 'I can well believe that officialdom has made a mess of her case – they can't find their own arses without a map – but what exactly do you think you can do about it? I'm sorry to say that having half-German blood is enough to put people behind bars these days. I even heard of an English boy put in the camp on the Isle of Man merely because he didn't have any papers. Didn't speak a word of the lingo, was as Cockney as they come and still the Home Office locked him up.'

Sebastian could hear the refusal circling and coming in to land.

'Write letters. Recruit the support of all your friends back home. Do your duty here. If you really want to help her, you'll do your bit to end this war sooner rather than later, not rush to her side to share her lamentations.'

At least Duff-Taylor didn't assume she was guilty – he could take some comfort from that.

'I'll look over the leave roster and see if I can shuffle a few things, but for the moment there is no break in that particular cloud.'

Swallowing his frustration, Sebastian nodded. 'Thank you, sir.'

The captain leaned his arm on his desk and drummed his fingers on the blotter, his method of puzzling out a tricky matter. 'I tell you what: I'll write to my uncle in the Foreign Office and ask him to look into her case. He's got connections. I don't know the lady but I believe I know my men: if she has your good opinion, then that is character reference enough for me. Give me the details and I'll see what I can do.'

This show of support made Sebastian feel slightly better. 'I'd be very grateful. Helen is the sweetest girl alive.'

With a slight smile, the captain waved a dismissal. Sebastian returned to his tent to start writing his letters.

Aylesbury Prison, 4 p.m.

Helen sat on the edge of her bed in the cell, body shaking. The experience of being searched by the rough female guard had been vile from start to finish. She had never undressed in front of anyone, and the woman had expected her to do it with all the brazenness of an artist's model. That was what she tried to think about as she complied: Sebastian's tales of sketching at the Slade, not this mortifying pat-down for treasonous materials. Even her plaited hair was unwound to check she wasn't smuggling in a stiletto. Once allowed to dress, she huddled in a corner while her suitcase was emptied, the lining slit, then the belongings bundled back inside.

'She's clean,' growled the woman to the male officer waiting outside. 'No contraband.' Together the two of them led Helen along a metal gantry to a cell on the top floor of the women's wing. They'd unlocked a heavy door onto a two-bed room and gestured for her to go in. One bed was clearly already taken, so Helen had slid her things under the second. The door closed on her without any explanation of what she was to expect.

Being alone without distractions allowed her worries to come out of hiding. At the moment, her biggest fear was that the other prisoners would eat her alive. She had no illusions how she would come across: a young, scared, well-to-do girl of supposedly German extraction – every fact a mark against her. The longer-term anxiety was that she could be here indefinitely. No charges had been made against her, but the government did not need them. Dislike and suspicion were enough. Only peace and the dropping of wartime regulations would change that, but the conflict had already dragged on for three and a half years; what was to say it wouldn't carry on for the same length of time or longer? She did not want to spend her next years staring at four white walls.

She looked down at her extravagant diamond engagement ring. The female guard had spent a second or two examining it, her expression avaricious. *What had she been thinking when she walked out of the house in Bloomsbury?* Helen wondered. She should have left this behind. If she waltzed around a women's prison with a king's ransom on her finger, she was asking for trouble. She should hide it again. With a little tugging, she slipped the ring off and attached it to the locket chain she wore around her neck. Tucking both under her clothing, she hoped neither would be noticed. If she got any visitors, she would ask them to take the jewellery home with them for safekeeping.

There was a rattle as the door was unlocked and a woman in prison uniform was let in, a thickset blonde who looked like she had seen the tough side of life, if her cynical expression was anything to go by.

'Heard I got myself a roommate. Just my bleeding luck to be saddled with one of the German baby-killers.' She kicked off her heavy clogs and stretched out on her bed, displaying legs roped with varicose veins. 'Keep to your side and keep quiet and we won't have any problems.' She closed her eyes, giving Helen a profile view of her heavy eyebrows, flushed square face, wispy hair. She looked exhausted.

Helen looped her arms around her knees. 'My name is Helen Sandford. I'm not German. I've never killed a baby – saved a few, mind.' It was exhausting to have to defend herself against ridiculous allegations; she wished it were all over – in the past – filed under finished business.

The woman cracked open an eye. 'You don't sound foreign. Why you here then?'

Helen shrugged. 'Because the men in the Home Office are idiots?'

The woman gave a salty laugh. 'Got that right. Where are you from then?'

'Suffolk.'

'Stone the crows: they've put me in with a country lass!' She sat up and extended a hand. 'Name's Marge Bailey. In here for running a house of ill repute.' She wrinkled her nose in amusement. 'As if the judges aren't among some of my best customers, but that's men for you.'

Helen shook her hand. It felt warm and work-roughened. She instinctively felt she would be safe with Marge. 'Pleased to meet you.'

'There are a few real Huns in here. You'd better steer clear of them.'

'Really? How many?'

'Oh, four or five. We've kept them in their place; they won't be lending the Kaiser a helping hand while they're in here.'

'Don't worry: I've no interest in them. I just want to be left alone by the government.'

'I sense a story.'

'Not a very interesting one.'

Marge gave a husky chuckle. 'We're in prison, staring

at blank walls; believe me, anything you say would be as good as a Saturday night at the pictures for me.'

Helen smiled. 'I worked as a nurse but got the finger pointed at me – wrongly, I promise you – for stealing morphine capsules. They worked themselves up into a lather about it and kicked me out. Since then they've convinced themselves I'm some kind of chief plotter, while all I've done is try to work to earn a living.'

'Lord, ducky, you don't want them sort after you. They make black white and white black; and they don't have a clue how real life is lived by us with no fancy education and money behind us.' Marge warmed to her theme, waving her fingers expressively as if addressing the ceiling. 'Men in power pick on people who they don't like, then try and make the accusations stick. I see it all the time. You'd think I was the first person ever to make a living off working girls if you'd been at my trial. I looked after my girls, I did. How else was I going to make ends meet after my useless husband ran off with the piano tuner.' Marge gave a jaw-cracking yawn. 'They've got me working in the laundry, so forgive me if I have a little nap. Been at it since dawn. Better than sitting in here on my bum all day, but still – I'm knackered.' Marge stretched out and fell instantly asleep, her whistling snores a strange music to keep Helen company.

I'm sharing a cell with a woman who ran a brothel, thought Helen with a bizarre desire to laugh. She hoped she had no false snobbery when it came to people – nurses treated all sorts – but never had she thought she would end up here. Marge seemed a good sort and could well be her first lucky break of the last few days. She wondered what Sebastian would think; she doubted he would share her opinion: he still cherished ideas of her being sweet and innocent.

Well, darling, she told his locket, *I'm in prison with a madam. Even you are going to have to rethink.*

The first time Helen had to emerge from her cell was for supper. Funny, she reflected, how somewhere to which she had been reluctant to come now felt like a safe haven. A bell rang downstairs and warders unlocked the doors. Marge woke up with another yawn, displaying a glint of a gold tooth at the back.

'What do we do now, Marge?' asked Helen, brushing down her wrinkled skirt. She wanted to hide behind the larger woman like a chick under a hen's wing.

'We line up outside, ducky, and wait for the signal to file down. They don't like us talking. It is allowed when we are at the tables but not when moving about.' Marge stretched her arms above her head. 'Come on, Suffolk. Stick with me and you'll survive.'

Relieved to have a guide, Helen followed her out to the walkway. Women in the same grey uniform as Marge stood waiting, hands folded behind their backs, feet apart. Further down, she spotted a couple of women dressed in civilian clothes. They were slouching on the rail; one was smoking a cigarette fixed in a long holder.

'The Germans,' said Marge under her breath. 'Consider

themselves a law unto themselves, as they're internees and not convicts.' She glanced at Helen's clothes. 'Like you.'

'Hardly.' Helen wondered if it would have been easier to don a uniform and disappear from notice.

At the blast of a high whistle, the women turned and filed down the stairs to join the queue to the canteen.

'Don't expect much,' muttered Marge. 'The cooks only know how to do stew.'

Helen wasn't feeling very hungry. A good thing, she decided, when she saw the watery brown stew, gristle floating on the surface. A few peas bobbed amidst the grease, like survivors of a U-boat sinking. Nobody was eating prime cuts these days, thanks to rationing, but it appeared women prisoners were at the bottom of the list for meat supplies. She took her tin plate and sat beside Marge at the long trestle table. The greasy smell of the food made her stomach turn over.

'Didn't think you'd take up with the German, Marge,' said a thin woman with sleek black hair and long pale fingers. She looked like the illustration of the witch in a child's book of fairy tales.

'She's not, Janet.' Marge scooped up the stew, wrinkled her nose, and then swallowed with the minimum of chewing. It seemed the best policy if you were actually going to eat the meal. Helen followed suit, telling her rebellious stomach to behave. 'She's from Suffolk.'

Janet scowled. 'You sure?'

Marge shrugged. 'Ask her yourself.'

'Well?'

Helen swallowed her mouthful, trying not to gag as the fatty mixture slid down. 'I'm from Haverhill originally. My dad's a solicitor's clerk.'

'So why have they put you in here?'

'Do I need to define government bureaucracy for you?'

Janet guffawed. 'No, love, you don't. You have my commiserations. Just keep away from the real Huns and you'll be all right. Strange bunch, they are: still plotting though there's nothing for them to do in here as far as I can tell. And stay clear of Big Hetty; she's got a screw loose.' She nodded at a muscular woman sitting on her own at the far end of the table. Her little eyes swivelled around the room with the restlessness of a searchlight. A cold shiver ran down Helen's spine.

'What's she in here for?' she asked. She had almost forgotten that there would be real criminals in prison, sitting alongside the harmless Marge and Janet.

'Killing her old man and his sister.' Janet took a mouthful of food. 'With a hammer.'

'She should be in an asylum but they wouldn't have her.' Marge broke her slice of bread into pieces, savouring each one, a kind of dessert after the foul stew. 'She's in a cell on her own now since she threw her last cellmate off the walkway.'

Seeing Helen's shocked expression, Janet added: 'The net caught her. She lived to tell the tale.'

'I think she was relieved. Better a short flight over the rail than a night with Hetty.'

'I'd jump if it were me,' admitted Janet.

'So you only get put with her if the guards really don't like you. She's their guard dog – the ultimate threat to make you toe the line. Keep your record clean and you'll not have to worry about that.'

Helen chewed on her bread, trying not to look at Hetty. The German prisoners sat together, chatting in their own language. From time to time, one would glance in her direction and offer a smile, but Helen ducked her head and kept eating. They had obviously heard that another 'German' was among their number, but were destined to be disappointed when they found her spoken German was pretty much drawn from the nursery. She resolved it was best to forget she knew any at all, as it would not do for Marge and Janet to turn against her. What was that legend? Scylla and Charybdis. She felt she sat between the teeth of the Hetty monster and the whirlpool of intrigue of the Germans. Best she stay on board with Marge and Janet and try to steer a clean course between them.

The following morning, Helen was not surprised to hear she had visitors. At last. Perhaps this nightmare would be over more quickly than she'd anticipated. The female guard waited at the door, keys swinging on her belt, as Helen quickly put on her shoes. Marge was already at the laundry so she had the cell to herself.

'Do you know who it is?' she asked the woman.

'Not my place to ask. I've just been sent to fetch you,' the guard replied sullenly.

Helen imagined it would be Aunt Dee-Dee, or maybe even Sebastian if he had had the good fortune of being granted leave to come to visit her.

The guard was staring at her. Helen rubbed her nose, wondering if she had a smudge on her face. 'Is something out of place?'

'Lost your ring already?'

Helen spread her bare fingers. 'No, I've just put it somewhere . . . for safe keeping.'

The guard gave a bark of laughter. 'Good idea, Sandford. You realize you are sleeping surrounded by thieves and whores. I'll look after it for you if you like.'

Helen had a shrewd suspicion she wouldn't see it again if she handed it over. 'No, no, that's not necessary, thank you all the same.'

'You never know when these things might go missing.' The guard tucked her thumbs in her belt. 'Don't say you weren't warned.'

'It won't go missing if no one knows of its existence, will it?' She gave the guard a hard look, but the woman's eyes skated over her and away. There was something more to these comments, something devious.

'Silence might be a luxury. The kind you have to pay for,' the guard said airily.

Fully expecting to be able to hand the ring over to her friends for safe keeping, Helen chose not to take the bait. 'I imagine so,' she said with equal lightness. 'Just as well I have it somewhere private and safe.'

The guard escorted her down to the visitors' room, a

plain square box with a locked door to the outside and another that led back to the prison.

'Sit down.' The guard gestured to her to take her seat at the wooden table. She sat facing two upright chairs, looking forward to seeing friendly faces opposite her. The guard went over to the far door and opened the slot.

'The prisoner is ready for her visitors now.'

18

With the sound of chains and keys on the other side, the door opened. In walked her parents. Cursing herself for her own stupidity at not anticipating that they would be told of her incarceration, Helen's heart sank to the soles of her feet. Neither party said anything as the visitors took the seats opposite her. Her mother, fair hair caught back from her face, seemed to crumple as she sat, her fingers clutching her handbag on her knees. Helen felt the familiar longing and frustration at seeing her mother. A pretty but spiritless woman, Geerta did not have it in her to come out of her husband's shadow and act as a defender to her daughters, being too battered by his violent nature and terrified of repercussions. She tried a smile at her daughter, but it wobbled and tears came to her eyes.

'Not now, Mother,' growled her father. He never addressed his wife by her Christian name, having subsumed her identity under her role in the family.

Helen turned her attention to her father. She hadn't seen him for a couple of years and he had aged in the interval. His hair had receded further up his forehead and gone steel grey. He had kept his bulk, but it was more fat than muscle: a lion gone to seed but still very dangerous. She knew that he had not come to comfort her – that did not lie in his repertoire. Whatever had brought him to visit would not be in her interests. She folded her hands in her lap and waited for the axe to fall.

'Always knew you'd come to bad but even I didn't dream you'd end up behind bars,' began Harvey Sandford.

'I'm interned. I've not been charged with a criminal offence,' she said quietly.

'Bleeding well should've been – stealing from a hospital on the front line! Should've been shot for that!'

'I did not steal anything.'

Harvey rolled on like a tank, crushing any obstacle in his path. 'I couldn't hold my head up in Haverhill for months after we saw the news reports. My daughter – a traitor! I almost lost my job with Bufton, Smithers and Felcher. If it weren't for my years of exemplary service, I'd've been out on my ear. Did you think of that when you flexed those light fingers of yours, eh?'

'Clearly that was my primary consideration at the time.' Helen couldn't resist sarcasm as he wasn't going to listen to her in any case.

'I'm ashamed of you, my girl. So's your mother. Aren't you, Mother?'

Geerta looked at her daughter and made a faint yes–no gesture that could have meant anything. Now Helen had had time to gather her thoughts, she was even more surprised to see her mother here. Helen had been interned for a supposed allegiance based on being half-German. Being fully German, Geerta's venturing into a prison for internees took some courage. Geerta had so far avoided official attention by living a blameless, quiet life in the country.

'I thought you were staying with Aunt Giselle?' Helen addressed the question to Geerta. Sebastian had told her that, last he had heard, her mother had gone to her father's sister.

'She is. Bad enough I married her. Can't have her in the public eye in Haverhill. She's living on the farm at Bures, aren't you, Mother?'

'Your aunt is very kind,' whispered Geerta. 'Are . . . are you all right, Helen?'

'I'm in prison for no good reason. It's not usually a definition of being "all right".' She couldn't help the sour note.

'I am so sorry.'

Helen sighed. 'I'm fine. I'm sure it will all be sorted out soon and they'll let me go.'

Harvey gave a scornful laugh. 'That's not what Mr Brown told me. Nice man, that Brown. Very apologetic that he had to break the bad news to me. Very reasonable.'

'Mr Brown has hounded me from one end of London to the other: in what way is that reasonable?' Helen drew a square on the table top with her finger, preferring not to meet her father's eye as she knew they would both lose their temper.

'He said you had a choice. You could agree to come home to my custody. I'd make sure you couldn't consort with any of your old acquaintances, keep you in the house. I told him it would be difficult for me, having my traitor daughter under my roof, but I promised to make sure you saw the error of your ways and had no scope to create more trouble.'

'I've not created trouble. It has been entirely in his imagination.'

Harvey rolled over that comment too. 'He said you've been fraternizing with a distinguished officer in the air force, putting a black mark against the innocent boy's record, preventing further promotion.'

Helen swallowed against the lump in her throat. She had not realized she had done that to Sebastian, as he had never complained that his advancement had been blocked. That was a new guilt to add to her conscience for being unable to let him go. 'I'm not fraternizing; I'm engaged to be married.'

Harvey gave a hoot. 'You forget how old you are, Helen. You can't marry without my consent until you are twenty-one.'

Stupidly, she hadn't realized he would try to play that card. 'Why would you stop me? You've never truly cared what I did.'

'I care for the reputation of the young man in question – one of our brave defenders. I wouldn't want him to marry in haste and repent at leisure like I've done.'

Geerta gave a sharp intake of breath.

'You are very cruel, Dad. Always have been.' Helen dismissed him by turning her shoulder away, reaching out and patting her mother's hands. 'Mum, you should stay with Aunt Giselle; you are better off there. Just as I'm better off in prison than in the jail he'd make for me.'

Harvey's hand shot out and cuffed her round the head. 'Ungrateful chit.'

Helen reeled but caught herself on the table. Geerta let out a little cry.

The guard cleared her throat. 'Sir, I cannot allow you to lay hands on the prisoner – I mean, internee.'

Tears shone in Helen's eyes but she kept them from falling. She hardened her heart against him; there was no point claiming kinship, as all he had for her were hard words and harder blows. She could fight back by showing him how little he mattered to her. 'Thank you for coming, but don't concern yourself about what happens to me. I find your concern quite painful.' She touched her burning ear.

Harvey got to his feet, pushing the chair back with a loud scrape. 'Come on, Mother. I wash my hands of her. Go to the devil in your own fashion, Helen. Don't crawl to me expecting help later when you realize your mistake.'

Helen did not rise, did not even look at him as he stormed out. She felt her mother's light touch brush her shoulder.

'Mother!'

Summoned like a dog off the lead, Geerta hurried out of the room.

The guard said nothing as she escorted Helen back to her cell. When they reached the entrance, she paused.

'Do you need something for that?' She gestured to Helen's reddened cheek.

'No, thank you. I'm used to it.'

'I'd be obliged if you didn't complain to the governor. That kind of business isn't allowed — manhandling the inmates.'

'I have no intention of complaining.'

With a sceptical humph, the woman locked the cell door behind her.

Her second visitation came in the afternoon.

'My, aren't you the popular one,' said the guard, escorting her to the governor's office rather than the visitors' room.

'Do you know who it is this time?' Helen asked, wishing to be better prepared than she had been for her parents.

The guard shrugged. 'An official of some kind. A suit from London.'

Helen was unsurprised when she entered the office to find Mr Brown behind the desk and the governor standing at the window.

'Miss Abendroth-Sandford,' Mr Brown said crisply.

'Mr Brown. Sir.' She nodded at the prison governor.

He gave her a nod in reply and returned to studying the yard under the window.

'Take a seat.' Mr Brown gestured to the chair opposite him. 'By now you will have met with your parents.'

Helen touched her ear, still tender from the morning's encounter. 'Yes.'

'You understand the nature of the offer I have made?'

'Yes.'

'And?'

'I refused it.'

'You'd prefer to remain in prison rather than at your parent's house?'

'Yes.' Let him draw what conclusions he liked from that.

'I am displeased.'

She didn't think that deserved an answer.

'You are putting a strain on this country's law enforcement resources at a time when we need them most. Do you feel no shame for doing that?'

Helen stared back at him, focusing on the slight sheen of sweat on his forehead. Was he married? she wondered. Was there a Mrs Brown who loved him? Somehow she doubted that.

'I see you are unmoved. In that case I have a final offer to make you. The government will cover the costs of your deportation if you sign a confession and agree not to return to these shores.'

'Deport me where? I'm English.'

'It is true there are obstacles to your removal to Germany . . .'

Like a battlefield on the border.

'But it has been suggested to me that you might agree to join your sister in America.'

Helen jolted to attention. 'You'd pay for me to cross the Atlantic?'

'Steerage class, of course, but yes.' He looked very pleased with himself for having found something to which she responded. 'I can smooth the way with the Americans.'

'And the price of this is a confession and promise not to return? To what would I be confessing?' Helen's mind was racing – a chink had opened up in the wall, freedom and Flora on the other side.

'Come, come, you know what you have done.'

'Yes: precisely nothing.'

'Stolen medicines, communicated with your masters to guide bombing raids, smuggled messages to the men interned in Alexandra Palace, compromised a decorated officer's loyalties. Need I go on?'

All of these had some slight connection to her activities, but he had then distorted them in the mirror of his suspicions. It struck Helen that really what Brown was after was a way of justifying the expensive surveillance he had kept on her. With no proof, he could only hope for her to do his work for him and confess to his invented crimes. Helen weighed her choices. Internees would remain under lock and key until the war ended – but how long would that be? The enemy were making advances at the moment and seemed to be prevailing, but with America joining in the fight it was possible the balance might swing the other way. This to-and-fro conflict might grind on for years. Did she want to spend her next few years 'inside'? Come 1920, or 1922, still in prison, would she regret not taking this escape?

Like a cat waiting by a mouse hole, Brown pounced on the doubt he saw on her face. 'You claim to care for Lieutenant Trewby. He would be much better off for having nothing more to do with you. Unfortunately, his family are active on your part and people are noticing his attachment to a traitor. Don't you think you should do the decent thing and cut the young man free?'

So here was the second motive: Brown wanted her gone, by her own choice, so he could silence the protests of Sebastian's family with irrefutable proof of her guilt. Making a false confession to purchase a ticket to New York was not something she could stomach. She had left Sebastian once already for what she thought was his own good; now in this much more serious case could – should – she do it again?

Phrased like that, it dawned on Helen what her answer would be.

No. She had promised. Even if it meant staying behind bars. Even if it ended with trumped-up criminal charges and her utter disgrace, forcing Sebastian to be the one to break the engagement as a result. This time it would be his choice, not hers. The decision gave her an exhilarating boost of strength like a gulp of brandy, harsh but powerful.

'Mr Brown?'

'Yes?'

'Do you believe in telling the truth?'

He nudged a piece of paper and a pen towards her. 'Naturally.'

'Then I will tell you my truth. You are entirely wrong about me. I have never betrayed my country – and that country, by the way, is England, as I owe no loyalty to Germany.' In her head, brass bands were marching, flags waving, as she did battle with this man. After hiding and ducking for so long, she felt euphoric to declare her position. 'You can't deport me as I am a subject of His Majesty and have the right to reside here, even if it has to be behind bars for the moment.'

'But, Miss Abendroth-Sandford –'

'No, Mr Brown, I am not taking your pieces of silver, even for my fiancé's sake. Lieutenant Trewby knows me far better than you, and he is perfectly capable of making his own decisions and has no need of your attempts to "protect" him. I assure you he won't be thanking you for them. As much as I would like to visit my sister, I will do so on my own ticket and on my own timetable, not yours.'

'And this is your final answer?' Anger turned Brown's cheeks a bee-stung red.

'Yes, it is. I know you set no store by my claims of innocence but you might consider that if I were the trai-torous creature you think, I would leap at the chance to wriggle free and go spread mischief elsewhere. I'd prefer to stay, as I know that I do not deserve to be here. Put simply: I am in the right and you are in the wrong.'

'Hah! But you are the one behind bars.'

She smiled wryly. 'I didn't say I expected life to be fair just because I'm innocent.'

'A hardened case.' Mr Brown sounded flustered as he addressed the governor. 'I know the Earl of Bessick by reputation. He won't welcome this schemer getting hold of his grandson once he realizes the truth.'

'So I'm not to expect the earl to be pounding on my doors next?' asked the governor, glancing at Helen with a puzzled expression, wondering how so small a person could cause so much trouble.

'You hold her under government authority, not your own. I'm sure you can deal with an irate earl if necessary. He's a spent force in the Lords.' Mr Brown stood up and gathered his papers. 'If you change your mind, the offer of passage to America might still be open. The governor will let me know.' He shook hands with the official in charge of the prison. 'See if you can change her mind, Governor. It would be the best for everyone.'

British Airbase, Carvin, France, 2 May 1918, 8 p.m.

As Sebastian put his plane down on the grass runway, the undercarriage bounced once on a rut before settling to a smooth taxi. He guided the Pup towards the canvas hangars, reviewing the details of his latest mission for his report. From what he'd seen from the skies, after the successful push in the spring and taking of several airfields, the German advance appeared to have mired in the mud, as so many of the Allied attempts had done in the past.

There had been little change to the positions he had mapped the previous week. The response to his flight's presence overhead had been less heated than before. The edge had been blunted on the Fokker crews since they had lost the Red Baron in April. The Allies had buried the baron with full military honours; such was his reputation on both sides of the conflict. The British pilots no longer felt overwhelmed by the superior strength of the enemy. The war scales were once more hanging in the balance position, waiting for the next grain to be added to the pans to change the side that fortune was favouring.

He cut the engine and climbed out. A mechanic waited to assist him to the ground.

'Bit of wear on the runway, Greeves.' He gestured to the spot where the undercarriage had hit the rut.

'I'll see to it, sir.' The mechanic tapped his forehead in acknowledgement.

Sebastian unwound his scarf and pulled off his leather helmet and goggles. 'All well?'

'Just waiting for Lieutenant Matthews to return. Everyone else got in before you.'

Sebastian frowned, trying to recall if he had seen the New Zealander. No one liked to hear of late returns; it rarely boded well.

Then the mechanic smiled, his sharp hearing catching the sound of an engine a moment before Sebastian. 'Ah, that's him now. Looks like he's seen a bit of action.'

Sebastian shaded his eyes into the setting sun and saw the silhouette of the plane coming in for the approach.

The radio cable was trailing from the back, which meant the winding mechanism had failed or been damaged. Hanging like that, it would cut like a scythe if anything got in the way; worse, it could snag on a tree and bring the plane to grief.

'I hope he realizes he's got a tail.'

'I'd say so, sir. See how he's coming in high.'

Both held their breath as the New Zealander put the plane down. The wire snaked in the grass behind but did not catch on anything, allowing him to come to a controlled stop. Sebastian had seen so many accidents on landing, he tended to be surprised if someone managed to land safely when the odds were against them. The mechanic gave a relieved huff of released breath.

'Oh, sir, the Yanks have arrived. A squadron fresh from training school. Thought you'd like to know.'

'Thanks, Greeves.'

'I hear the mess has voted you cultural ambassador.' Greeves started walking towards the slowing plane. 'Seeing how you are half and half, like.'

'Wonderful.' Sebastian raised a hand to acknowledge Matthews in the cockpit, then headed back to his billet.

When Sebastian entered the mess later that night, he could feel the uneasy atmosphere. When other recruits from overseas had come, they had been absorbed in their ones and twos, part of the Empire; there had been American volunteers before, who had slotted into the existing structures – but these airmen were a different business, having their own chain of command and not being exhausted by four years of battle. The five pilots in the mess looked impossibly optimistic and shiny, their uniforms straight out of the quartermaster's stores. Their expressions were friendly, but the other men were regarding them somewhat suspiciously. Foolish though it may be, there was a bubbling resentment that Uncle Sam was going to march in and take credit for a win when it had been the blood of other men that had really kept the war from being lost, good men like Charlie and the many other friends Sebastian had seen die. Sebastian rubbed his eyes, pushing away the irrational feelings. Of course it was good the Americans were here. They were risking their lives just like everyone else and should be made welcome.

'Ah, Trewby!' called Captain Duff-Taylor. 'Meet the new men. Their squadron has been posted alongside us to learn the ropes of air combat.' He quickly ran through the names. 'Trewby here has an American father.'

The senior man, introduced as Captain Grossman, held out a hand, his even white teeth gleaming in his golden-skinned face. He could be a poster boy for a health tonic. 'Hey, I believe I know your family, Trewby. Big in finance.'

'Yes, that's my father. Theodore Trewby of Trewby Holdings.'

'Pleased to meet you. I believe my uncle once worked for the New York office of your father's firm.'

'Did he? An extra reason then to welcome you to our

mess. Drink, anyone?' Sebastian asked, showing the new men where the pilots kept their supplies.

The five Americans and Sebastian settled down on the two old sofas near the grand fireplace. Matthews, Benn and a couple of the other pilots drifted over to make conversation, leaving Sebastian to talk to Grossman.

'So, Trewby, how long have you been at the front?' the American asked.

'A lifetime.' It felt like it most days when all he wanted was to be in England demanding Helen's release. 'Since late 1915. I was at the Somme but invalided out. Returned as a pilot last year.'

Grossman swirled his wine and took a sip. He grimaced.

'Not much better than vinegar, is it?' Sebastian smiled. 'I think we drank all the good stuff last winter.'

'It'll do. We've heard stories about the Somme. Bad, was it?'

'Hell.'

'And what's it like to fly against the enemy?'

'Better than the ground campaign. At least it's a fair fight up there.'

Grossman nodded. 'My men are good fliers but none of us have combat experience. And from what I've seen; your machines are streets ahead of ours.'

'We all have to start somewhere. We've been refining the machines as we go – needs must.'

'I guess so. Well then: to a swift victory!'

Sebastian raised his glass. He had lost hope some months ago, but now he allowed just a little to creep back in. The energy of the new men did change the atmosphere in the mess; the tired old hands finally had someone else to help carry the burden. The resources of America, both men and materials, felt limitless compared to the exhausted ones of Europe and Empire. Maybe it would be enough.

Aylesbury Prison, 4 June 1918, 11 a.m.

Alone in the cell, Helen cast the newspaper aside. Depressing: the lines were back to where they had been in 1914. All the lives lost in the interim had been wasted. She stared at the shiny white tiles on the wall, vision blurring with tears as she remembered the men she had treated in France, the ones who had died on the operating table or later in their beds on the wards. She wanted to scream with frustration; instead she punched her pillow. Why was her generation being spent so recklessly by the men in power, like a box of dud matches, each struck once, then discarded as useless? She lived every day in fear of hearing that Sebastian had become one of the casualty figures. Rationally, she knew the war would have to end, but now she was beginning to think it would be more like the Hundred Years War of history than the short sharp campaign they had been promised, where just one more push would make the difference.

The prison was quiet at this time of day, inmates going about their business in the various departments that provided employment, the internees left to their own devices. She had long since made it clear that, even isolated as she was, she did not want to fraternize with the German group. Odd how Mr Brown's insistence that she was a spy consorting with the enemy's agents had resulted in her being brought into contact with those who very likely were; it would have accomplished the very thing he feared if she had been so minded as to accept their overtures.

The female prison guard she now knew was called Stokes appeared in the doorway.

'I've orders to move you in a few days, Sandford.'

'Move me?'

'Governor's orders.'

Helen had been quite comfortable with Marge and had no desire for a change. That was probably the point. No one wanted her comfortable. 'Where to?'

Stokes cleared her throat. 'To Big Hetty's cell.'

'What!' Helen felt as though she had just tumbled down a flight of stairs.

'My orders are to move you unless you change your mind about taking the government's offer to deport you.'

Helen clutched her locket. She didn't even have the ring any longer to bribe the guard, having sent that to Aunt Dee-Dee in the care of the solicitor they had appointed for her. 'No, please!'

'Orders is orders, Sandford. I'd be getting myself out of here if I were you.' Stokes turned on her heel and left Helen to her thoughts.

Her brain felt as though it was on strike, marching in

circles, waving a placard demanding help. She wiped the newsprint off her fingers on a handkerchief and gripped the cotton like a lifeline. She had to face up to the reality of her position. Even if she survived Hetty – which she sincerely doubted – going by the news from France, she could be here for years yet. None of Sebastian's family or her friends had been allowed in to see her, as her visitor privilege had been restricted to her relatives and her solicitor for fear she would contaminate the hearts and minds of loyal Englishmen. That meant she saw no one. Her letters were opened and censored, arriving looking more like black-and-white chessboards than correspondence. It was no life.

Did she really have a choice?

She got up and paced the cell, rubbing her arms, trying to decide what she should do. Finally, she returned to her bed, picked up her pen and began to write.

Dear Sebastian . . .

19

Duff-Taylor stopped Sebastian as he was on his way to the hangar, helmet in hand, flying jacket already on.

'Trewby, some good news. Command wants three of our Pups flown back for the trainees. They are to be replaced by a new delivery of Sopwith Camels.'

'Yes, sir.' Sebastian wondered what this had to do with him. He was due to take the morning patrol and the day looked as though it would only worsen weather-wise.

'I need three pilots to fly there and back. I'm prepared to authorize you to take a short leave of absence while you complete the handover.'

So Duff-Taylor had come through with his promise – that truly was great news. 'Thank you, sir.' Sebastian's mind was already whirling with the possibilities. 'When would you like us to leave?'

'Immediately. Barnsley can lead the patrol. I'm sending Matthews and Benn along with you, but you're in charge. See Horrocks for a map of where you are to put down.'

Sebastian saluted and turned on his heel to fetch a few belongings from his billet. He passed Matthews on the way.

'We're heading for Blighty. Pack an overnight bag,' he called.

'Right with you!' Matthews rubbed his hands together.

Sebastian stopped en route to tell Benn his good fortune and found Grossman playing chess with the Britisher.

'What's going on?' the American asked, sensing Sebastian's eagerness.

'We've been given a short leave back home. Plane delivery. We set off immediately.' Sebastian knew they had not a moment to spare if he was to do anything for Helen in the time allotted. 'Hurry up, Benn.'

'Some guys have all the luck.' The American grinned. 'Say hello to your sweethearts for me.' He began packing away the chess pieces.

'Sore point, Grossman. Trewby can't. They've put his girl away for having a German mother,' said Benn, shoving a few things in a duffle bag. Sebastian had made no secret of Helen's predicament, asking all the pilots he knew to use their contacts back home to make a noise on her behalf.

Grossman shook his head. 'That's crazy. My father's from Germany – emigrated to the States in the nineties. Are they going to bang me up in jail too?'

'Given half a chance they might.' Sebastian headed for his tent.

'Hey, hold up, Trewby!' He heard Grossman on his heels.

'I'm in a rush, Grossman.'

'Sure you are. I take it you're going to try see your girl?'

'That's the plan.'

'My father's posted to the Embassy in London. You're half American, correct?'

Sebastian wasn't sure where this was going. 'I am.'

'Give him a call.' Grossman scribbled a number on the back of a cigarette pack. 'He'll help get you in to see your girl. Diplomats can open doors closed to others, particularly now the Brits need us in this fight.'

'He'll help?'

'I'm sure of it. He won't like to hear of a girl being persecuted for something she can't help.'

Sebastian shook Grossman's hand. 'Thanks.'

'Think nothing of it. You'd do the same for me, I've no doubt, if the tables were turned.'

Sebastian jogged the rest of the way to his tent. While he had been out, his servant had delivered the post. A letter from Helen lay on the top. With a whoop of delight, Sebastian picked it up and gave it a kiss.

'Seeing you very soon, my darling,' he said, sliding it inside his flying jacket. There would be plenty of time to read that when he landed; right now he had to cross the Channel before the weather took a turn for the worse.

2 p.m.

Sebastian abandoned his colleagues and the planes at the Upavon airfield, and then jumped on a train for London. He had already telegraphed his father and left a message for Grossman senior, but he only had the rest of this day and the next to get to see Helen before he had to fly back.

He hoped that would be enough to get the red tape cut. Sitting down in First Class, he felt an envelope crunch within his jacket. Unfastening his inside jacket pocket, he took out the letter. He ran his thumb over her familiar handwriting, wondering what she would have to tell him today. It was an art finding new things to mention that would pass the censor.

He broke the seal.

Dear Sebastian,

She had crossed that out and started again.

Dearest love,

As ever, I hope this letter finds you well. I am writing because I am in more of a fix than ever. Mr [censored] has given me a choice: either I leave for America immediately or I will be moved to a cell with Big Hetty. I think you will remember that I told you about her. The poor woman is as dangerous as a rabid dog. Orders came down today for me to be put in with her if I don't take up his offer of deportation. I really don't know what to do. I have to admit I'm scared.

Sebastian swore, checking the date of the letter: two days ago.

I know you are working to get me free but I am no longer certain I can wait. I do not know what you would prefer me to do.

I'd prefer you to keep safe, he thought.

> *But I have promised you in the past not to leave you. I therefore have decided to [censored].*
>
> *I hope you will think this is the right decision. I pray for you every day and send you my love.*
>
> *Yours*
> *Helen*

Sebastian held the letter up to the light, wondering if he could tell what the key sentence contained before the censor had struck it through. He could see no reason for the deletion other than spite: she had hardly been on the point of revealing a national secret. Had she decided to take the way out that Brown had offered? Was he rushing to break down prison doors only to find she was already gone? He wished he didn't doubt her, but she had fled once before from his family home and disappeared for months. And maybe he should be hoping she had taken the way out offered, as the very last thing he wanted was for her to be in danger? The problem was that, if she had agreed and confessed to things she hadn't done in order to get out, she would never be able to live in England again and they would have to reconsider their whole future.

The train drew into Paddington Station. Sebastian was the first to hop out and hurry to the Underground. His plan remained the same, no matter what the censored letter hid: collect reinforcements and kick up such a fuss that

Mr Brown of the Home Office would regret the day he decided to go after Helen Sandford. The official may have thought he could get away with browbeating an unprotected nineteen-year-old girl; now he had a decorated officer in the Royal Air Force to reckon with – and Sebastian had learned a thing or two about conducting a war.

Sebastian held his briefing in his club. His father was the first to arrive and gave his son a tight hug.

'It eases my heart every time I see you fit and well,' Theo said heartily. 'I am so sorry about your friend, Charlie. He was a good boy.'

Sebastian swallowed against the lump in his throat; he missed Charlie every day and it did not seem to be softening with the passage of time. It made him more determined than ever to make sure he didn't lose Helen. 'Yes, he was.'

Theo took a seat in the armchair and accepted the cup of tea offered to him by the waiter. 'I should warn you: your grandfather is here.'

'The earl's in London?'

'Yes, but I mean *here* here. He's coming up, but I thought I'd give you time to prepare first. He has taken a keen interest in your girl.'

'I thought he would not approve of her, seeing how she's not from our class.'

'In the normal course of events that would be true, but Mr Brown made the mistake of ignoring your grandfather. And nothing annoys him more than a jumped-up paper-pusher not giving the Earl of Bessick his due.' Theo gave a sour smile and took a sip of his drink. 'Brown's done you a huge favour really, as it's brought the earl round to your side when ordinarily he would have tried to block the match.'

'Sebastian, my boy!' The earl was cutting a swathe through the late afternoon crowd of members who had dropped by the club for tea and sandwiches. 'Got the Hun on the run yet?'

Sebastian knew the only way to handle the earl was to answer him in kind. 'Not yet, but I've given him a few lumps, sir.'

The earl swatted him on the back. 'Of course you have. A true sprig off the old family tree. Thought I'd see you back earlier to send that wretched Brown fellow about his business.'

'I could not get leave before today, sir.'

'Duty first and whatnot. Very good.' Giving a nod of approval, the earl subsided into the armchair Theo had vacated for him. At over eighty, the earl was now a stooped version of his former self, a crop of untamed white hair and a pair of shrewd dark eyes. He held together the last scraps of magnificence adorning his family title through sheer will-power, having found his income unable to keep up with the expense of a country house and a family of three unmarried grown-up children. Only Lady Mabel, Sebastian's mother, had succeeded in marrying – and that had been to an American. It had taken the earl over a decade to look on the match as an asset rather than a shame.

'I can't abide these new people who think that the old guard no longer count.' The earl picked a large biscuit from the tea-tray and took a bite. He crunched it like a dragon devouring an annoying huntsman. 'If anyone is a traitor to the traditions of this country, it's him – not your girl, who as far as I can tell has done nothing wrong.'

'She hasn't, sir.'

'An Englishman's daughter, even if her father is only a clerk, but an educated sort – the kind that comprises the backbone of this country.'

Sebastian bit his tongue. Helen was worth twenty of her father.

'Of course, she isn't good enough for you, but you've made your choice and a gentleman sticks by his word. And you are in the cadet branch, so you can be spared.'

They all understood that if it were the earl's son, Tolly, angling after a middle-class girl, then the earl would not be so tolerant of her.

'Thank you, sir.'

'So how are we going to take down this upstart, Theo?' The earl slurped his tea, leaving a little garland of biscuit crumbs on his moustache.

'I've called in some favours, and made an appointment with Brown's superior in the Home Office tomorrow morning as soon as I heard Seb was coming back.'

'Favours?' Sebastian asked.

'I haven't been idle since March. I've been manoeuvring to make myself indispensable to Lloyd George. I reminded the Home Secretary that I am lending the government rather a lot of money, money that is going to pay for boots and bullets. Now is not the time for them to offend one of its creditors.'

The earl waved his biscuit. 'Excellent. Money talks in this world. Sir George Cave is a good enough fellow for a Tory, but he needs to be told what's what. Has the political instincts of that teaspoon.' He gestured to his saucer.

'We need to roll out all our big guns if we are to defeat the Browns of this world. The man's a menace: believes he is right and won't hear any arguments to the contrary.' Theo fiddled with his cuff-links. For all his calm tone, Sebastian could sense that he clearly wasn't entirely convinced he had done enough to win the day.

'I'm serving with a captain from Kentucky called Grossman. His father will help.'

'Grossman? From the Embassy? That's good. I know him a little socially. Having him with us will make Sir George sit up and take notice. I have long suspected that Brown is now after Helen because to admit he has no case would be to own up to a serious misuse of government resources. He is willing her to be guilty to save face. If we make it more awkward to keep her locked up, then I suspect they would be happy to set her free.'

That was if she hadn't already taken the escape Brown had corralled her into accepting. 'I hope you are right, Pa. They're putting her under intolerable pressure to fold.'

Theo rubbed his son's knee. 'Don't worry, Seb. It's taken us a while to gain this ground and I'm sorry for that, but now we have reached the gates, let's not retreat.'

'Damned right we won't back off from a fight!' spluttered the earl.

Sebastian toasted them with his teacup. 'To victory.'

20

Helen crouched in the corner of Big Hetty's cell, arms around her knees, as she attempted to make herself as small a target as possible. Her roommate was currently smashing up the contents of the cell. The enamel wash-basin flew and hit the wall, falling to the ground with a clang. Helen's mattress was next. Hetty seized the cheap cotton case and tore it apart, spilling the stuffing. Two guards stood in the doorway, empty hands spread.

'Please, Hetty. Calm down. We're not going to harm her. The governor wants to see her.'

'Nooo!' shouted the woman. 'She stays with me!'

Helen had been in the cell since the previous night, having resolved to bear it so as not to break her word to Sebastian. She had been fully prepared for a brief and brutal attack; instead, Hetty had decided Helen was hers, a replacement for her little girl whom she was no longer allowed to see. It had been terrifyingly unnerving to find herself cuddled against that matronly bosom, and have

302

her hair brushed and plaited with such care, when Helen had expected fists and abuse. Hetty had insisted she go to sleep early while the older woman sang her lullabies in an oddly tuneful alto.

Sleep? As if that was going to happen. She had pretended until Hetty had dropped off, and then crept into this corner.

The poor woman was entirely mad and very pitiful. She should be receiving psychiatric care, not a prison sentence. And now the governor had sent word that he wanted to see Helen, doubtless to see if she had changed her mind after a dose of the Hetty shock treatment. For once, it suited Helen to stay in her corner and let the guards work out how to deal with this. She was in no rush to see the governor just to repeat her refusal.

'You will not touch my little girl!' howled Hetty, backing up so that she stood in front of Helen, blocking any view of the door. 'I say when she comes and goes. She's my girl – mine – not yours!'

If Helen hadn't been so scared that Hetty's jealous love of her 'little girl' might swing against her, she would have been amused to see the guards struggling to cope with the determined prisoner. Served them right.

'You all right, Miss Sandford?' called Stokes.

'Yes.' Helen dared not say any more in case it sent Hetty off on another unpredictable path.

There came the sound of more voices by the door and a low discussion as the guards debated their next move;

the governor himself had arrived, but clearly had no desire to take the lead. Hetty patted Helen roughly on the shoulder. Helen flinched but no blow came.

'Don't worry, sweet, I won't let them hurt a hair on your head.'

'Um, thanks, *Mother*.' She'd heard that from a parent before and knew not to trust that vow.

'Helen?'

Helen rubbed her ears. She thought she'd heard Sebastian but that was impossible.

'Helen, are you hurt?'

It couldn't be! 'Sebastian? No, no, not hurt. I'm well.' Joy and relief burst from her.

Hetty growled, swinging around to deal with the new threat to her cub.

Helen quickly reined in her high spirits as Hetty took them so ill. 'I mean, my mother here is taking good care of me.'

Hetty unclenched her fists.

'Perhaps your mother might let you out for a moment?' Helen could hear the fear in Sebastian's voice. He couldn't show Hetty that he was scared of her; that always primed the woman for attack. How could she persuade Hetty to let her out? Her Sebastian was just outside but she couldn't reach him, couldn't touch him. She wanted to wail with frustration, but didn't dare make a peep.

Hetty stabbed a blunt forefinger into her own chest. 'I say when she comes and goes. I'm her mother.'

'Of course you do, Mrs . . . um . . . Hetty,' Sebastian said humbly.

Peeking round Hetty's tree-trunk legs, Helen could see him standing in the doorway. The guards had retreated on to the walkway.

'Please be careful, Sebastian,' warned Helen. It wouldn't take much for Hetty to rush him and push him over the rail as she had others who had annoyed her.

'You know this boy? I've not seen him before,' said Hetty, her muscles bunching as she made ready to remove the threat from her door.

Quickly, Helen reached out and grabbed her hand. 'Yes, Mother: he's a friend. From . . . from school. He wants me to go with him.'

Hetty gave a warning rumble.

'To play, Mrs Hetty,' Sebastian said swiftly.

'Play? What kind of games?' asked Hetty, the seesaw of her mood banging down on the side of interest.

'Oh, lots of splendid games.' Heavens, this was bizarre. Helen could see Sebastian struggling to think of playground amusements. 'Marbles. Conkers.'

'Them's boys' games.' Hetty folded her arms. 'My little girl don't play those.'

'Dolls. We are playing dolls. I've a tea party all set up.' Sebastian could see he had caught her imagination. 'There's real cake.'

'Cake? I like cake.' Hetty licked her lips.

Helen got slowly to her feet, moving fluidly, every

inch calculated not to alarm. 'I'll bring you back a slice. Let me go – just for a few minutes.'

'Please may she come out and play?' Sebastian repeated, echoing the age-old childhood request.

Hetty spun round, arm raised over Helen's head. Helen tensed, expecting a blow, but Hetty only wanted to straighten her collar and pat her on the head.

'Go play with him. He looks a nice boy.'

'Thank you, Mother.' Helen slid out from behind her before Hetty remembered that boys in their twenties were very unlikely to have dolls' tea parties. She hurried to the door. 'I won't be long.'

As soon as she stepped through, the guards closed the door and locked it. They could hear Hetty humming inside, clearing up the mess she had made of her nest.

Stokes mopped the sweat from her brow. 'That was a close-run thing, Sandford.'

Helen leaned back against the wall, shaking now the immediate danger had passed. 'Oh God, oh God. I didn't think I was going to get out alive.'

Sebastian took her in his arms and hugged her tight, beyond words.

'Keep that wretched prisoner in her cell for the rest of the day,' ordered the governor.

Fury boiled up in Helen's chest, beyond suppression. 'Is that all you can say? You put me in there with her! You started this!'

The governor cleared his throat, looking over Helen's head. Helen didn't care if she got put in solitary for insubordination: enough was enough! 'That woman needs to be in an asylum, not a prison. You all know it!' After weeks of minding her manners, Helen's outburst caught everyone by surprise. 'Call yourself public servants? You are a disgrace to your uniform, using her as you do!'

Sebastian gripped her arm, warning her to be silent. 'Darling.'

To Helen's amazement, no punishment came her way for her insolence.

'I'll look into it,' said the governor. 'Carry on with your duties.' He waved away the rest of his staff. He nodded once to Helen. 'Miss Sandford.' Then he walked away.

Why hadn't he reprimanded her? And why was she being allowed to stay with Sebastian?

'What's happening? Why are you here?' asked Helen. He framed her face with his hands and kissed her soundly. For a moment the prison receded, leaving just the two of them. 'I am so pleased to see you – I can't tell you how much.'

'Is there anything you need from in there?' Sebastian nodded at the closed door.

Helen shook her head fervently. 'I wouldn't go back in there if you paid me. They can't make me after that incident.'

'You aren't going back in there.' Sebastian buried his face in her neck, relishing the fact that he had her safe at long last.

'What do you mean?'

'As of ten o'clock this morning, you are free to go. The Home Secretary himself agreed to it.'

Helen reeled. Only his arms around her stopped her from crumpling. 'You're not . . . you're serious?'

'Completely. The guard there is waiting to escort us out. My father, grandfather and even the American Embassy laid down the law to the bureaucrats and they decided to set you free.'

She squeezed him tight, a little scared he might vanish and reveal this had been some crazy dream and she'd wake up in Hetty's cell again. 'You're telling me the truth?' Helen guessed Sebastian himself had also had a key part to play. 'Thank you, thank you.'

'No, don't thank me. I should have got here sooner but they wouldn't let me. I'm sorry it took so long.' He leaned forward and kissed her again, part apology, part promise. Lips softened, deepening the kiss. On his touch, Helen shivered as a stream of silver ran through her veins, a shimmering, precious current of delight at being held by the man she loved after so many months apart. He smelt so wonderful: of the outside world, fresh air, with a faint trace of tobacco from the train. The kiss had a slightly desperate edge, both knowing that this was only a moment stolen from the war; life was so fragile, especially for a pilot. Helen thought that if she could have crawled inside him, never to be separated again, she would have done. Instead, she had to content herself with the embrace.

There was a shrill wolf-whistle from down below. Marge had spotted them. They broke apart.

'Oi, Suffolk! Care to share?'

Jolted back to their inappropriate location for a reunion, Helen chuckled and waved. 'Get your own man, Marge. This one is taken.'

'Too right,' whispered Sebastian, squeezing her round the waist.

'They're letting you go?' called Marge, correctly interpreting the escort who was still waiting for them.

'That's right.' Helen tugged Sebastian into a walk. They passed the Germans hanging around the balcony with nothing to do as usual. '*Auf wiedersehen*, ladies.'

'Well, good luck to you then,' shouted Marge. 'I hope never to see you in here again.'

'Me too. All the best.'

Marge tapped her forehead in a mocking salute to the lieutenant.

Sebastian steered her to the door leading to freedom. 'Who is that?'

Helen smiled as she anticipated his reaction. 'A rather interesting businesswoman called Marge. I'll tell you all about her when we get out of here.'

Just when she thought she had finally slipped free and clear of the Home Office's grasp, she saw Mr Brown waiting in the visitor's foyer. She clutched Sebastian's arm.

'Tell me it's not him. I can't bear it if he finds another excuse to lock me up!'

Sebastian patted her arm. 'Sorry, love, but I had to bring him with me. The Home Secretary demanded Brown see to it personally after our little intervention in his office this morning. Brown is probably on the fast track to some obscure post in the colonies. Personally, I'd prefer to plant him a facer, as Reg might put it, but he's made himself useful persuading the governor to let you go with me without involving your parents.'

Mr Brown stepped forward to intercept them.

'Miss Sandford?'

'I see you've finally got my name right.' Helen slid on her gloves in preparation for going outside.

Mr Brown ignored that. In fact, he looked as though he was chewing razor-blades rather than issuing an official pardon.

'The Home Secretary has asked me –'

Sebastian coughed. '*Ordered* him.'

'– to apologize on behalf of His Majesty's government for any inconvenience that may have been caused to you during the time of your internment.'

Helen raised a brow. 'Inconvenience? Is that what it's called?'

'We are at war, miss.'

'Funny, I hadn't noticed. Had you, Sebastian?'

'What? Me? So *that's* what all the machine-guns aimed at me are about!'

Mr Brown didn't appreciate their sarcasm. 'He also wishes me to assure you that any mark against your character has been expunged from the record. Should you wish to return to nursing, or pursue some other war-related work, there is nothing to prevent you.'

Sarcasm died a quick death. Helen's throat suddenly constricted with the urge to cry. 'I can?'

'Yes.' Mr Brown gave her a curt bow.

'Thank you.'

Her soft thanks disconcerted him. He coughed. 'Yes, well, it seems that maybe I have misjudged some of the actions that were attributed to you. If that is the case . . .'

'It is the case,' said Sebastian severely.

'Then I add my own sincere apologies. I was only doing what I thought was my job.'

Helen nodded. It was the defence of men in power throughout the centuries. 'Perhaps, sir, next time, you might think twice before assuming someone's guilt.'

'Indeed.'

The guard who had been so rude to her on her arrival opened the outer door. 'There you are, sir, miss. Lovely day, isn't it? Good luck. So glad you didn't turn out to be one of them spies.'

Helen couldn't bring herself to thank him. She had to learn to accept that much of the hostility had not been personal, but it was odd to get friendly smiles after hatred. 'Goodbye,' she said instead, stepping over the threshold.

In a patch of sunshine outside, she turned to face Sebastian. He was smiling down at her; his implacable faith, his caring strength, all his wonderfulness at her fingertips.

'I love you more than words can say,' she said simply.

He slid her engagement ring on to her finger. 'There. Back to how it should be. I love you too, Helen Sandford.'

Helen stood at the window of the studio watching two men hang bunting from the lamp-posts. People were spilling out of the houses as the deadline for Armistice ticked closer. Already they had begun removing the black-out paint from the bulbs. That night, the street should be ablaze with its pre-war light. She took the first free breath she had managed since Sebastian had joined up three-and-a-half years ago. Finally, she would not have to worry if this was his last day on earth. The war was over.

Aunt Dee-Dee came to stand beside her. Finishing the Actaeon had purged some of the sculptress's grief. They could talk about Charlie now with fondness, laughing at some of the memories, crying over others. The loss still hurt but the ache was something Aunt Dee-Dee could bear. Helen wondered how many other women were standing at windows at just this moment, torn between celebration and mourning. No, Helen corrected herself, celebration was the wrong word. What the country felt was relief. With a million men dead, no one with any sense could consider it a war won.

'I wonder how long it will take for things to get back to normal?' mused Aunt Dee-Dee. Two children ran by, flags trailing behind them like colourful tails.

'Normal? What's that?' The bunting was hoisted high, swaying in the chill breeze. Had the bunting been in an attic throughout the war or had someone sewn it that autumn, knowing the end was approaching? Helen wasn't sure if she could have done that; it would have tempted Fate to assume victory.

'You're right: there is no normal.' The sculptress opened the window so they could hear the bells and cheers of the city. 'I think we've smashed the moulds of the old life. It's no good expecting us all to be poured back into the same shapes.'

Aunt Dee-Dee had welcomed Helen back when Sebastian had brought her to London from Aylesbury, apologizing that she had not prevented her being taken in the first place. Helen had tried to persuade her that there was nothing anyone could have done, but Aunt Dee-Dee had made it a personal campaign to plague the Home Office with letters of complaint at the abuse of her friend and invasion of her household.

There was a scratching at the door and Rolly came in, carrying his lead in his mouth.

'Ah, your summons.' Aunt Dee-Dee patted her on the shoulder. 'Go out and enjoy yourself, Helen. There will be plenty to see on the streets today.'

Helen gave her a quick hug. 'I wish Sebastian were here to share it with me.'

'He will be soon, my dear.'

'And Charlie.'

'I know. I wish he were too.' Aunt Dee-Dee sniffed and dabbed her eyes.

Muffin entered, carrying the tea-tray. 'I found some raisin biscuits to mark the day.'

'Aren't we pushing the boat out!' Aunt Dee-Dee smiled bravely, eyes still tearful. 'I guess it is too soon to hope that rationing will be over. Helen's not staying. She's off to see what's happening for us and will report back.'

'Have fun, dear. Don't let any sailors kiss you.'

'I thought that was part of the fun,' said Aunt Dee-Dee, trying to inject a little of her old spirit into the proceedings.

Saluting her landlady commander, Helen fastened the lead on the Labrador and ran down the stairs. 'Come on, Rolly. Let's go see what peace looks like.'

7 p.m.

The planes did not fly that day. The Armistice was being signed and all hostilities were to cease, even a patrol over the front lines. The pilots sat in their fleapit of a mess in Houthulst, drinking bad wine and wondering what came next.

'This is wrong,' said Benn, thumping his chair down on the bare floorboards. 'It's more like a wake than a party. We should be roaming the streets of London, gathering in Trafalgar Square, kissing pretty girls; instead we're squelching through mud with only other chaps for company and wine that tastes worse than engine oil.'

Tomlin, a grim Scot, laughed darkly. 'Drunk a lot of oil in your time, have you, lad?'

Benn toasted his friend. 'My share. So much of it flies in your face up there –' he gestured to the skies – 'that I guess I've drunk a pint at least.'

Sebastian swirled his drink. His mind kept going to other mess gatherings, other men he had known. So many gone. He hadn't expected to be here among those who made it over the finish line.

'What are you going to do, Tomlin, now it's over?' he asked, trying to jog his mind down a more positive path.

'Back to Glasgow. I'm hoping I can keep up the flying now I've a taste for it. Might be a future for civilian flights, don't you think?'

'Maybe. Hard to know what the future looks like, sitting here.' The world immediately outside the door had been flattened. If you were to guess the rest of the century from that evidence, you would think humanity would go backwards, return to cavemen bashing each other with clubs. 'What about you, Benn?'

'I'll go back to college to pick up where I left off. I want to be a barrister. It won't matter I'm a few years late.' Benn left unsaid the thought that there would be many gaps to fill. 'Trewby? Don't tell us: you are rushing back to your girl.' The mess teased him about his frequent exchange of letters with Helen, though from the support they had given him over her wrongful internment, he knew he had their approval.

'Yes, back to Helen. I'll have to decide if I return to art school or do something else. Not sure art is enough any more.'

Tomlin grunted. 'I don't know, lad. I think you should give it serious thought. Someone needs to bear witness to this stupidity.'

Sebastian was surprised. He would have put money on Tomlin scoffing at artists. 'You think so?'

'Aye. If your lass doesn't mind the life, you should do it.' He winked. 'Benn here will buy a painting when he's a rich lawyer, spare a few pennies for the starving artist.'

'Starving but talented artist,' corrected Benn. 'Yes, I'll buy a few daubings from you if they aren't too ghastly. Are you any good?'

'I don't know. Haven't done much recently.' The thought of trying to pick up where he left off, as Benn intended with his legal career, was terrifying.

'Ah well, I'm sure the knack hasn't left you,' said Benn, comfortable with his own plans and assuming others shared his view. 'We've survived this, so I think we can survive anything.'

Their flight leader came into the mess. 'Hurry up, chaps. The Chinese have found an old stash of German signal flares – we're having fireworks!'

Abandoning their cups, the pilots hurried outside. The little blue-uniformed Easterners who did most of the building and clearance work were darting around, setting light to the flares; another group had lit a drum full of lumber to make a bonfire, casting a warm orange glow over the muddy grass of the field. The rockets shot up into the sky and popped in a white bloom of light, a red, and then a green – not as pretty as Guy Fawkes Night but no bad simulation considering the materials at hand. The pilots and Chinese workers applauded and whistled, for a brief moment united in their appreciation.

Sebastian hung back where it was still dark, letting the lights dazzle him, leaving a trail to linger on his sight. Since the healing time with Helen after her release – just a matter of hours before he had had to fly back – he had gradually begun to allow himself to hope that those he had lost also somehow lingered, in some afterlife or maybe just in the hearts of those that had known them. Having entirely lost faith after Charlie's death, belief was creeping back. He wondered if it was simply too hard a habit to break, or maybe an instinct as deeply rooted as survival. He didn't know if he was ready yet to consider God, if there was such a being, but at least he was convinced of the reality of love and was ready to value life as more than the sum of flesh and bone.

Rockets burned. There went his brother, Neil, and his friend, Des – both lost in the Med; Captain Williams, his commander on the Somme, the men he had led and lost in no man's land; Charlie and so many other pilots – he sent a wish for each one with a flare. Better than the hasty ceremony in a battlefield graveyard: this was going out in style.

Sebastian took out his notebook. He had the theme of his first work clear in his mind. By the light of the bonfire, he began to sketch the faces.

21

Bewley House, Somerset, 31 July 1919, 1 p.m.

Helen stood in front of the pier-glass hardly able to believe her reflection. Finally, after months of ticking off the dates on a calendar, the day had arrived and they were to be wed. Helen had happily agreed to do the deed in the church that served Sebastian's family home, as the earl demanded, so she was fully expecting his side of the nave to be stacked with friends and well-wishers, hers to be conspicuously empty. The Cooks would be there, Muffin, Mary Henderson and her fiancé, a charming doctor from Leeds, Molly Juniper, a friend from her nurse training days, and Toots with her elderly husband, who turned out to be an acquaintance of the earl, but that was all. Her sister, Flora, remained in New York, her own marriage to a local businessman due in September. Cary Cosgrove did not know his wife-to-be was not a widow as she claimed so Flora had decided, for the sake of little Des, her illegitimate child, that it was best to stay away from those who knew her from before. In her last letter, Flora had sent love and said that she wished she were there; Helen believed her sister's regret was genuine, but it was hard to tell with Flora.

'You look lovely, dear.' Aunt Dee-Dee peeked in behind her at the mirror in the guest bedroom and straightened the bow on her own red chiffon outfit. She looked like a raging fire next to Helen's ice-white lace confection of a dress, a gown the sculptress had insisted on designing and paying for. Helen knew it scandalized the earl that she had chosen Aunt Dee-Dee to walk her down the aisle, but it was the right decision. The lady had been a better parent to her than her own, so fully deserved the honour. Helen did not expect Harvey and Geerta to show, even though she had informed them of the time and place. She would have liked her mother there – could have borne her father if Sebastian's relatives kept him away from her – but they had not replied to her letters.

Not all could be perfect in her happy ending. In a world scarred by war, it would feel wrong if it were, she decided.

'Ready?' Muffin, in her capacity as bride's attendant, fussed with the long veil that had come from some coffer in the earl's attic. She had fastened it with a thin band of flowers to Helen's heavy fall of hair.

I do look like a pre-Raphaelite painting after all, thought Helen, remembering the first conversation she had ever had with Sebastian in his studio, when they had discussed the artists of the last century and their preference for models with thick wavy hair and medieval gowns.

Sebastian's own paintings were now very different; he was developing a brutally direct style of portraiture that was making critics in London sit up and take notice, not always flatteringly. Sebastian shrugged off their comments, saying those who had gone through the war with him would understand.

'Yes, I think I'm ready.' She picked up the posy of white roses, draped the train of her dress over one arm, and followed her two escorts downstairs.

Sebastian's younger brother, Steven, gave him the thumbs-up from the door to the church, signalling that he had spotted the bride approaching. Sebastian turned to Reg Cook, his controversial choice for best man. Once upon a time, there could have been others in his place – Neil or Charlie – but when he came to pick, he didn't want any of his grandfather's approved choices, but decided the man who had backed him up on the Somme and engineered his reunion with Helen was the right person to have beside him. He knew it was a torture to Reg, feeling the earl's beady eye on the cockney's every gesture. The earl had taken Reg aside and warned him not to open his mouth in front of any of the county set and give away his lowly origins; Sebastian, however, knew that by the time they reached the champagne-drinking part of the proceedings, Reg would have bounced back from his momentary cowing and forgotten all warnings. He was rather looking forward to that.

'Did you feel like this when you married Elsie?'

'Feel like what, sir?' Reg tipped his pretty wife a wink as she wrestled the twins back on to the pew seat to their left. Maddie held the youngest competently on her knee while Joan sucked her thumb, leaning against her big sister.

'Like you've swallowed live eels?'

'Nah. I felt like I was king of the world that day.'

'I might work my way up to that later. I'm just worried that I'll make a hash of it.'

'She's a good'un, your girl. Nothing to worry about.'

Sebastian appreciated the cockney's plain good sense, but he couldn't help the jitters of nerves. They had waited so long for this day and were both about to set out with not a clue how to be happily married.

Reg studied his expression and sighed. 'Put it this way, sir. Did you know what you were doing when you led us over the top?'

'Definitely not.'

'But we all thought you did. You acted like you knew, so we followed. I reckon marriage might be a bit like that: set out acting confident and the rest will follow.'

'You know, Cook, that might be the best bit of advice I've ever been given.'

'You can pay me later.'

Sebastian chuckled.

The organist started the wedding march and the congregation stood. Sebastian turned to watch Helen walk down the aisle on Aunt Dee-Dee's arm, her posy of flowers quivering a little in her hand. She looked exquisite – like the glimpse of a shy doe among white blossom. Perhaps the thought was fanciful, but if a chap in love couldn't be fanciful on his wedding day, then when could he be? Everything dropped into place inside and a feeling of rightness settled over him like a cloak. He smiled at her – and she smiled back.

'*My face in thine eye, and thine in mine appears,*' he whispered the lines from their favourite poem, '*And true plain hearts do in the faces rest.*'

She must have read the words on his lips as her eyes sparkled.

Breaking with yet another tradition, Sebastian reached out and ran his finger down her cheek. '*Good-morrow to my waking soul,*' he murmured.

With a sigh, she leaned into his palm and did not open her eyes until the vicar cleared his throat, calling them to attention.

A peal of bells broke the summer's afternoon. Mr and Mrs Sebastian Trewby processed out of the church to the good wishes of their friends and a shower of rice from enthusiastic children. Sebastian stopped Helen at the lych-gate. The sun darted in and out from behind clouds, making the shadows race.

'Helen, do you remember your promise to me?'

She gazed up at him, a questioning expression in her eyes. 'Of course! I've just made my vows before all of our guests.'

He shook his head with an I'm-up-to-no-good smile on his lips. 'Not that. You said, some time ago now, that you would come fly with me if I managed to survive the war.'

Helen wrinkled her nose. 'I suppose I was hoping you had forgotten about that. All right, maybe sometime, in the future. When I've mentally prepared myself.'

'What about in the near future?' Sebastian tugged her round to show her the two-seater biplane he had bought when the RAF retired some of its aircraft. It was decorated with white ribbons and a garland of flowers.

She pulled back. 'But I'm in my wedding dress!'

'I know.' He reached up, unfastened the band holding the veil and passed it to a grinning Steven. 'Look after that.' Reg handed him a long overcoat. 'Slip this on, darling.'

'Are you joking?' She put her arms down the sleeves.

He tapped her nose. 'You promised. Think how much fun it will be to throw the bouquet from up there. There: all buttoned up.' He picked her up in his arms to the cheers of the onlookers and carried her over to the plane. Some of his RAF friends and Captain Grossman of the US Army Air Service were there to help her into the front seat.

Grossman winked as he handed her the leather helmet. 'You'll love it, I promise.'

'There's a lot of promising going on around here,' she muttered darkly. 'Sebastian Trewby?'

'Yes, Helen Trewby?'

Her new name took her aback. She liked the sound of it. 'Sebastian Trewby, I promise to get my revenge for this.'

'I do hope so.' He gave the nod to Grossman to swing the propeller.

At the last moment, Reg passed her the bouquet. 'Get one of these scheming young men with that, me darling: that'll put a kink in their tail.'

Laughing now, Helen gripped the bouquet as the plane bumped down the grassy runway Sebastian had had mown the day before.

'We always take off into the wind!' he shouted.

The plane picked up speed, then, as smooth as a salmon leaping, took off from the ground. Helen didn't want to get too near to the side of the cockpit as they climbed, but had to peek over to time her bouquet missile. She had aimed for Grossman but, forgetting the wind, the posy carried to hit a startled Aunt Dee-Dee squarely on the chest. She had to laugh at that; the gods of mischief were out in force today.

Sebastian turned the plane to fly off over the Quantock Hills, a swelling shoulder of green earth shrugging off woods near the summit. Her initial fears gave way to wonder. She trusted Sebastian completely; of course, he would not put her in danger. It was amazing – the world was so neat from up here. Bewley House looked like a doll's dwelling, the fields like the ones she had made as a child to play with wooden farm animals. She turned to look back at Sebastian. He had his pilot's face on, the one concentrating on the signals the plane was sending him. He loved this – she could see it in his expression. She was pleased she had agreed to this madness, even if it risked her wedding dress.

He glanced up and noticed her gaze on him.

'All right?' he shouted. The words were whipped away but she could read his question in the shape of his mouth.

She grinned and made the OK sign.

'Ready to loop-the-loop then?' He circled his finger in the air.

'Sebastian!' Her protest became laughter as he swung the plane to a steep bank to the right. He had just been pulling her leg. Thankfully. Otherwise, he might not have made it in one piece to the wedding night when she got her hands on him.

'Maybe next time,' he shouted. 'I'll make an aviatrix of you yet!'

For these brief moments, swooping through the clouds, Helen could believe that a new world really had dawned, that the war was over and the peace would last.

'I love you.' Facing him, she mouthed the words.

He read her meaning even though the engine noise and wind prevented him hearing. 'I love you too.' He pointed to his heart.

Then, stealing his bride for a few more minutes before they had to return to the party, Sebastian set a course eastwards towards the limitless horizon.

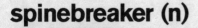

081L

He just wanted a decent book to read ...

Not too much to ask, is it? It was in 1935 when Allen Lane, Managing Director of Bodley Head Publishers, stood on a platform at Exeter railway station looking for something good to read on his journey back to London. His choice was limited to popular magazines and poor-quality paperbacks – the same choice faced every day by the vast majority of readers, few of whom could afford hardbacks. Lane's disappointment and subsequent anger at the range of books generally available led him to found a company – and change the world.

'We believed in the existence in this country of a vast reading public for intelligent books at a low price, and staked everything on it'
Sir Allen Lane, 1902–1970, founder of Penguin Books

The quality paperback had arrived – and not just in bookshops. Lane was adamant that his Penguins should appear in chain stores and tobacconists, and should cost no more than a packet of cigarettes.

Reading habits (and cigarette prices) have changed since 1935, but Penguin still believes in publishing the best books for everybody to enjoy. We still believe that good design costs no more than bad design, and we still believe that quality books published passionately and responsibly make the world a better place.

So wherever you see the little bird – whether it's on a piece of prize-winning literary fiction or a celebrity autobiography, political tour de force or historical masterpiece, a serial-killer thriller, reference book, world classic or a piece of pure escapism – you can bet that it represents the very best that the genre has to offer.

Whatever you like to read – trust Penguin.